PANIC ON THE RIVER

Jason Lowell was at the poker table, getting ready to fold a pair of nines, when he felt the floor shake and then tilt, as though the *Argo* had been lifted by a giant hand. From the commotion rising from the lower deck, he caught the single most terrifying word in the language of riverboatmen:

"Fire!"

Men were coming to their feet all over the room. In a few moments, they would be surging toward the doors, each man feeding the other's panic. Jason beckoned to the head steward.

"Put two or three of your best men in the strong-room. *Armed*. This could be a trick to distract our attention. Send three or four others to check every stateroom and make sure no one is asleep. Passengers to assemble here at once."

He was thinking of the girl Elizabeth—and of the sinister men down in the steerage—as he rose to salvage what he could from the ruin of all his hopes . . .

The Making of America Series

THE WILDERNESS SEEKERS
THE MOUNTAIN BREED
THE CONESTOGA PEOPLE
THE FORTY-NINERS
HEARTS DIVIDED
THE BUILDERS
THE LAND RUSHERS
THE WILD AND THE WAYWARD
THE TEXANS
THE ALASKANS
THE GOLDEN STATERS
THE RIVER PEOPLE
THE LANDGRABBERS
THE RANCHERS
THE HOMESTEADERS
THE FRONTIER HEALERS
THE BUFFALO PEOPLE
THE BORDER BREED
THE FAR ISLANDERS
THE BOOMERS
THE WILDCATTERS
THE GUNFIGHTERS
THE CAJUNS
THE DONNER PEOPLE
THE CREOLES
THE NIGHTRIDERS
THE SOONERS
THE EXPRESS RIDERS
THE VIGILANTES
THE SOLDIERS OF FORTUNE
THE WRANGLERS
THE BAJA PEOPLE
THE YUKON BREED
THE SMUGGLERS
THE VOYAGEURS
THE BARBARY COASTERS
THE WHALERS
THE CANADIANS
THE PROPHET'S PEOPLE
THE LAWMEN
THE COPPER KINGS
THE CARIBBEANS
THE TRAIL BLAZERS
THE GAMBLERS

THE
GAMBLERS

Lee Davis Willoughby

A DELL/JAMES A. BRYANS BOOK

Published by
Dell Publishing Co., Inc.
1 Dag Hammarskjold Plaza
New York, New York, 10017

Dell TM 681510, Dell Publishing Co., Inc.

ISBN: 0-440-02786-1

Printed in the United States of America

First printing—November 1983

CHAPTER ONE

Marie-Claire Aubray stepped noiselessly across the room to the tall window and pulled the right-hand shutter open. The morning light, dappled by an overhanging tree, caressed her shoulder, brushed across a small high breast, and lightened the flawless cocoa color of her belly before losing itself in the valley of her thighs. Almost without awareness, her hands gently followed the path of the sun's warmth down her body. The touch, and the shivers it brought, reminded her of her nakedness. She took a lace mantelet from the back of a chair and settled it around her shoulders. The white lace had been brought across the ocean from Venice and embodied weeks of labor by the tiny fingers of convent orphans. Though it was no weightier than a cobweb, its presence comforted her.

From the courtyard, scents of crepe myrtle and oleander wafted up to her, their fragrance all the more intense in the humid air. A cockatiel, the prize of Madame Latrobe's collection of tropical birds, screamed from its cage. Marie-Claire leaned forward to gaze out the window. Across the rooftops, the three spires of the cathedral were dark against a sky of pale blue. She recognized that sky. The day would be stifling hot. By four o'clock a thunderstorm would come to rattle the windows and turn the streets of the Vieux Carré into pits of foul-smelling muck. Even the banquettes, elevated above the roadway, would quickly gather a thick layer of mud from the boots of pedestrians.

She gave a small sigh and pushed the shutter closed. One day, perhaps one day soon, she would have a carriage of her own. She could see it in her mind; it would be deep maroon with a thin, elegant gold stripe, and she'd have a boy in maroon and gold livery to drive it. She would laugh aloud and snap her fingers at the rain then. But until that day came, she did not dare risk her hems or her fragile slippers. When the streets were wet, she remained indoors. It was the smallest part of the trick life had played on her.

Marie-Claire's father had been a wealthy cotton broker who claimed a hundred years of Louisiana aristocrats as his ancestors. Her mother was his quadroon mistress. Such liaisons were common, even usual, in New Orleans society. Marie-Claire had been raised in luxurious surroundings, and in the ordinary course of events she would have been well provided for. But when she was barely fourteen, her father took part in an affair of honor in St. Anthony's Garden, just behind the cathedral, and was killed. Still in his thirties and a noted fencer, he had not thought to make a will. His widow, whether through ignorance or malice, denied any knowledge of Marie-Claire or her mother. Later that year, Marie-Claire's mother was taken by the yellow fever, leaving the child orphaned and penniless, but very beautiful.

She found a refuge in the establishment of Madame Latrobe, an old friend of her mother's. She was a guest of the house, not an employee. Both she and Madame expected that she would catch the eye of some young aristocrat who appreciated beauty and understood what was owed to it. Until then, she was free to practice the arts her mother had taught her with whomever she pleased, as long as she was discreet.

A tap on the door, and a small boy came in carrying a tray. Like all Madame's house slaves, he was of the very blackest black obtainable. He wore billowy blue trousers that tied at the ankles, a red sash at the waist, and a red cap with a tassel that brushed his bare shoulder. Madame had designed the costume after an engraving in one of the novels she imported from Paris.

The aroma of coffee and chicory filled the room as the boy carried the tray across to a table near the window. After a single glance he did not look again at Marie-Claire, although they were good friends. He seemed unaware of her lack of clothing, or perhaps uninterested. But several times his eyes edged toward the other person in the room, then skittered away. He looked up at Marie-Claire with a question on his lips, but she made a fierce face and gestured to the door.

Carefully pouring from the pots of coffee and scalded milk, she filled two cups and carried one across to her companion. He was seated at her dressing table, staring at himself in the mirror. To her mind, he was worth a stare. His body was compact and well-muscled and his skin was as light as the milk she had just poured. Light brown hair fell carelessly, almost down to his shoulders, and his hands, with fine tapering fingers, were as soft and well cared-for as her own. But anyone who took all that as evidence of an unmanly character had only to look at his eyes to realize the mistake. Those steel-blue eyes seemed to regard the world without illusion and without pity. All that saved them from being inhuman was a hint of sardonic humor.

As he stared into his own eyes, his hands shuffled and reshuffled a deck of cards. The motion was so easy, so unstudied, that it appeared to be nothing more than a nervous habit. Still not looking down, he dealt four cards face-down and turned up the fifth, then repeated the sequence three more times. When he glanced at the table, he saw that the four cards showing were the four aces. His expression did not change, but Marie-Claire sensed a tiny movement in the muscles of his shoulders, a slight relaxation that was as close as he would come to expressing satisfaction.

He noticed the steaming cup. "Ah, *café au lait*. Thank you." Then, with a wave toward the cards, he remarked, "A pass I learned last evening by watching a dealer at Allen Jones' house on Royal Street. Simple enough once you notice the secret."

She stroked his shoulders and upper arms. "Simple for you perhaps, Captain Lowell," she said mockingly.

He leaned back, resting his head lightly between her breasts. "Jason," he said, "and I've told you before, I'm no captain. I don't hold with ranks and titles unless they're fairly earned."

"Very well, then *Jason*." Bending forward, she ran her soft hands down over his bare chest. As they crossed his waistline, he caught and held them. For a moment she struggled to free them, then shrugged in submission. "But I do not understand why you are no captain. The *Argo* is yours, *n'est-ce pas?* All the world knows it as Jason Lowell's steamboat."

"I own the *Argo*, but I don't command her. A boat can't stand more than one commander, and on the *Argo* that man is Captain Clement."

As he spoke, he turned toward her and released her hands. With a giggle, she reached lower and found what she was seeking. "Very well," he said after a few moments. He stood up and carried her toward the big, rumpled bed. "But no more than an hour, mind you. We leave for St. Louis this afternoon, and I have much to do before then."

Instead of replying, she raised her head and sank her small white teeth into the fold of skin where his neck and shoulder met.

The Negro doorman, decked in a uniform of sky blue with enough gold braid for a fleet-load of admirals, sprang forward and tugged at the handle while Duncan was still several paces away. He nodded in reply to the black man's murmured "Mornin', Colonel," and entered the St. Charles Hotel. He was still uncomfortable around slaves. He was certain that their outward servility and apparent stupidity was a sly, deliberate disguise. The doorman, for example, surely knew that a young man of twenty-three was not likely to be a colonel, even in the title-crazy South. Wasn't there a faint hint of mockery, then, in his greeting?

Servants were different in Duncan's native Boston. For a start, they did not *serve*; they *helped* or *obliged*, as if to make it very clear that they were free and independent. Having wealth, they implied, might allow their employers to hire their services, but in no way did it make them their betters. Jed, the hand on Duncan's father's farm, reacted to an order by thinking it over, then giving his own opinion of its worth. Duncan's father made a point of listening, too, because in fact Jed had a primitive wisdom about the land. If he thought some plan a mistake, it probably needed rethinking.

How different it was in the South! Duncan recalled his conversation, two nights before, with a cotton planter from near Jackson, Mississippi. They had been eating dinner at adjacent tables in the Restaurant d'Orléans, the most famous place in town for Creole cuisine. The planter, overhearing Duncan's conversation with the waiter and intrigued by his New England drawl, invited him to join him for a *café brûlot*.

They watched in silence as the proprietor lit the alcohol under the metal bowl, stirred sugar, orange peel, and spices into the heated cognac, then added strong, hot coffee. After a first sip of the fragrant drink, the planter, who had introduced himself as Richard Maxwell, observed, "You're quite a ways from home, Mr. Sargent."

Duncan explained that he was making notes for

a book about travel on the Mississippi River. "The river carries the lifeblood of our country, sir, but I am sorry to say that many cultured, educated people in Boston and New York and Philadelphia are not even quite sure where it is or where it flows."

"A worthy project, Mr. Sargent. May I ask if you come to us burdened by any strong political opinions?"

Duncan hesitated. He had known that he would face this question. Boston was known and detested throughout the South as the birthplace of abolitionism and the home of Garrison's inflammatory newspaper *The Liberator*. Anyone from that town was suspected of being an agitator. But though he had anticipated the question, he had not decided how to answer it.

"No, sir," he said finally, "I do not think so. But I must admit that I am made uneasy by the peculiar institution of this region."

"Slavery, you mean. It would surprise me if you weren't. It's not what you were brought up with. But I think a closer acquaintance might convince you that our system is both efficient and humane. More so than the system that forces young girls to spend fourteen hours a day tending the looms of Lowell and Lawrence."

"Are you . . . that is. . . ."

Maxwell guessed Duncan's question. "Do I own slaves myself? Yes, sir, I do. About six hundred of them, working three separate plantations."

Duncan's eyes widened. That represented an enormous fortune. "How can you supervise so many people?"

His companion laughed. "I? I have foremen to

do that. I send them my instructions, and they see to carrying them out. They know very well that if they fail to do so, I can find another man for their post in five minutes who *will* follow orders.''

"You don't live on your plantations, then?''

"Why, no. I have houses, of course, but we spend most of the time in the city. My kids are young still, and I think it's important for them to have the company of those of their own station. They're off visiting my wife's people in Baton Rouge just now, and I don't much care to take my meals alone.''

As they were leaving the restaurant, Maxwell said, "May we have the pleasure of your company for dinner on Saturday next, Mr. Sargent? My wife will have returned before then, and I'm sure she would be glad to hear whatever you can tell her of the fashionable world back East.''

Duncan's regret was genuine. "I've made plans to leave the day after tomorrow,'' he explained, "for St. Louis. Friends there are expecting me, or I would be glad to put off the journey and accept your kind invitation.''

"No, sir, I wouldn't hear of it. Which boat do you take?''

"The *Argo*. I was told it's quite up to date.''

"Surely, surely. Are you a sporting man, then?''

Duncan looked puzzled. "I hunt, and I play a tolerable game of billiards. Why do you ask, sir?''

"Your boat, Mr. Sargent, your boat!'' He laughed at Duncan's expression. "Surely they told you that Jason Lowell's steamboat is the fanciest gambling house afloat! Oh, the *Argo* has luxury and speed enough, but what sets her apart is the gaming. I've heard Lowell brag in his quiet way that he'll supply a partner for any game of chance known. And the prime part is that all the games are on the straight, by Lowell's personal orders. Even the faro game is square, they say. I'm damned if I know where you'd find another square faro bank between here and Chicago.''

"Really? I had no idea."

"The natural result," Maxwell continued, "is that anyone who likes to gamble but prefers to have a fair chance of winning, and who is obliged to travel to Natchez or Memphis or beyond, lays his plans around the schedule of the *Argo*. I reckon Lowell is onto a good thing, yes sir. No flies on that fellow. I'll be surprised if he doesn't take up a deal of space in your work.''

"My . . . ? Oh, yes. Yes, no doubt."

Maxwell raised his tall beaver hat. "Good night, Mr. Sargent, and a pleasant journey. If you are back this way, I hope you'll call. If not, I'll look for your book." He turned right, toward Royal Street, and strolled away, leaving Duncan lost in thought in front of the restaurant. Finally he turned the other way, admiring for a moment the exquisite cast-iron balconies of the Le Prète mansion before striding off in the direction of his hotel. The conversation had given him a lot to consider.

Why had his friends urged him so strongly to travel by the *Argo*?

"Boy! See that our luggage is put aboard the *Argo*, at the foot of Lesperance Street, by three o'clock."

The order, delivered in the ringing tones of a

practiced orator, carried clearly across the lobby of the St. Charles. Duncan Sargent, alerted by the name of the steamboat he was boarding in a few hours, turned his head in time to hear the porter say, "Yassuh, Senator."

A tall man with a great mane of white hair sweeping back from his forehead was standing in the center of the lobby. In spite of the heat, he was wearing a black frock suit with vest and a high collar already limp from the humidity. He gazed around the room as though the other patrons of the hotel had been assembled especially for his private entertainment.

Duncan recognized him. He was Senator Junius Stephenson. He was famous for having stated, on the floor of the United States Senate, that he would gladly strangle a baby in the cradle if he knew that it was destined to grow up an abolitionist. He was also said to have killed half a dozen men or more, some in duels and some in less formal circumstances.

His eyes met Duncan's, and paused for a moment, as if committing his features to memory, before moving on. Duncan felt, to his own dismay, a prickling sensation at the top of his forehead, along the hairline. He told himself that it was the heat, but he was careful not to look at Stephenson again. Drawing a silk handkerchief from his coattail pocket, he dabbed at his forehead and turned his attention to the Senator's companion.

A greater contrast was hard to imagine. The girl could not have been more than sixteen or seventeen, with a figure so slight and unformed that she might have passed for a rather tall child. She was dressed for travel in a gown of pale blue silk with flounces of dark blue velvet on the bell sleeves and a white cap tied with ribbons of matching blue. The gown, of course, had the fashionable crinoline skirt that widened from her tiny waist to fully four feet in diameter at the floor. Duncan was forcibly reminded of a candle-snuffer. He was inclined to smile, until he looked at her face.

Her features were regular enough, though the nose was a bit small and the eyes a bit wide-set by current taste, and the ringlets that hung down on either cheek were a soft brown with highlights of gold. She was certainly far from plain, and at another time he might even have considered her a beauty. But all he could see now was the terror in her face, a terror so chronic that she seemed unaware of it. He saw it in the paleness of her cheeks, in the pinched look of the wings of her nose, in the skittishness of her glance. When the Senator turned to speak to her, she flinched as though she expected a blow. Yet Duncan did not believe that it was the Senator who caused her fright, because immediately afterward she nestled closer to him and clung to his arm.

Duncan tugged at one of his bushy sidewhiskers. It was a habit he had when he was weighing his course of action. If, as it seemed, Senator Stephenson was to be aboard the *Argo*, it was very likely that the girl would be as well. Duncan would have further chances to ponder their little drama and penetrate its meaning. For the moment, though, he would have to leave them. There was a warehouse off Bienville Street that had a more urgent claim on his attention. Rapping his stick on the counter, he told the clerk to have his portmanteau sent to the *Argo*, then strode across the lobby. His path to the door took him very close to the two he had been watching. As he passed, the girl looked up. For a moment he believed he saw a hint of hope in her face. Then the light died.

"Charlie, you won't forget that we've got to be all packed and ready by three, will you?"

Charles Brigham was at the washstand, leaning forward to bring his face within inches of the mirror. Carefully he brushed his index finger across his upper lip once more. It was rough, wasn't it? Almost bristly. He stared harder. In his bag was his father's set of razors. He longed to bring them out, but he knew that Lizzie would say something about it. She always seemed to have something to say.

"Charlie dear, did you hear me? We have to get ready."

He straightened up and practiced a look of defiance. This involved narrowing his eyes, flaring his nostrils, and curling his upper lip. He wasn't quite happy with it yet, but he did see improvement.

"Charlie?"

He stalked over to the door between their rooms. "Durn it, Liz, I hear you. You don't have to keep saying it over and over." He meant to sound stern, but the effect was somehow peevish instead.

His sister was four years older than he. Her dark eyes, finely molded nose, and clear forehead warred with the tired downturn of her lips. She finished pinning up her long dark hair and turned to face him. "But, Charlie," she said in a mild tone, "you didn't answer."

He looked past her shoulder, in the direction of the window. Why did he have so much trouble meeting her eyes? It wasn't fair! "It's not fitting," he mumbled, "a man taking orders from a girl. If anyone heard the way you talk to me, they'd think I was a child."

Lizzie looked at him with both laughter and fondness in her eyes. The fondness won; she banished the laughter and said, quite seriously, "I'll watch for that in the future, indeed I will, Charlie. But I don't think it is quite proper to refer to me as a girl, either. I believe that on my twenty-first birthday I became a young lady."

He searched her face for signs of mockery, but she hid them well. "All right then," he said, "but you'd better get all those things of yours packed. We have to be ready by three, you know. I hear the *Argo* is an awful popular boat, and we don't want last choice of staterooms."

The scar began near the center of his forehead, passed over the left eye, and curved across the left cheek before vanishing in a thicket of sidewhiskers. The slaves of the warehouse gang looked at him sidelong as they passed and cowered, though he didn't seem to pay any attention at all to them. They were working hard, one to each end of the two-hundred-pound crates of farming equipment. The sweat was carving gullies through the dirt that caked their bare backs and turned their ragged jeans black.

The scarred man reached into the pocket of his flower-embroidered silk vest and drew out a gold hunting-case watch. He said nothing, but the gesture alone was enough for the warehouse foreman.

"Hurry it up, you lazy bastards," he shouted. "If you don't get those crates loaded in five minutes, I'll see the color of your backbones, by God!" He flourished a short whip, which had been made from the cured skin of a bull's penis, to emphasize his order.

Five crates were still in the warehouse. Three were quickly brought out and hoisted atop those already on the wagon. But as the men were lifting the fourth, it slipped from their sweat-slicked hands.

"AIEEAH!" Simultaneous with the crash of splintering wood, the slave on the left let out a terrible scream, then continued to shriek rhythmically. The others stared at him, frozen with shock, while the foreman ran to the front of the wagon to help the carter control his panicked horses.

The scarred man stepped forward. "You! At that end! You, take that corner! Fast, damn you! *Heave!*"

The crisp orders broke their immobility. In moments they had lifted the heavy crate off the injured man, who had mercifully fainted. They looked down in fascinated horror at his mangled feet. One turned away to be sick. The dark blood pooled and sank into the dust of Bienville Street.

The scarred man was inspecting the corner of the damaged crate. Finally satisfied that it was sound, he looked around. "Here," he said, "you're not done yet. Drag him out of the way and get that last crate loaded. And be quick about it, or you'll remember this day for the rest of your lives."

He watched closely as they carried the heavy

wooden box from the warehouse and secured it on top of the others. Then he sprang easily up onto the seat next to the carter. "The foot of Lesperance," he said, and drove off without a backward glance at the warehouse or the crippled stevedore, who had regained consciousness and was shrieking again.

As the loaded wagon vanished around a corner, a stocky, well-dressed young man with bushy sidewhiskers stepped out from between two buildings. He hesitated for a moment, and gazed around as if he was uncertain of his route, before setting off westward along the levee. He was humming under his breath.

CHAPTER TWO

The Mississippi at New Orleans made a great sweeping bend around three sides of the town before resuming its ponderous journey to the Gulf of Mexico, a hundred miles south. It was the river that gave the town a reason for existing, and it was the river that constantly threatened that existence. The spring crest had already passed, but even now the water stood at fully fifteen feet above the level of the streets. All that saved the town from a swift return to the days of Noah was the line of yellow clay levees encircling it.

The waterfront had its own life, its own customs. The foreign ships tied up nearest the Gulf, near the old French Market. The brigs and barkentines and full-rigged ships made a forest of masts and yards as they waited, three and four deep, for their cargoes of baled cotton and cane sugar. The sailors, whether Limey or Lascar, Chinaman or Dago, found entertainment—and willing help in spending

their pay—on nearby Gallatin Street, which boasted
the most cosmopolitan brothels in the Western
Hemisphere and perhaps in the world.

Next along the riverfront were the raffish coasting vessels—the schooners, sloops, and luggers—
that linked the town with Texas, Mexico, and the
rich islands of the Caribbean. Beyond them, lining
the levee like a wall of white-painted wood, were
the steamboats. The smoke from their tall chimneys blackened the sky, and the hissing of steam,
the clangor of bells, and the shouts of teamsters
and stevedores dinned in passersby's ears.

The riverboats came in every size and variety:
tiny shallow-draft sternwheelers that crept up narrow bayous to pick up a bale or two of cotton and
leave off a pound of coffee and a bolt of calico
cloth at a swamp-isolated plantation; the larger boats
that braved snags and sawyers on the passages up
the Red River to Natchitoches and up the Arkansas
to Ft. Smith; and huge sidewheelers with flaring
decks that could move five thousand bales of cotton stacked four deep and so high that only the
pilot house and smokestacks reached over them.

The queens of the river, by everyone's estimation,
were the fast packets. The construction was light,
flimsy, and cheap, because the hazards of the river
claimed them quickly, but their furnishings dazzled even the most sophisticated passenger. Their
grand saloons displayed Turkish carpets fit for an
Ottoman palace, great chandeliers of Bohemian
crystal, and carved wainscotting of rare woods.
Each stateroom door might sport its own painting
of a quaint scene along the river. In the staterooms,
French plate mirrors in hand-carved, gilded frames

reflected marble-topped tables and walnut chairs upholstered in deep-cut velvet and, in the bridal suite, a square grand piano of the finest make.

Some of the packets followed routes that took them eastward at Cairo and up the Ohio River to Louisville, Cincinnati, and even Pittsburgh. Others continued up the Mississippi to Hannibal, Rock Island, and Prairie du Chien. But the fastest, the most luxurious, ran between New Orleans and St. Louis, making as few stops as the gross appetites of their wood-fired boilers allowed. Jason Lowell's *Argo* was one of these.

Jason strolled down Lesperance Street and climbed the levee. The air reminded him of a Turkish bath. He was still wearing the black broadcloth suit and handpainted vest he had donned the evening before, for his visit to Marie-Claire, and under them his shirt of Egyptian cotton was soaked. He was looking forward to returning to his suite of rooms on the *Argo* for a cold sponge bath and a change to lighter clothes.

Around him, conversations went on in all the languages of a great seaport, and in a few, too— like Cherokee, Choctaw, and several Creole dialects —that would draw baffled stares in Liverpool, Shanghai, or New York. Jason barely noticed. An elderly Sicilian woman with a basket of fruit on her arm called him by name and offered him a wizened apple. A tamale vendor with a wooden leg tugged at his forelock sailor-fashion. A boy dealing monte, who looked no more than thirteen, paused with the lady in his hand and gave Jason a wink. Jason accepted the apple and returned the salute and the wink, but the exchanges did nothing to soften the steel in his gaze.

His thoughts were still back with Marie-Claire. He suspected that he would not see the lovely octoroon girl again. She was nearly seventeen; it was time for her to find a man who could place her at the head of her own establishment. She would not have any trouble finding one. She had youth, beauty, social graces, and, as Jason knew very well, a bubbling reservoir of unrefined passion. Those qualities would bring her servants, carriages, costly gowns and jewels, and a recognized, if irregular, position in society. Her children would bear their father's name, though without the right to it, and would be sent off to Paris for their education. Jason knew the system, had known it before he met Marie-Claire, and he had no particular quarrel with it. Why, then, was he grinding his teeth as he thought of her situation?

As soon as he asked himself the question, the clarity he applied to other people's deceits penetrated his own. He had come to like the girl, not just as a bedpartner, but as someone whose spunk and determination he admired. She deserved better than the prospect of being some rich bastard's sex toy, but her ancestry, the taint of Negro blood in her veins, made that the very best she might expect. Jason was no abolitionist, but he had never learned the essential hypocrisy of the Southern white either. He despised the man who, over dinner, proclaimed the eternal innate inferiority of the African, then after dinner crept out to the slave quarters to indulge his lusts on those who had no power to refuse him.

He laughed aloud, a chilly laugh that had no humor in it. The national habit of turning almost any situation into an aspect of the slavery issue had affected even him, it seemed. The simple fact was, he felt a degree of jealousy toward the man who was wealthy enough to afford Marie-Claire on a permanent basis. Politics had nothing to do with it; if he himself had that kind of wealth, he might well take the girl as his mistress without another thought about the injustices of her position. But he didn't, and that was the end of the story. All his money was tied up in the *Argo*. The boat made a handsome profit, and the gaming tables added substantially to that, but the river was like Lady Luck, fickle to the core. An instant of inattention by the pilot, an indetectible weakness in one of the eight huge boilers, even a single spark finding its way to the painted woodwork, and the steamboat, its palatial fittings, and its passengers might become nothing more than another disaster story in the *Daily Crescent*.

Stepping out of the path of a rattling wagon, he stood back a moment to look over his steamboat. As always, the sight improved his spirits. To his mind, she was the handsomest craft on the Mississippi. Her shear made her seem to float on the water like a swan, and like a swan, she was glistening white from hull to hurricane deck. Around each deck was an ornamental railing of fretwork filigree, and the spark arresters at the top of the stacks were shaped like giant acanthus leaves and painted gold. The wheelhouses that jutted out from either side of the hull displayed the boat's name, in gold-leaf letters fully six feet high, and above the name a painting of an ancient Greek galley, the first *Argo*, embarked on the quest for the Golden Fleece. The man who had done those paintings had since left St. Louis for Paris, where his canvases of buffalo hunts and Indian encampments were the talk of the boulevards; according to the newspapers, one had even been bought for the collection of the Emperor.

A faint breeze stirred, and thunder grumbled in the distance. The boat's burgee, a long triangular flag with her name in red on white, flapped limply at the top of the jackstaff and told the waterfront that the *Argo* meant to leave that day. Jason edged through the tangle of wagons waiting to put cargo aboard and reminded himself to tell Starbuck, the first mate, to clear a path for the passengers, who provided most of the boat's profits. He was careful never to interfere with the operation of the boat when she was under way, but tied up at the levee, she was more a business than a steamer—and he ran the business himself.

In an alcove off Jason's sleeping cabin was a big copper hip bath, but he had no time for that. Stripping off his sweat-soaked clothes, he lathered himself, then stood patiently while his manservant Francis sluiced him down with cool water. A fresh ruffled shirt and a suit of white linen were laid out on the bed for him. On a steamboat, with its constant shower of cinders and black wood ash, wearing white was an extravagance, but one that made a statement about his position in the world. It went with the diamond stickpin that winked from his shirt front and the engraved gold cigar case in his coat pocket.

Refurbished and refreshed, he stepped out onto the gallery that ran around the perimeter of the texas deck. Leaning on the mahogony railing, he looked down at the bustle on the levee. The trickle of passengers was becoming a stream. As four o'clock approached, it would become a flood, or so he hoped. He lit a long thin cheroot, fanned the smoke away with a languid hand, and gazed idly at the western sky, where a dark thunderhead towered. Lightning sparkled in its folds as it moved slowly toward the city. Already a peculiar yellow light was altering the look of everything and beginning to work on the spirits of the people who thronged the levee. The teamsters shouted less and glanced uneasily over their shoulders at the immense stormcloud, while the black stevedores rolled their eyes in superstitious dread of the uncanny atmosphere.

"I hope it holds off 'til we're on our way," a voice said, "else some of our high-stakes fellows might decide to stay snug in their rooms at the St. Charles for another night or two."

"It'll hold off," Jason replied without turning. His younger brother Augustus was about the only person in the world he really cared about. He would know Gus's voice even amid the shouts of an excited crowd at a close horse race. "Look at them now, think a little rain would faze them?"

He waved his cheroot in the direction of a hired carriage just pulling up on the roadway. Its passengers were both middle-aged, with bodies that showed the effects of years of eating well. The rear-facing seat was piled high with cases and boxes of pigskin with gold mountings. A knot of waterfront idlers, scenting money to be made, crowded forward to offer their services, but the coachman drove them back with a few well-placed flicks of his whip, then stretched around to take a glittering coin from one of his fares.

"They'll eat double portions of every delicacy we have on board," Jason continued, "but they'll drop twenty times the cost of their food at the roulette and poker tables and brag about their losses for the next three months."

Gus chuckled. "To their friends, maybe; but they'll tell their wives they came out ahead. I recognize the one in the high hat, by the way. He's a railway promoter out of Chicago, name of Lionel Hornby. Said to be close with Vanderbilt's crowd. Reckon he won't miss whatever he loses at the tables, if that's the case. I wonder if he had anything to do with that bridge at Rock Island."

Jason knew what Gus was referring to. Steamboaters up and down the river had been talking for months about the railroad bridge being built across the Mississippi from Rock Island, Illinois, to Davenport, Iowa. Its five spans, at the foot of the rapids, were to provide the link between the East and the newly opened settlements of the Great Plains. In April the first train had rumbled across the completed bridge. Two weeks later, the packet *Effie Afton* was caught by a swirling eddy and hurled against one of the bridge's timber piers. The steamboat caught fire, and soon the flames spread to the wooden bridge. On the river, the news was met with unconcealed glee. The general sentiment was that the destruction of that damned bridge would have been worth the loss of three or four boats.

"If he did have any part of it," Jason replied, "he would be wise not to boast of it. He might find himself taking an unexpected lesson in swimming. Do you know the other man?"

Gus shook his head. "No, but there's a face I know. That's Senator Stephenson. The tall red-faced man with the white hair, over next to that dray. That's a pretty girl on his arm, isn't it? His daughter, I suppose."

Jason glanced in the direction his brother indicated, then looked more closely. Part of his skill at the card table lay in his trained ability to notice the subtle changes in an opponent's posture and understand their meaning. The tilt of a head, the set of the shoulders, the tightness with which a man held his cards—all of these carried messages to someone who could read them. That first glance had told him that the senator was in a stew about something and trying to hide it. And the girl, to Jason's eye, looked nearly scared to death, though Gus didn't seem to have noticed.

Why was Stephenson standing around in the midst of the hubbub, instead of taking the girl to her stateroom? He could be waiting to see that his luggage arrived safely, but then wouldn't he be looking at the arriving traffic? Instead, he seemed to be studying the lines of the *General Monroe*, which was tied up just west of the *Argo*. Twice some roustabouts who were unloading a dozen heavy crates from the dray nearly collided with him, but he barely noticed them. Nor did he seem to hear when his young companion spoke to him.

He simply stood there, like a piling, and let the traffic of the wharf flow around him.

The more Jason examined the scene below, the odder it became. Senator Stephenson and his young lady were not the only ones acting peculiarly. There was the young man with muttonchop whiskers who was leaning with folded arms against a stack of cotton bales and staring fixedly at . . . the senator? the girl? From his vantage point, Jason couldn't tell which. And was there some understanding between Stephenson and the man with a scarred cheek who was overseeing the unloading of the dray? Several times their eyes seemed to meet, but they didn't speak.

As the last of the wooden crates was dragged from the dray and carried aboard, the man with the scar walked toward the senator and said something in an undertone. The girl shrank back, almost hid behind her escort like a small child confronted by a stranger. The scarred man must have noticed, because even from a distance Jason saw his neck redden, but he chose to ignore it by turning abruptly away from them and striding up the stage onto the boat. A few moments later, Stephenson and the girl followed. The young man with the muttonchops was a few paces behind them.

"Gus, the man with a slashed cheek and that lad with the whiskers—find out, and tell me tonight. Oh, and the girl with the senator, who is she?"

"Right," said Gus. His unofficial role on the *Argo* was peacekeeper and troubleshooter. He had an eye for both live ones and fakers. If he said to accept a man's i.o.u., Jason accepted it, whatever his own doubts; and if he said not to, it didn't matter how impressive the man's credentials might look, he got no credit from Jason. It hadn't always been that way. When Jason first bought the steamer and brought his brother out to help him, he went against Gus's advice several times, and always with what seemed to be excellent reasons. On the wall of his office he kept a reminder of one of those occasions: a letter of credit for £1000, drawn on the Rothschild Bank in London, properly countersigned by Sir Robert Chapman. Forged, of course, and utterly worthless, just as Gus had warned him it would be. Gus had also managed to hunt down 'Chapman' on the boat's next call at St. Louis, but he found the English confidence man in a miserable state. Addicted to the game of faro, he had bucked the tiger' once too often and lost everything. Even his fine Savile Row clothes, so essential to his profession, were at the pawn shop. Gus, instead of giving him a beating as he had meant to, took him around the corner and stood him a drink. Jason had laughed at him, but the laughter contained both affection and respect.

Now Gus took a close look at each of the passengers Jason had pointed out. The one in the lead, with the scar, looked slightly familiar. "Right," he repeated. "I'll bring you whatever I have after supper. I'll have the list by then, too, and we can go over it together."

As his brother turned to go, Jason felt the air stir coolly against his damp forehead, then become still again. A few fat raindrops hit the wooden deck above him like isolated taps of a snare drum. Below, on the bank, tiny craters appeared here and there in the thick dust. The passengers, arriving now in a gathering stream, glanced upward, then pressed on more hurriedly.

At the top of the levee, Elizabeth Brigham paused to turn her eyes back toward the Garden District. Twenty blocks of houses stood in her way, but in her mind she saw the little pink cottage on Third Street, just off Prytania. It was the only home she had ever known.

On a warm spring afternoon like this, she would have been seated on the raised gallery that encircled the house, embroidering a handkerchief or reading the latest novel by Mr. Dickens. The air, cooled by the screening palms and live oaks and scented by a dozen sorts of flowering shrubs, was more pleasant there than anywhere in town, to her mind. Her father had often said the same. About now she would start listening for the sound of his horse, carrying him home from the Custom House. She was always there to greet him when he dismounted.

The scene before her blurred. She groped in her reticule for one of those handkerchiefs she had spent so many idle, memorable hours over. It was not likely that she would be doing much fine needlework in the wilds of Kansas.

"Durn it, Liz, will you come along!"

Her brother's voice broke in on her sad memories. She furtively dabbed at her cheeks and eyes, then turned to him. "I was just remembering, Charlie," she said. "We may never see New Orleans again, you know. I wanted to treasure up the sight."

He didn't seem to hear. "First you rush me about until I can't think straight, and then you start dawdling like this. Come on now; people are start-

ing to look at us queerly. Do you think I want
them saying I've got a sister who's touched in the
head?''

Without waiting for an answer, he stalked away
in the direction of the boarding stage of the *Argo*.
After a last glance southward across the rooftops,
Elizabeth followed him. As she stepped onto the
plank ramp, she looked up and met the eye of a
tall man dressed in dazzling white who was leaning on the railing of the texas deck to watch the
scene on the levee. Something in his gaze, an air
of supercilious amusement, made her angry. She
tightened her lips, then blushed when he bowed
gravely in her direction. Lowering her head to
place the brim of her bonnet between them, she
hurried off after Charlie.

Four o'clock.

The big brass bell set up a nerve-frazzling din.
Below, the stokers flung fat pine logs into the
roaring furnaces, then followed with shovel-loads
of powdered resin. The flames leapt up fiercely.
Skeins of thick black smoke billowed from the tall
stacks. Rousters and stevedores broke into a trot,
hurrying to get the last of the cargo aboard before
the twin stages were raised.

Samuel Bowles, the pilot, strolled along an elegant corridor, paused to shoot a stream of brown
tobacco juice at a nearby spittoon, and mounted
the stairway to the upper deck. He was the most
important person on the boat. He knew it, and he
knew that Captain Clement and Mr. Lowell knew
it. It was his job to be familiar with every sandbar,
snag, and shallow, with every sunken log lurking

to tear the bottom out of a steamboat, between New Orleans and St. Louis. On a starless night, in thick fog or driving rain, one glance told him where he was and how to steer. He and his kind were the idols of every boy between St. Paul and the Gulf.

The pilothouse reflected his dignity. Perched atop the highest deck of the boat, its wide plate-glass windows, blue roof with gilt filigree lightning-rod, and carved mahogany nameboards told the passing world that this was the place of command, the seat of power. He entered easily and climbed up to his high leather bench, glanced around, and let loose with another stream of tobacco juice.

"Afternoon, Mr. Bowles."

"Afternoon, Cap'n."

Captain Clement made an elaborate show of consulting his watch. "Shall we proceed, Mr. Bowles?"

The pilot nodded regally and spat once more. "As you wish, Cap'n." He turned to a scared-looking boy in his late teens who was trying to hide in the corner. "Jem, you take the wheel. Lively, boy! You'll never make a pilot if you can't look sharp."

The captain was out on the deck, shouting orders down to the men on the bow. First one, then the other long landing stage was hoisted up to vertical and made fast. The two thick hawsers that secured the steamboat to the levee were slipped from the bollards and tossed aboard.

"Set her back on the starboard. Now the larboard." Bowles spoke quickly but calmly, and his orders were relayed by the bells to the engineer three decks below. Valves were turned and levers thrown; steam expanded in the giant cylinders and pushed against the pistons with the might of a thousand horses; and the great paddle wheels, fully forty feet in diameter, began to turn. Slowly at first, then with quickening pace, the long white craft slipped out into the river. As the current caught the stern, she began to curve downstream. "Stop the starboard; now come ahead slow. Stop the larboard. Now, young Jem, when we go ahead, you shave those boats as close as you'd shave your chin on your wedding day. All ahead forward, full steam!"

He reached up and pulled the wooden handle just above his head, then flinched as the mighty whistle of the *Argo* cut loose a blast that could be heard on Lake Pontchartrain. From the hurricane deck of the *Governor Morris*, a bunch of men whistled back derisively and made impolite gestures. Bowles ignored them, but his apprentice, unnerved by the closeness of the boats he was passing, steered a trifle farther out toward the center of the river.

The pilot noticed at once. "Shave them, I said," he cried, and took the wheel. "Like this." Jem watched in terror as the *Argo* passed within a few feet of the moored steamboats. "It's the current," Bowles finally explained. "The easy water's close ashore and the current's outside, so we hug the bank going upstream and stay well out coming down. Now take the wheel, and *shave those boats!*"

Jason watched the departure from the texas deck.

Once the long line of tied-up steamboats dropped astern and the *Argo* was well on its way, he went back to the purser's office. His path took him through the Ladies' Cabin and the Grand Saloon, and his appearance started a number of conversations.

"See that?" a hardware dealer from Natchez said to his neighbor, a drummer in dry goods from Chicago. "That there's Jason Lowell, who owns this boat. One hell of a card player, and as cold as a well-digger's ass."

"Lowell, huh? Any relation to all those rich Lowells back East?"

"What do *you* think? The story I heard is that he was raised in the lap of luxury, sent to Harvard College and all, but he couldn't keep himself away from the poker table. Finally his sorrowing family sent him out here and put up the money for this here steamboat on condition that he never show his face in Boston again."

"I'll be—" the drummer said, watching Jason's retreating back. "What they call a black sheep, huh? Maybe I'll try to get into a game with him before St. Louis. I admire a man who's dedicated to poker."

Jason overheard a snatch of the conversation as he passed, enough to let him guess the rest. Its only visible effect was to make the glint in his eye and the slight twist of his mouth more ironical. He had heard the stories before, had even helped them along by occasionally quoting Ralph Waldo Emerson in a manner that hinted at years spent in Concord, Mass., at the sage's feet. It gave people a thrill to play cards with an aristocratic ne'er-do-well, and anything that encouraged people to play cards was fine with Jason.

Only he and Gus knew the truth, and Gus was too young to remember the worst years. Jason remembered them only too well.

CHAPTER THREE

By standing on his tiptoes, the boy could just see over the window sill into the saloon. The interior was dim, except for a small area to his left where two oil lamps cast a flickering light. He gasped. On the table near the lamps was a box of highly polished wood, with a painting on its lid: a Royal Bengal tiger—long, lithe, and powerful, with its haunches coiled to leap. He had never seen anything so beautiful. It reminded him of stories his mother had told, stories of chests full of magical treasure. Surely no one would dare to put anything less than treasure in a box like that.

Reluctantly he pulled his eyes away from the wondrous box and looked around the saloon for his father. He was at the bar, talking to a stranger, making broad gestures with his arms. The boy's mood darkened; he knew the signs. As he watched, his father slapped a hand against the pocket of his vest, then reached for the bottle waiting on the bar. The stranger covered his glass, refusing to accept the offered drink, and crossed the room to the brightly lit table. He was a short man, thick through the middle, and his black suit, cut a little oddly, flared out from the waist like a skirt. His boots, worn outside his trousers, reached almost to his knees, and the brim of his hat was wider than any the boy had seen before. For a little town in southern Ohio, he was only slightly less exotic than a Barbary pirate would have been, pantaloons, scimitar, and all.

The stranger was unfastening the clasps of the box. The boy scrabbled his bare feet against the rough stone wall and found a toehold. His new perspective let him see the man lift the lid with its remarkable decoration and draw out a large sheet of enameled oilcloth. Unfolded, it displayed two rows of playing cards and another dramatic tiger. After spreading it on the table, he added a frame with wire-strung beads, several stacks of ivory rectangles the size of dominoes, and a brass box with an open top.

"Gentlemen," he said in a peculiar accent, "the bank is now open for business. Who among you is ready to buck the tiger?"

The boy's father crossed the room with glass in one hand and bottle in the other. His face was already flushed. Setting the bottle down, he drew some coins from his vest pocket and exchanged them for a stack of the ivory counters, which he placed at different spots on the oilcloth layout. Other men did the same. The stranger produced a deck of cards from his box, shuffled it, and placed it face-up inside the brass frame.

"The soda's a seven, gents, seven is dead." He drew out the top card, put it to one side, and drew out the next, continuing his commentary. "And the first loser is jack, and four wins on the first turn. Deuce loses, and deuce wins—a split, gentlemen, and so early in the game, too. The lady loses, and eight's a winner. . . ."

With some of the cards the stranger put more chips down on the layout, and with others he picked some up. The boy was unable to figure out the rules of the game, but before long he understood one thing about it: his father was losing heavily. When his chips were gone, he handed over more coins, accepted the new stack of ivory, and refilled his glass. Both the whiskey and the chips were gone in a few minutes.

Duty and fear wrestled for the boy's spirit, and in the end duty won. His mother had told him to fetch his father home, no matter what. He had already put it off much longer than he should have. He jumped lightly to the ground and padded around to the front of the saloon. No one challenged or even noticed his entrance; they were all held by the game of faro. He crossed the room and stopped just behind his father, who was fumbling through his pockets.

"I'll have to play on credit," he was saying. "I meant to bring more cash, but I must have forgotten. You don't need to fear for the money, I'm a well-known man in town and own my own store. I'll take ten dollars more."

The boy bit his lip to keep from crying out. Ten dollars was as much as most men made in a month!

"I'm sorry, sir," the stranger said smoothly. "I

told you at the beginning that this is strictly a cash game.''

"But I have the cash! I forgot to bring it, that's all!''

"Then maybe you'd best go to your store and get it. I reckon the game will go on a while without you.''

The other players laughed, not kindly.

The boy reached up and tugged at his father's coat.

"You! What are you doing here? Go home!''

The boy flinched at his tone, but said, "Momma told me to bring you home to supper.''

"Go home, I say! I'll come when I'm good and ready.'' He gave the boy a shove, perhaps harder than he meant to. The boy landed painfully on his bottom and let out a ludicrous squeal.

From the floor, he met the eyes of the stranger, and thought he saw sympathy there. But the other men, his own fellow-townspeople, were laughing at him. The sound enraged him. Jumping to his feet, he yelled, "Momma told me that men who drink and gamble at cards will be damned straightway and burn in Hell forever! And I hope it's true!''

"Sass me, will you, you little bastard! I'll learn you manners!'' The backhand blow caught him just under the right ear and lifted him off his feet. A table leg stopped his career across the floor. The next he knew, Jack Scott, who cut firewood for the steamboats, was bending over him, wiping his face with a wet, smelly rag.

"He's coming around now,'' Scott said. "You

hit him awful hard, though. I'll tell you, you keep that up and you'll kill him sure enough.''

"So what?" his father growled. "He's mine, ain't he? Didn't I give him the gift of life? Hain't I fed and clothed him for ten long years?''

The words were slow and slurred. The boy had trouble understanding them. He sat up on his elbows, wishing that the roaring in his head would go away. His cheeks were wet, but he knew that if he cried aloud, the response would be a kick in the side. Added to the pain in his head, and in the shoulder that had struck the table leg, was that in the spot on the lower lip he was biting to help keep himself silent.

His father was leaning heavily on the table now, staring at the stranger from a distance of only inches. Oily beads of sweat dotted his forehead. "Here,'' he said suddenly, "I'll tell you. Give me ten dollars in chips, and you can have the brat.''

"Me?" the man scoffed. "What would I do with a boy?''

"Work him to death or drown him; I don't give a damn. But give me the chips. Give me the chance to get even. My luck's been bad all night, but it's turning now. I can feel it. I feel it, I tell you!''

He lurched forward, tipping the table. Ivory chips clattered on the floor. One of the players caught a lamp just as it started to fall.

The other men, whose game was being spoiled by the ruckus, grabbed the boy's father, dragged him unresisting to the door, and tossed him into the dust of the street.

The boy, still lying on the floor, looked once

more at the stranger. This time he could not mistake the sympathy in the gambler's face. Silently
the boy swore an oath to himself: the next time his
father struck him, he would wait until he was
asleep, load the varmint gun, and blow his head
off. He didn't resent the blows; after all, the Bible
preached that parents had a duty to beat their
children. But his father had shamed him in front of
the stranger, and that he could never forgive him
for.

Outside, his father was crumpled against the
wall, snoring noisily. He tried to wake him, then
to lift him—both without success—so he gave up
and walked home. His mother was standing in the
doorway, lamp in hand, staring into the dark. She
got mad when he told her what had happened, but
not real deep-down mad. She only gave him half a
dozen switches across the legs, not too hard, and
sent him to his bed in the attic with no supper.
And a little later she came up the ladder with a
slab of cornbread and a slice of fatback for him.

The air was chilly. He bolted down the food and
burrowed back under the covers to search for the
warm spot he had left when he sat up, but his kid
brother had already taken it over. His jaw still
hurt, but not enough to keep him awake. As he
drifted off, he saw that splendid tiger again, but
this time it was alive, sidling through tall grass
with its long tail swishing from side to side. It
turned its head to look at him, and it seemed to the
boy that its eyes were the eyes of the stranger,
fierce, but somehow understanding.

The pounding on the door woke him. He crept
to the edge of the attic floor and peered down. His

mother, blanket-wrapped, was talking in a low voice to someone he couldn't see. She stiffened, then stepped back to open the door wide.

"You'd best bring him in," she said in a louder tone. "I can do what's needful. The Lord giveth and the Lord taketh away; blessed be the name of the Lord."

Jack Scott and another man came in, carrying a long bundle that dripped on the floor. They set it carefully on the bench near the fireplace and stepped back. The woman bent over and pulled aside the concealing cloth. From above, the boy stared in horrified fascination at the unblinking eyes of his father. One arm flopped limply toward the floor, but his mother lifted it and crossed it on the sodden chest, then did the same with the other.

"How did it happen?" she asked grimly.

"Don't rightly know, ma'am," said Scott. "I was going home and I heard a splash from the direction of Scotch Creek. Tom and me, we hurried over and looked around, but we didn't have a light, so it took us some little while to find him. He wasn't breathing when we fetched him out. I figure he must have missed his step on the footbridge and maybe hit his head when he fell. I'm sorry to be the one to bring you bad news like this. If you like, I'll send my woman over to give you a hand."

"No, thank you. I'll lay him out myself. It's my duty as a wife. But if you'd pass a word to Mr. Bowring about this, I'd appreciate it. I reckon he can come by in the morning it he needs measurements."

After some foot-shuffling and muttered expres-

sions of sympathy, the two men left. The boy
ducked his head back as his mother stood with her
back against the door and looked around the little
house, then disappeared into the kitchen. Moments
later she was beside the bench again. She set a pail
of water near the fire and started undressing the
corpse. She had a difficult time of it, disentangling
water-logged clothes from uncooperative limbs, but
finally she was done.

Taking a rag from the pail, she began to wash
the body. The boy watched intently. He had seldom seen his father naked, and he was amazed to
see how insignificant he looked. His mother handled him with the same matter-of-fact care she
would have used scalding a freshly slaughtered pig.
Ice gathered in the pit of the boy's stomach. He
wanted to cry out, to protest, but an unformed fear
clamped his tongue—a fear that he would be laid
out beside his father. Shivering, he crawled back
to bed and wrapped himself around his sound-
sleeping brother. Through the darkness, the eyes
still stared at him, but he refused to meet them,
and in time he slept.

A number of townspeople came by the house
after the funeral to pay their respects. Some, those
who had small accounts outstanding at the store,
brought food—a ham, pans of cornbread, even a
pie made with the last of the winter apples. When
they left, Lawyer Bascom stayed behind. He was
the richest man in town, and he sat for it in the
state legislature. Now he was sitting in the good
chair, clasping his hands in front of his ample
paunch. His fingers were white and pudgy. They

reminded the boy of a drowned man he had once seen after a steamboat explosion.

"Well, ma'am," the lawyer began, "have you given thought to the future?"

"The Lord will provide."

"I certainly hope so, for it is certain sure that your man didn't. I mean no disrespect of the dead, ma'am, but the only thing he was worse at than keeping a store was playing a hand of cards. Do you have folks to turn to?"

"My brother and his family are at Cincinnati. Are we . . . Will there be anything left?"

Bascom hesitated, looked away. "Oh well, I reckon even after the bills are settled, there'll be your fares to Cincinnati and something over to help set you up. Yes, I think I can promise you that."

She knew that he was lying, that whatever sum he gave her would be from his own pocket. She supposed that properly she should refuse the charity, but she knew that she did not have enough courage to do so. If she had had only herself to think of . . . But there were her sons. "I'm glad to hear that," she said, looking down at her boots. "I'll write to my brother tonight, to warn him that we're coming."

The boy, forgotten in a corner behind the dresser, heard this with both excitement and dismay. The prospect of traveling all the way downriver to Cincinnati on a real steamboat was so grand that he had trouble catching his breath. But Cincinnati also meant his cousin Harry. Harry, two years older than he, was a bully and a sneak. The last time he had come on a visit, he had gotten mud and dung all over the boy's Sunday suit, then threatened to pinch his earlobes if he told.

After a sample, the boy had decided that a whipping from his mom was easier to take, but it left him with a fierce hatred of the bigger boy, all the fiercer because he didn't dare let it be seen. Now, listening to his mother talking to Lawyer Bascom, he made another vow: that before he went to live under the same roof as Harry, he would throw himself in the river. What did a few moments of swallowing water matter, compared to endless months and years of misery?

It took three weeks to wrap up the affairs of the store and to get a reply from Cincinnati. One day, when he came home from helping Jack Scott stack cordwood, the boy found his mother sitting on the floor gazing into the bed of coals in the fireplace. Near her right hand was a neatly folded letter. He looked at it in fright, remembering his vow.

"Is something the matter, Momma?"

She looked up and tried to smile. "No, pet, nothing. I was thinking, that's all. About you, and how fast you're growing up. Why, you're nearly a man already, aren't you?"

"Today I carried three logs at a time. That's pretty good, isn't it. But they weren't very big ones," he added. "Not like what Jack carries."

"That's very good, and I'm proud of you. I think it's time we started to look for a trade for you. What would you say to helping Mr. Scott in his wood yard all the time?"

A rush of thoughts swept through the boy's mind and collided with each other. To be a man, with a job and wages of his own, was something, and to be free of the specter of Cousin Harry was even more, but if it meant parting from his mother and little brother, and missing a steamboat trip to Cincinnati? Where would he live? Who would stroke his forehead if he caught the fever?

And behind these thoughts were others, less formed, too complex perhaps for him to shape into words, but powerful nonetheless. His father had been a failure, and failure had killed him. He had never taken the trouble to learn to do anything well. He had come to rest in a small river town much as a water-logged elm trunk might come to rest on a sand bank. The drunkenness and gambling and brutality were the signs of a decay that set in long before the process was completed by the eight inches of water in Scotch Creek.

The boy was determined that he would not go that way. He meant to make something of himself. He knew he was pretty smart and willing to put in hard work, but beyond that he sensed a calling, a destiny far wider than haggling with steamer captains over the price of firewood. He was going to go far, to see the world, to set his mark on it—but when? how?

The answer did not lie in the woodyard, or anywhere in the village. He was sure of that. But Cincinnati was a big, important place, a good place to look for one's destiny, even if it meant putting up with Harry.

"Can't I go with you instead? I think I'd like that better."

Her hand reached out to touch the folded letter and returned to her lap. "I'm afraid not. Your uncle writes that he has room only for me and your little brother. In a little while, when I've gotten on my feet again, I'll send for you, but you should be very grateful that Mr. Scott is willing to take you in and give you work. It's a kindness on his part.''

''I don't want his kindness! I don't want to stay here! I don't want you to go away!''

She stood up abruptly and turned away. ''It is not for us to question or dispute God's ways,'' she said in a flat voice. ''You will go to Mr. Scott's home tomorrow, as soon as you've helped get our things down to the landing.''

''Momma!'' he wailed, and hurled himself at her.

She turned to clasp him in her arms. ''There, pet, there,'' she murmured. ''I'm sorry as can be, but there's no helping it. We must face our trials bravely and trust in the Lord. It's only for a little while.''

''It's not,'' he sobbed. ''I'll never see you again!''

''Stuff and nonsense! We'll be together in Cincinnati before you know it!''

But the next day, as he stood on the bank watching the *Laura Webster* disappear around the bend, he knew that he was seeing the last of his family and his childhood.

Jack Scott's kindness took the form of stuffing the boy with food at every meal, although the constant toil of cutting and moving wood kept him from getting pudgy. By the start of summer, he was two inches taller and strong enough to toss a four-foot log onto the top layer of a cord. There was excitement enough, too, waking in the middle of the night to the whistle of a steamboat that needed to wood up. He would rush to help the deckhands pass the firelogs aboard, then watch the boat fade into a line of white foam and twin trails of orange sparks from the tall chimneys.

At those moments, he remembered. His life was passing him by. His destiny was receding from him. He was nearly eleven years old, and he was stuck in a woodyard in a backwater village. Worse, he was beginning to believe that there was nothing else, to forget his conviction that he was meant for higher things. The walls were starting to close in.

But those thoughts came only at night. By day he was a cheerful and willing helper, always ready to smile at a joke or dodge a playful cuff. When he wasn't working, he fished and swam and robbed birds' nests, or lay belly-down on the bank and watched the river flow by. Once he swam out to a passing keelboat and hitched a ride downriver, then spent most of the night finding his way back. Jack had whipped him for that, more to persuade him not to do it again than as punishment for having done it the once.

His mother wrote him twice. Both times she spoke of her brother's kindness and her own gratitude to him, and of the trials of a poor widow in a strange city, and she urged him to be a good boy and a good worker and to remember his master in his prayers every night. Nothing was said of his coming to Cincinnati. She seemed to feel that she had settled him and given him a wonderful start in life. Certainly she gave no sign of knowing that he felt cast out and abandoned. The effect of that silence, whatever its cause, was to magnify those feelings unbearably.

The crisis came two days after the second letter.

Over breakfast Jack described an idea he had had, which was to raise the boy's wages by a few cents a day, but also to hold back the increase and put it toward buying a share of the woodyard. "Why, in five or ten years you'll practically be a partner," he enthused. "Just about the time you'll be thinking of settling down with some pretty little girl, I reckon. What do you say to that, hey?"

He choked out some words of thanks. After the meal he vanished to his secret place, a tiny clearing in the heart of a bramble, high above the river. Five years? Ten years? He felt himself sinking into deep, clinging mud. In moments it would reach his face and he would die, though his form might go on cutting wood and piling it by the landing for five years or ten years, or forty years.

No! Once again he swore an oath, a very particular, especially binding oath, to go out into the world before it was too late for him. Somewhere out there, beyond the marshes and forests that encircled the village, his destiny was waiting.

Whee-oop! Whee-oop! From upriver, the demanding whistle of a steamer sounded twice, frightening a flock of waterfowl into flight. He sprang to his feet, swung around the outer edge of the bramble on a handy limb, and set off for the woodyard at a trot. The boat, a small sidewheeler, was already nosing toward the bank. Half a dozen rousters stood in the bow, ready to jump ashore and pass the wood aboard.

Jack emerged from the forest, his felling axe on his shoulder, and gave a shout. "Morning, Cap'n! What do you need?"

"Five cords if it's hard and dry, seven if it's not," the captain shouted back. "How much?"

"All hardwood, dry as a bone, and only two-fifty the cord."

"Two-fifty!" The captain grabbed the cap from his head and flung it to the deck. "You iron-jawed, brass-mounted, copper-bellied old grave-robber, I'll see you in hell and this boat at the bottom of the Kanawha before I give you a cent over two dollars!"

Jack stood silently, arms folded. He had been through this exchange a hundred times. Two-fifty was a fair price, and the next woodyard was nearly an hour downstream. He could afford to wait out the captain's stream of colorful abuse, which was now touching on his ancestors, his appearance, his companions, and his peculiar practices with sheep, goats, and chickens. The captain was warming to his subject, no question, but Jack had known keelboatmen who could give him a half-hour's start and still talk him to a standstill.

Some of the passengers had come out on deck to watch the fun and cheer on the captain. One of them caught the boy's attention. He moved closer, shaded his eyes with his hand. In his mind he heard the distant growl of a tiger on the hunt. It was, no doubt about it, the stranger with the wonderful wooden box that night his father died. The stranger looked around and met his gaze. For a moment something stirred in his face, then he glanced away.

At that moment the boy decided. It was a sign, the stranger turning up like that just when he had sworn to go forth and find his destiny! People in the Bible were always getting signs, and people in the tales his mother used to tell, so why shouldn't he? And the one thing he knew for certain was that it was the worst kind of luck to disregard a sign.

Jack and the captain concluded their bargain, as they both had known they would, and the rousters started carrying the wood on board. The boy pitched in, as always, and waited for his chance. A moment came when he was the only one near the growing woodpile behind the number-one boiler. Dropping the log, he scooted into a dark corner and made himself very tiny. Several sets of feet approached and then passed his hiding place, and once a heavy log thudded down inches away, but he made no sound. It seemed forever before the signal bells tinkled and the huge cylinders chuffed to life, but finally he heard the rhythmical splashes of the wheels and knew that he was on his way. Only then did he wonder if Jack would be mad at him for running away. He hoped not; Jack had always been nice to him.

He stayed in hiding all day, coming out only to snitch some cornbread and later to pee over the side of the boat. Once he judged it was dark enough, he started to explore. The only lights were coming from the two main cabins on the saloon deck. He crept up to a door and looked through the glass, to find the tiger of his memory and dreams only two feet away. The stranger was seated at a table, drawing cards from the brass box, just as he had that night, and four men were across from him, watching closely and placing their ivory squares on the oilcloth board.

No one looked up; no one noticed the small face pressed against the glass.

By shortly after midnight the last pigeon had lost his appetite for the game. Jonathan Curtis sorted the chips and stacked them in their compartments, added the cards, the shoe, and the casekeeper, then carefully folded the layout and placed it across the top before closing and clasping the mahogany box. He patted the tiger before picking up the box. In his leisure time he favored a good game of poker, but faro was his living.

The only light in his cabin came through the louvers at the top and bottom of the door. He set the faro box on the table and was about to take off his frock coat when he heard a rustling noise across the room. Quickly, silently, he put his hand to the back of his neck and drew the long, sharp dagger that lay hidden under his collar.

"Just hold it right there," he said quietly, "if you like wearing a whole skin."

With his free hand he pulled a packet of loco-foco matches from his pocket and lit the candle. Huddled in the far corner, staring at him white-faced, was a young boy in rough homespun. His face seemed familiar, but Curtis could not quite place it.

"Looking for something to steal, boy? I hope you swim well, because my way with thieves is to throw them in the river, and I wouldn't want your drowning on my conscience."

The boy opened his mouth; his throat moved convulsively. Finally he said, "Oh no, sir, I ain't no thief. I come here to go along with you. I want to learn your trade."

The gambler gave a snort of disbelief. "Go along with me? Come on, now, who put you up to this? Your pa?"

"Pa's dead. He drowned after he lost all the money to you. He never was much good at cards or anything."

Something stirred in Curtis's memory. "Around Christmas, was it? Sure, we passed the town today. You were loading wood; I saw you. Well, you'll have to work your way back. *I'm* not forking over for your fare."

"I'm not going back. I want to go with you."

"You can't, and that's flat."

"I want to learn how you deal the cards you want to, and make two of the same come up in a row, and pull two out at a time without anyone seeing."

Curtis stiffened, alerted by the scent of danger. Was someone listening at the door, waiting to hear him admit that he had gaffed the game? Plenty of professionals before him had vanished off a steamboat in the night, some to escape with their victims' losses, and some to become fish food. "I can't figure where you heard about stuff like that," he said cautiously. "I deal a square game; everybody knows that."

"But I saw you!" the boy protested. "I was out on deck, watching through the door. You were awful good at it. I knew you would be."

"Keep your voice down!" Something in the boy's face, the open, unfeigned admiration, convinced Curtis. "What makes you think I want a boy along?"

"I could be awful handy. I could carry your

He had always intended to set something aside, to make some provision for his two children, but he'd generally put it off in favor of more immediate expenses. Then, one day, when he climbed down into the hold of a coasting schooner out of South America, a poisonous serpent struck his calf. He swelled up, turned black, and died before sunset.

They had to sell the house on Third Street, of course. What remained after paying their father's debts would not have supported two young people for very long in a luxurious city like New Orleans. Family friends had offered Charlie clerkships in a bank, a shipping company, and a marine insurance firm, but each time he'd put off his decision until it was too late. Liz had an impression, which she quickly banished as pure fantasy, that he somehow found the offers insulting. That was impossible, for what could he expect? He had never much taken to school, and he certainly had no experience in business. Perhaps he had sensed that the offers were rooted in charity and had declined out of a very proper pride.

A sudden lull in the chattering around her drew Liz back to the present. She looked up and saw the man in white who had caught her attention as she boarded the boat. Seen up close, he was not nearly so tall as she had thought, but he crossed the Ladies' Cabin with the air of the Grand Turk visiting one of his lesser harems. She watched furtively, with an interest that she found somewhat shameful.

She had already discovered, from an overheard comment, who he was: Jason Lowell, the notorious gambler. That was part of the fascination. In the system of values she had been taught, gentlemen might gamble for amusement, and generally did, but only riffraff and scum gambled for a living. Yet Lowell certainly did not appear to be scum. In fact, he had the look of a fine, if haughty, gentleman. She had often read about the glamour that highwaymen in olden days had cast over their noble victims; now she felt that she was near to understanding it.

He glanced down as he strode past her divan. In the instant before she lowered her eyes, he appeared to sense the direction of her thoughts and find it amusing. His expression seemed to invite her to join him in laughing at such silly conventions. She felt her cheeks and forehead grow quite warm. She was very glad when he continued across the cabin and out the door to the promenade.

The moment he left, the buzz of conversation swelled to new levels.

Elizabeth looked over at the clock. It was nearly six, and where was Charlie? They had not actually made any arrangements to meet, but naturally he would come to take her in to supper. The menu suggested that it would be a very formal and elegant occasion, and she was not sure that she could face it unsupported. When she looked around the Ladies' Cabin, though, she had to wonder. Some of her fellow passengers looked as out of place as a billy goat at the bishop's garden party.

The door at the far end opened and a steward in a white jacket rang a brass handbell. Everyone rushed forward at once, and soon a crowd jammed the doorway. Liz waited for it to clear, looked

around once more for her brother, and then followed the others.

The dining saloon ran nearly the length of the
boat, with a single row of large round tables stretching down the center to infinity. Oil lamps, a dozen
to each hanging fixture, blazed; their light re-
bounded from tall gilt-framed mirrors, glinted off
polished silver and crystal, added depth to dazzling linens. Black waiters ran along the aisles
bearing huge platters and tureens.

Elizabeth stopped to one side of the doorway.
The scene dazed her—not only the scale of it,
though that was daunting enough, but its unreality.
Every seat was filled, every head bowed over its
plate, every jaw working at top speed. The only
sound in the gigantic hall was the shrill clatter of
silverware against china.

"Would you allow me to escort you to your
place, madam?"

The hint of mockery in the voice told her its
owner's identity even before she looked up. She
wanted to refuse, to reject his forwardness, but she
didn't quite dare. She needed help to get through
the ordeal of this meal, and the only person she
knew, the one who should have helped, was not to
be found.

"Thank you," she said simply, and rested her
hand lightly on his arm. She knew that people
were turning to look, but she avoided the curious
eyes by looking straight ahead. Her escort led her
down the entire length of the cabin to a small table
at the end set for six. Somewhere in the middle of
that long, almost stately walk, the faces of the
other diners had faded into a featureless mass. She

no longer cared what they might say or think. Let them think what they liked. At that moment there was only one man on the whole boat whose opinion she cared two pins about.

He held one of the vacant chairs for her, then bowed. "May I introduce myself, madam? Jason Lowell, at your service."

"How do you do. I am Elizabeth Brigham."

"Charmed." He bowed a second time. "Will you permit me to join you, Miss Brigham?"

The ridiculousness of the request made her smile. "Please do, Mr. Lowell. I believe this is your table. And your steamboat as well, I understand."

He smiled in reply. His teeth were remarkably white and even. They reminded her of the silent laughter of a fox. The image brought a flutter to her midsection, like a feather brushing across her skin.

Lowell introduced the others at the table: Captain and Mrs. Clement; Count de la Fevre, from France, who was looking over investment opportunities in cattle-raising; and Mrs. Beverley, the grande dame of a wealthy Memphis family. The Count and Mrs. Beverley were in the midst of a discussion about breeding racehorses. Lowell listened for a moment, then asked Captain Clement a question about recent changes in the course of the river. That set off a long explanation, full of references to Island 37 and cut-offs and rainbow reefs.

It seemed to Liz that theirs was the only table in the whole enormous room at which there was any conversation at all. Looking around, she understood why. The meal was being served boarding-house style. Each dish arrived on a single platter, from which the diners helped themselves. Anyone who stopped to talk risked getting less than his share of some delicacy or missing it entirely. The natural result was that everyone ate with the concentration, ferocity, and manners of a half-starved hog. She watched, appalled, as a well-dressed man at a nearby table ate a large piece of roast beef, then sucked the gravy from his fork and plunged it into a bowl of candied beets, only narrowly missing his neighbor's hand.

Lowell's voice broke into her thoughts. "Have you been on a visit to New Orleans, Miss Brigham?"

"No, sir. I lived in New Orleans for most of my life. My brother and I are on our way to live with our uncle, in Kansas."

"You must be saddened by leaving so fair a city for so wild a place." He seemed to notice her black gown and the jet beads at her neck for the first time. "A recent bereavement, I fear?"

"Yes, sir, my father."

"My sympathies," he said politely, but she thought that his voice hardened. After a short pause, he turned to the Count and began to discuss the rules of some nearly-forgotten card game. She sensed that he was rebuking her, but she could not imagine how she had offended him. Hurt flowed into anger, which in turn hardened into the conviction that he was no gentleman. Blinking away angry tears, she turned to Mrs. Clement and asked her about life on a steamboat. A few well-turned questions were enough to keep the captain's wife talking cheerfully for the rest of the meal.

Only once did she look at Jason Lowell again, when the time came for her and the other ladies to withdraw while the gentlemen smoked and drank and gambled. His bow was correct and his face was grave, but she retired to her stateroom convinced that he had been inwardly laughing at her.

She found Charlie waiting for her. The room stank of his cigar.

"I suppose you feel proud of yourself," he began.

"Charlie—"

"I don't know why it is that every time I get the chance to make something of myself, I get pulled down again. It's not right, that's all!"

"What do you mean, Charlie?" She crossed the room to where he was standing and put her hand on his shoulder, but he shrugged it off and turned away.

"What do I mean?" he said roughly. "I'll tell you what I mean all right. I mean you, parading up and down during supper hand in hand with a slick damned Yankee, that's what! But I suppose you don't care if folks, big important folks, take you for a loose woman. I don't suppose you thought how it would look or how it would reflect on me. I just wish you would think about me for a change, Lizzie. It's hard enough being an orphan, without my own sister bringing disgrace down on me." He sniffled once, loudly.

Elizabeth was silent, struggling to gain control of her emotions and her voice. "I don't think you're being very fair, Charlie," she said at last. "I did look for you, but you must have gone ahead without me. It was very kind of Mr. Lowell to find me a place, and I'm grateful to him."

"I waited 'til they rang the bell," he replied

sullenly, "but you had to be late. You got to be wide-awake on a boat like this, I tell you. If I hadn't gone on ahead without you, I wouldn't have gotten at the same table as Senator Stephenson."

"Senator Stephenson? Is he the big important folks who took me for a . . . what you said?"

The boy sniggered. "He used a different word, but I reckon the meaning was about the same."

"And what did you do when you heard him say such a vile thing about your own sister?"

"Do? Why, what do you think? I made as if I didn't know who you were, of course. I'm no fool." He paused, as if expecting her to congratulate him. "That's what I came to talk to you about. The Senator is a mighty 'cute man, with friends in a lot of places you wouldn't expect, and he seemed to kind of take a shine to me. But if you come around oh-Charlie-ing me, he's going to catch on pretty fast. Now you don't want to spoil my chances, do you?"

She made a low, incoherent noise.

Her brother persisted. "I don't suppose you'd do anything as low and selfish as that, would you, ruining a fellow's big opportunity to get ahead? Of course, you wouldn't. So you just keep away 'til we get to St. Louis. And keep away from that Yankee gambler, too."

Elizabeth could scarcely breathe with the pain. She felt as if she had been orphaned all over again. "Oh, Charlie," she cried softly.

"There! That's just the kind of thing I mean."

Shortly after supper Gus came to Jason's cabin with disturbing news.

''Pennyman tells me that three fresh decks were stolen from the bar sometime after we sailed.''

Jason's lips tightened to a thin line. The playing cards used aboard the *Argo* were specially made up by a reliable company in Philadelphia. The backs featured a steel engraving of an ancient Greek trireme, which was surrounded by a floral border almost as intricate as the borders on a dollar bill. Jason considered the cards almost impossible to imitate; that was the point.

The stewards had firm orders to collect all used decks at the end of the evening and throw them in the furnace. Jason was aware that passengers sometimes bribed a steward to pass a used deck to them, as a souvenir of their journey. He winked at the practice, as long as the cards were clearly used. But if someone took the trouble of stealing new, unopened decks, it could mean only one thing: he meant to gaff a game.

There were dozens of ways to do it. He might make tiny, almost imperceptible dots or scratches on important cards, or he might roughen pre-selected spots with emery dust. By shaving the sides or ends, he could count on finding the high cards in the deck. He might even find ways to alter the back design, to make the deck into 'readers.' Each time a particular method became widely known, other, more subtle tricks were devised. But all of them required the time, and privacy, to prepare the cards.

''Who is on board that we know?''

Gus shrugged. ''Knoxville Pete and his punk. The Major from Chicago. A couple of smaller sharks. No hard-time card mechanics that I recognize.''

Jason massaged his eyebrow with his thumb, a sure sign that he was worried. The success of the *Argo* rested partly on its reputation for square games. Of course, the passengers tried to cheat each other and the house, but the house played square. Let word get around that the play was dishonest, and the boat might as well be on the bottom of the river.

"Have you done anything yet?" he asked.

Gus was pouring himself a shot of whiskey. He turned and said, "No, I figured I'd bring it to you first."

"Good. If this fellow sees us watching, he'll just leave the rigged deck in his vest pocket or boot top until we ease up, then ring it into the game. I want to give him time to bring it into play; then, once I've spotted him, we can decide what to do with him."

"What he deserves is a swimming lesson."

"You know my feelings about that," Jason said sharply. "Violence is the favorite tool of cowards and fools. I have yet to come across a problem that couldn't be dealt with some better, smarter way, though I admit that the threat of violence is sometimes very useful, particularly when dealing with fools and cowards. They recognize the language."

"They damn well better," replied Gus. He was obviously unpersuaded. "But you're the boss. Do you want to go over the passenger list now?"

The *Argo* carried a maximum of 150 cabin passengers; the usual number was closer to 125. The six or eight hundred miserable immigrants who bought deck passage were of no interest to

Jason or anyone else. Gus had done his usual thorough job, concentrating on the men.

"First off, the young filly with Senator Stephenson isn't his daughter, the way I thought. Name's Melissa Wainwright, of the shipping family. Her maid says the Senator is her guardian, whatever that means." He scowled down at his notes. "Those fellows you asked me about. The one with the chopped-up mug is listed as Luke Shuttlesworth of Joplin. He booked his cabin at the same time as the Senator, but not next to him. The other one, with the moss on his face, is named Duncan Sargent. Talkative sort, hails from Boston, says he's writing a book about the Mississippi. His bags cost a lot but have seen a lot of use."

"Hm. Shuttlesworth . . ." Jason frowned into space. "Nope. Whatever it was, I lost it. All right, who else?"

"I pointed out Hornby to you. His friend is big in Chicago real estate, name of Asbury. No limit with them, I'd say. We've got another live one on board, too: Captain James Bolling. Owns a good deal of the Texas coast and thinks nothing of putting fifty acres of prime bottom land into a poker pot if he fancies his hand. The rest is the usual mixture of planters, merchants, and brokers, flush enough to enjoy a lively game if the stakes aren't too high. We'll do all right, I reckon, though nothing like that trip last fall."

He glanced pointedly at the large diamond, the 'headlight,' that sparkled on Jason's shirt front. It was a reminder of an evening that gradually turned into a personal battle between Jason and a rich sugar planter. They had begun with poker, moved on to all-fours, then to backgammon and *vingt-et-un*. Jason could have crooked the game at any point, but it was a matter of pride to him to play straight. The planter was good. By three in the morning, he had all Jason's cash. At his suggestion, they cut for high card, the stakes being Jason's diamond, which he'd taken a liking to, against the money Jason had already lost. Jason cut first, to the five of clubs. His heart sank. But then the planter cut to a trey. By the time the two exhausted men stumbled off to their cabins, Jason was ahead over six thousand dollars.

He was also in trouble with his brother. "You're the one who taught me that getting in too deep is the mark of a sucker," Gus had railed. "What if you'd lost the cut? What was your stake going to be then? The *Argo*?"

"I couldn't quit while he was ahead, Gus. It would have ruined my reputation. Half the people who ride this steamboat want to say they lost money to the famous gambler Jason Lowell. It's like going a few rounds bare-knuckle with the Jersey Chicken. But once the Chicken loses his championship title, he'll be forgotten before Christmas. He has to keep on winning to survive. So do I."

"No matter what?"

"No matter what. It's part of what they expect for their money."

Gus had not been convinced, but he knew when he had a chance of changing his brother's mind and when he didn't. This time he didn't. He dropped the argument, except for occasional little reminders. In any case, no player of the caliber of that sugar planter had come aboard the *Argo* since, so perhaps it didn't matter so much.

Jason ignored the jibe. "Let me see," he said, elaborately casual, "do you have someone named Brigham on your list?"

"Yup," said Gus, scanning his papers. "Two of 'em. One's a little piss-ant who thinks he's got the world by the tit, and the other's that fine-looking gal I saw you take in to supper." He laughed at his brother's confusion. "Their pa was an official with Customs, died a little bit ago. Can't have left them a whole lot, even if he had sticky hands. The piss-ant seems to be hanging around that Shuttlesworth fellow. Want me to keep an eye on him?"

"Um-hum." Jason poured himself a glass of claret. "And keep yourself handy about eleven tonight," he added. "I figure on spotting our would-be sharper by then."

"Right." Gus left and Jason unlocked his patent desk to bring the *Argo*'s accounts up to date. It was a task he refused to trust to anyone else.

By ten o'clock the Grand Saloon seemed almost austere—no laughter, no idle conversation, only the murmur of men engaged in serious occupations. Cigar smoke grayed the air and made the far end of the room look a dozen miles away. Little knots of men devoted themselves to roulette, chuck-a-luck, and *vingt-et-un*, but their numbers were tiny compared to those playing faro and poker. It was the younger men, those craving fast action and constant risk, who gathered under the tapestry tiger.

The true, mature worshippers of the goddess Chance found a place at one of the poker tables.

Jason took a slice of baked ham from the cold buffet and a glass of chilled hock from a passing steward, then began to stroll around the saloon. He returned bows and greetings, stopped now and then for a few words with an acquaintance, and seemed to take only the most casual interest in anything that was happening around him. In fact, he could have told, within very close limits, how each table was doing, who the big winners and losers were, and who was likely to make a ruckus if he ended up a loser. He could also have told which of his dealers—and there was one—was cheating both the passengers and the house. The whoreson would have the opportunity to try his skills on the rascals of Natchez-under-the-Hill come tomorrow afternoon.

It might have looked as though Jason was distributing his interest impartially among all the games, but he wasn't. Logic told him that the man who had stolen the decks was most likely playing poker. *Vingt-et-un* was a possibility too, but only if he had made the cards into distance readers. Since the deck stayed with the house dealer, shaving or spotting it would not have helped him at all. No, he was at one of the six poker tables. But which?

Jason tried to imagine how he himself would play it. The best situation would be a game with a couple of heavy bettors who were good players, but not as good as they thought, and acquaintances, perhaps, naturally inclined to compete with each other and to forget the stranger at their table. He would feed both of them good hands, fan the betting, and let them win, then put in the gaff. Each would get his best hand of the night and gradually put everything into the pot, hardly noticing the fellow across the table who was calling every raise. Then, lo and behold, the fellow turns out to be holding a hand that beats both of them, and rakes in the pot.

Did any of the tables fit his picture? He crossed off Table 6 at once; it was a friendly game for small stakes. The stakes were higher at 1 and 3, but the players seemed pretty evenly matched in both skill and funds. Gradually his attention focused on Table 2 and Table 5. The tycoons from Chicago, Hornby and Asbury, were facing each other across Table 2, tossing ten-dollar gold pieces into the center as if they were nickels. But which of the others might be the gaffer? He studied each player in turn, but without coming to any conclusion.

Temporarily thwarted, he turned to Table 5. He did not recognize any of the players, but two of them, middle-aged men sitting side by side, certainly had enough money to attract a crook and didn't seem shy about risking it. There seemed to be a friendly rivalry between them as well, judging by some of the jibes passing back and forth. He leaned against a nearby column, and though he appeared to be scanning the room, he was actually following the play at Table 5 closely.

Across the table from the two rivals sat a burly man with a bushy black beard, long black hair, a black cigar, and no forehead to speak of. After a number of hands, Jason realized that one of the rivals took the pot each time Blackie dealt. It wasn't evidence you would hang a dog on, but it was enough of a hint.

He strolled away, signaling Gus with his eyes. They met at the buffet. "Table 5," Jason said tersely. "The two gents in seats 2 and 3. Know who they are?"

His brother's eyes scanned the room, without hesitating as they swept over Table 5. "I forget the names," he said, "but they're both planters. Big houses in Vicksburg and broad acres out somewhere in the countryside. I can't see either of them trying to snake a game."

"Nor can I. But who's the big dark man across from them?"

"Beats me," Gus confessed. "Never saw him before."

Jason thought for a moment. "Find out his name from the stewards and search his stateroom. *Quietly*. I don't want any fuss if I can help it."

Gus slipped away. Jason sipped a glass of soda water and watched the suspect table from a distance. A few minutes later Gus returned, looking grim. Turning slightly, so that his body blocked the view of the rest of the room, he showed Jason a small brass box. An ivory-handled steel blade pivoted along one edge, and the adjustable card-holder across the bottom was marked off in 1/64th's of an inch. Jason knew what it was; he had its cousin back in his desk. Its supposed use was to trim the edges of cards that had gotten frayed. In reality, it was the most accurate method of shaving cards indetectably.

"We found one of the stolen decks, too," said Gus. "Still unopened. He must have operated on the other two already. I'll get a couple of the men to take care of the bastard.''

''Wait. Put the shaver back where you found it. I'm handling this in my own way.''

Gus looked as though he dearly wanted to argue, but after a long moment he nodded and walked away. Jason immediately put him out of his thoughts. His mind was fully occupied with a series of lightning calculations. Chance, probabilities, and odds were the raw stuff of his occupation, not only the known, finite odds of games with formal rules, but the more tenuous probabilities of human action. Anticipating an opponent's moves was better than half of being a successful gambler. And in this instance he was trying to predict the moves of another gambler, who would, in turn, be trying to predict his own.

Even from across the room he could sense that the mood at Table 5 was becoming more feverish. His instinct told him that Blackie had put in the chill. He waited two or three minutes, then strolled past the table. As he thought: the two Vicksburg men and the crooked gambler were the only ones still in the game, and the pot was enormous, at least two thousand dollars. He continued to stroll on through the door to the pantry, then watched through the glass as the three men laid down their cards and Blackie raked in the pot. Jason's first calculation was that the gambler would not dare leave the game for a while after his *coup*. From the way he settled back in his chair, that seemed to be confirmed. The stage was set for Jason's move.

Once more he strolled past the table, then turned back to put one hand on the back of a vacant chair.

"Any of you gentlemen mind if I join you for a few hands?" he asked. "I find a little poker does wonders to compose the mind."

One of the planters spoke up. "We'd consider it a privilege, sir." The others murmured agreement. Blackie at first looked slightly alarmed, but then his face—what could be seen of it through the full beard—took on a cast of expectancy and even gloating. Jason's second calculation was confirmed.

For the next few hands Jason played a conservative game, twice folding his hand after he failed to improve on the draw. The level of betting was fairly high, but not outrageous. Then he was dealt two pair and filled it on the draw. The bet was to him. He pushed ten dollars in. The man to his left tossed in his cards, but the two planters stayed in, and Blackie raised ten. Jason raised him back; the betting went around once more, and Jason's hand took the pot. He didn't much care about that—it contained no more than three hundred dollars—but the win also meant that he got the deal.

A single touch told him that they were still playing with the gaffed deck. His next task was to discover which cards the gambler had shaved. As he shuffled, he brought some of them near to the top of the deck and the others to the bottom. By a combination of second-dealing—holding back the top card and dealing the one underneath it—and bottom-dealing, he gave himself five of the marked cards. When he examined his hand, it contained three kings, an ace, and a queen. After the betting, he discarded the three kings and dealt himself three more of the shaved cards, which proved to be the fourth king, another queen, and an ace. He closed his hand and ran his fingers absent mindedly along its edges, until he was sure that he understood how to distinguish the court cards from each other. Then, on the next raise, he folded.

His left-hand neighbor won the hand with two pair and dealt a hand that became a spirited duel between the Vicksburg men. There was nearly a thousand dollars on the table by the time the stouter of the two showed his four treys, to triumph over his neighbor's full house of tens and queens. The play was desultory for a couple of rounds, but then the deal went to Blackie. Jason's third calculation was about to be put to the test.

He opened his hand to find a pair of aces, a queen, and two small cards. Nothing in his expression or posture changed, but inwardly he smiled. He bet the hand conservatively, though both Blackie and the stout planter bumped back and forth a few times, then discarded two. As he anticipated, he drew another ace and a queen. The betting began again. The planter had not improved his hand, it seemed, but Blackie was pressing the pace, raising in steps of twenty, then fifty dollars. Jason stayed with him, but with smaller raises, until he had three or four hundred in the pot, then called. Blackie, of course, was holding four kings and raked it in.

On his second deal, he did not dare try another gaff. Jason was easily able to ring in the cards he had earlier put in a hold-out—a spring steel clip attached to the underside of the table by a sharp pin—and take the hand and the deal.

The next move called on all Jason's skill as a card mechanic, including the new pass he had learned only the night before. What he was trying was nothing less than using the gambler's gaffed deck against him, without making him suspect what was happening. He counted on having two factors in his favor. First, Blackie's easy victory two hands earlier had probably made him a little contemptuous of Jason's skills. Second, the plan was calculated to arouse a small degree of suspicion, then disarm it. Jason compared this in his mind to the technique of inoculation, by which a weak and curable strain of a disease prevented a later, stronger attack.

Jason dealt. From the corner of his eye he saw Blackie's fingers tighten infinitesimally as he spread his cards and saw two aces, two queens, and a king. Then, as he took in the implications of the hand, he relaxed. Either the deal was straight and his pairs a coincidence, in which case he held what could turn into a very strong hand, or the dealer had discovered the shaved cards and tried to use them, but had used them badly, in which case he held an unbeatable hand. He hesitated another moment, then opened for twenty dollars.

Jason raised ten and was surprised to find the others staying with him. In fact, one of the planters raised another ten. Then Blackie came back with twenty more, and Jason bumped ten again. His left-hand neighbor folded at that point, as did the second of the planters, but the betting went around twice more before the draw. Already the pot contained over five hundred dollars. A few spectators started to gather.

Blackie took one card, of course. Both Jason and the planter took two. Blackie's face didn't move when he studied his hand, but he opened for fifty dollars. Jason raised fifty, and the planter threw in his cards. It was a head-to-head contest now.

The bearded man raised back for a hundred, only to meet an equal raise from Jason. He looked at his hand again, then pushed a stack of double eagles into the center. "And raise five hundred," he said.

The spectators murmured in excitement, and more of them assembled.

Jason fumbled with his coins. "I'll see that," he said slowly. ". . . And raise you one thousand."

This time the spectators gasped.

Jason's opponent turned pale. He knew now that somehow he had walked into a trap. But he was thoroughly caught. If he folded, he lost everything, but all of his cash was already in the pot. He still believed that he held the winning hand, if only he could play it out. Reluctantly he drew his watch from his vest pocket and unwound the chain from his neck. "That's a Jeurgunsen repeater," he said. "Got a solid gold case and a one-carat diamond set in the stem. I paid a thousand for it in St. Louis six months ago, and four hundred more for the chain. All right with you if I shove it in?"

Jason nodded, and the gambler placed it next to the stacks of gold coins. "That's it then," he said. "I'm holding a full house, aces over queens."

He started to reach for the money, then froze as Jason laid down four kings. "You . . . !" He pushed up out of his chair and found a steward at one elbow and Gus at the other. Jason stared at him hard-eyed, daring him to make an accusation. He saw it now; Jason had either palmed the king he'd discarded or had rung in a fifth king. The game had been controlled all the way. But the only way he could explain how he knew that was by confessing that he had gaffed the deck. He knew the kind of treatment he could expect then.

"Were you about to say something, sir?" Jason asked in a chillingly gentle voice.

The gambler bowed to his fate. "No, sir, just that that last hand cleaned me out. I'll have to bid you gentlemen good evening."

"Or perhaps farewell," said Jason. "Didn't I overhear earlier that you were traveling with us only as far as Baton Rouge?" He glanced at his own watch, another Jeurgunsen. "We should arrive there in another hour or so. Thank you for an interesting game, sir."

Later, after making certain that Blackie left the *Argo* at Baton Rouge, Jason visited the cabin shared by the two planters from Vicksburg. By now they were pretty sure that they had been cheated. Even so, they were astonished when Jason returned what they had lost. One of them was so pleased that he pledged to do his best to lose it all again at roulette before the boat reached Vicksburg.

CHAPTER FIVE

"For the visitor from our Atlantic states,
the first shock is the River itself. Nothing, no
verbal description or painter's daub, prepares
him for its sheer immensity. Nor—"

Duncan Sargent looked up from his notebook as
Senator Stephenson and his young ward approached.
Duncan had found a place for his chair on the
shady side of the boat, where he was cooled, too, by
the breeze of its passage. Unfortunately, many other
passengers, those who were not already gaming,
favored that stretch of the promenade as well.
Most often he found himself resenting the interruption, but not this time. The Senator was a fit
object of study himself, and the girl added an
element of mystery and romance.

Her name was Melissa, he knew. He had asked
his steward. Melissa Wainwright. What an odd
pairing: Melissa, from the Greek, after the nymph

who first taught men the use of honey; and solid Anglo-Saxon Wainwright, or wagonmaker. Her name wedded romance to practicality, Attic grace to British industry. In college Duncan had always been drawn to poetry; the dry facts of natural philosophy repelled him. He occasionally wondered if the result was not an incurably flighty mind, one more interested in pursuing an intriguing train of associations than in getting on with the job.

But what was his job, after all? To write his book, certainly, but wasn't taking an interest in his fellow passengers an important part of that? And particularly one whose political and moral views were so peculiar to the region as Senator Stephenson's. Where else in the world could you find a man of wealth and education, a man esteemed by his constituents and respected by his neighbors, who proclaimed that the highest achievement of civilization was the establishment of chattel slavery?

The Senator and Miss Wainwright were nearly upon him. Duncan nodded cordially, with just the degree of reserve proper to shipboard acquaintances. The girl lowered her eyes shyly, but the Senator, politician to the bone, touched the brim of his slouch hat and said, "Good day, sir."

"Good day, Senator. A fine day, is it not?"

"Indeed. I don't believe I have had the honor . . . ?"

Duncan was on his feet by now. He bowed. "The honor is mine, sir. Duncan Sargent, at your service."

"Mr. Sargent. This is Miss Wainwright." Duncan bowed again. "You're not from this part of the world, are you, Mr. Sargent?"

Once more he found himself explaining his project, extolling the importance of the river and the need to educate Easterners about it. The Senator shook his white-maned head dolefully.

"No easy task, Mr. Sargent, no easy task. I have been contributing my mite to that great goal for many years now. But I fear that your fellow Yankees have been incurably prejudiced by the radicals and agitators in their midst. How they can countenance the presence of men who knowingly preach treason and servile rebellion, I fail to understand. But I have seen it; I know it. Why, at this very moment there is an organization in the state of Massachusetts that openly proclaims its goal of overthrowing the elected government of a part of the United States!"

"Are you referring to the Immigrant Aid Society, Senator?" said Duncan. "I had understood that its aim was to help poor families who wanted to settle in the Kansas Territory."

Stephenson's face reddened. "Poppycock, sir, pure poppycock! Poor families, indeed! Abolitionists and communists like themselves, the sweepings of the vilest gutters of the Old World, sent with the sole purpose of ravaging the homes of worthy settlers of true American stock! I tell you, sir, behind all the fine words and pious phrases you'll find one overarching purpose: nothing less than the mongrelization and destruction of the Anglo-Saxon race. They know full well that as long as we remain true to our blood, we are unconquerable. So they choose this method to prepare our downfall. That is the real battle of our day: to preserve our racial heritage unsullied!"

"May I use your words in my book, Senator? I think there is a grave need for the people of America to understand your views fully."

"Of course, Mr. Sargent, of course. How far do you go on the *Argo*? To St. Louis? So do we. Perhaps we shall find an opportunity to talk further."

Throughout this conversation Melissa Wainwright had been standing at the railing, looking out over the river. A breeze tugged at her wide straw hat, and she reached up with both hands to hold it down. The movement brought her bust into sharp definition, as it strained against the light material of her gown. Duncan stole an appreciative glance at her, then was shocked to realize that Senator Stephenson was doing the same, but more openly. Why, the old he-goat, thought Duncan; his own ward, too!

"Look, Uncle Junius," said the young lady, unaware that Uncle Junius was already looking. "Can that be Natchez? Annabelle Leigh, at school, was from Natchez, you know, and she always declared that it was on the noblest site for a town in the whole country. We all thought she was just being loyal, but I declare it *is* a fine-looking place, isn't it?"

Duncan and the Senator joined her at the rail. To the east, across the expanse of water, a line of bluffs rose greenly to a height of two hundred feet. Along the top, white mansions, widely spaced, faced out across the vista of river and sky. Farther up, the buildings seemed thicker, but they too were shaded by fine trees, carefully placed, and surrounded by elaborate plantings of azaleas, dogwoods, and magnolias.

"A fine city indeed," intoned the Senator. "A triumph of our Southern culture, made possible only by those social institutions which give leisure to that class most fitted by nature to use it well."

Duncan smiled inwardly and wondered if the Senator would succeed in finding a justification of slavery in, say, a steamboat explosion. Aloud he said, "A very noble prospect, Miss Wainwright, and healthy, too, I imagine, raised as it is above the miasma that rises from the river."

"Miasma, sir?" exclaimed the Senator, quick to sense a Yankee slight against the South. "The noisome slums of your Northern cities may create miasmas, but the mists of our rivers invigorate and nourish! We are creating here a new breed of mankind, far removed from the degraded and servile races of Old Europe. You may say we are rough; perhaps we are, but so are our bears and mountain lions. They are independent, sir, and quick to rile. They are not to be toyed with. Nor are we, sir; nor are we!"

As he spoke, the *Argo* changed course and arrowed toward the landing at the foot of the bluff. A large collection of rough shacks came into view, clustered around the wharf and the road up the bluff. This was Natchez-under-the-Hill, home to one of the largest collections of thieves and cutthroats on the Mississippi. The saloons, gambling hells, and whorehouses never shut down, and their brawls spilled constantly onto the street. From time to time the citizens of the upper city tired of this eyesore and tried to wipe it out. Their usual method was to hang anyone who refused to leave, then put the houses to the torch. But each time, after a year or so, the ginhouses and cribs were back again, flourishing as ever.

Senator Stephenson didn't seem to notice the area at all. He was occupied in telling Duncan about a few of the more notable residents of Natchez.

"Why, there's a gentleman, sir, whose name I forbear to mention, who has devoted his wealth and talent to the breeding of fine Arabian coursers. The sport of kings, you know, and this gentleman has created a stable of racehorses unequaled by that of any crowned head of decadent Europe. If you will believe it, sir, every stall in his barn is paneled in handcarved mahogany, and the drinking troughs are of Italian marble. Above each stall is a nameplate of engraved sterling, and within is a fine, large mirror so that each horse may gain a proper appreciation of his own excellence. I defy you, sir, to find such an *écurie* elsewhere in the civilized world."

To Duncan, the stable the Senator had described sounded remarkably like the cowshed created at Versailles by Queen Marie Antoinette, not long before she lost her crown and her head to an enraged populace. But he knew better than to express such a thought aloud. In any case, he was more interested in watching a curious drama taking place on the wharf.

A large band of men, perhaps twenty-five or thirty of them, was clustered together, meeting the curious glances of passersby with bellicose glares. Duncan had never seen a more obvious lot of ruffians and desperadoes. As he watched, four or five more came running down Silver Street to join the band. Then a giant of a man, fully six feet six and wide in proportion, appeared from the deck of the *Argo* and started passing among them, handing out what looked like ten-dollar gold pieces. Moments later the entire group was ambling up the gangway, laughing and joking among themselves.

Duncan was not the only observer. Gus Lowell was standing on the curved stairway that rose from the main deck to the boiler deck. From there he was able to see what Duncan, up above, could not. Moments after the steam derrick put the *Argo*'s landing stage in place, a huge man whose tiny eyes huddled under a shelf of bone bulled his way through the stream of disembarking passengers and took a position on the forward deck. There he waited, as unaffected by the commotion around him as a boulder in a mountain river, until Luke Shuttlesworth stepped up beside him and said a few words in an undertone. After a further short exchange, Shuttlesworth passed over a wash-leather bag. By the way they handled it, it looked heavy. The giant then went ashore, to return a few minutes later at the head of a gang of bravos, while Shuttlesworth, still watched by Gus, observed from the shadows.

Two levels higher, Duncan Sargent had bade Senator Stephenson and Miss Wainwright good afternoon and returned to his deck chair. He sat for a while, watching the bustling corruption of Natchez-under-the-Hill and the stately sedateness of Natchez-upon-the-Bluff recede into the distance. The last hour had given him a good deal to think about. Finally he opened his notebook and took up his pen.

". . . Nor is one acquainted with the Hudson, the Delaware, or the Potomac prepared for the appearance of the River, neither green nor blue, but an unsightly yellow-brown, sluggish and foetid, for all the world like an ill-kept barnyard after a week of rains. The mere look of it seems enough to induce a low fever."

As he listened to his brother's report, Jason practiced moving a five-dollar piece from one side of his fingers to the other. The trick was to do it without any apparent motion of the hand. "They took deck passage, I suppose?"

Gus nodded. "To St. Louis. The last I saw of them, they were down there striking holy terror into all the Micks and Dutchies."

"St. Louis . . . You don't know anything of their leader? Not Shuttlesworth, the big fellow."

"They call him Mangan. Not much help there. I'll tell you this: every one of 'em looks like he'd chop up his ma to help pass a rainy afternoon, but this Mangan wouldn't even need the excuse."

The gold coin vanished, to be plucked from Gus's left nostril. He didn't even blink; Jason's sleight of hand was an old story to him. "Well," said Jason, "if they're off on a filibuster of some kind, it's no concern of ours. I'd as soon keep an eye on them while they're on my boat, though. I don't want trouble coming on me unexpected."

"Hmm. There's one of the deck hands who seems a likely fellow. A Paddy, name of O'Donnell. Paddies are dab hands at conspiracies and such, so suppose I tell him to watch those buckos and report to me?''

Jason was about to say, ''Good idea,'' when there was a knock at the door. He nodded, and Gus opened it. The girl he had taken in to supper the evening before was standing there, looking appalled by her own boldness. Bingham, that was the name. Elizabeth Bingham.

''Oh, I— I beg your pardon, sir,'' she faltered. ''I didn't think— Of course, you're occupied. I do apologize for disturbing you.'' She started to back away.

''You're not disturbing me at all, Miss Bingham,'' said Jason quickly.

''Brigham,'' Gus said in an undertone. ''The name is Brigham.''

''Miss Brigham,'' Jason added, as smoothly as if he had just substituted an ace for a seven. ''My associate was just leaving. Won't you come in?''

She hesitated, then entered the cabin. Gus bowed and closed the door on his way out. The click of the latch startled her, and for a moment she looked inclined to turn and run. Her eyes roamed the cabin, pausing at the elegant parlor suite, the reed organ, the small mahogany dining table, and the formidable patent walnut desk, then skittering away from the door that so apparently led to Jason's sleeping quarters.

''Will you take a glass of sherry, ma'am? Or may I send for tea?''

''Nothing, sir, I thank you. I—I think I have come on a very foolish errand. Perhaps I should—'' Her dark eyes sought the door.

Jason moved toward her. The energy of his aura

affected her like a pith ball in the presence of a strong magnet. She took an unconscious step backward, then another, then stopped as the edge of a chair touched her calves. "Won't you sit down," he said, "and tell me what the trouble is?"

She felt quite helpless: helpless to leave, helpless to explain herself, helpless to deal with the troubles that assailed her one after another, like waves battering an exhausted swimmer. She sank into the chair because she could not think what else to do.

"Here, drink this," he commanded. "You look quite pale." She took the tiny glass and found herself staring intently at his ruffled shirt. The expense! she thought. He must keep a laundress just to iron the ruffles! Still wondering at the extravagance, she tipped the glass up and swallowed its contents, then came close to choking. The liquid burned her mouth and throat, but seemed to evaporate entirely before it reached her stomach. It left her with a faint taste of plums in her mouth and a warmth that spread from her chest throughout her body.

"What was that?" she gasped.

He smiled. "A cordial from one of the European provinces of the Turkish Empire. I find it a sovereign remedy for faintness. It has brought color back to *your* cheeks, I'm glad to say. Would you like more?"

"No, thank you," she said hastily. "No, I can't stay, really I can't. It's very kind of you, though."

"Not at all. If you have other engagements,

Miss Brigham, perhaps you will tell me how I may serve you.''

Once more he projected that aura of masculine power. When she was very little, her father had often lifted her in his arms and tossed her into the air. She had loved the giddiness of it, the illusion of flight, but there was a darker undercurrent to the game, an affirmation of her inability to resist him, whatever he chose to do.

This was quite different, of course. Mr. Lowell might be rather attractive, in a dandified way, but he was in no way to be compared to her father. She was overwrought, that was all, and the sooner she made her request and received the inevitable refusal, the sooner she could return to her stateroom and take a rest.

''I am traveling, sir, with my younger brother,'' she began, looking down at her hands. ''As I mentioned to you last evening, we recently lost our father; our mother has been gone for many years. I tell you this not to elicit sympathy, but to make our situation clear. We are not wealthy in the goods of this world. For some time to come we shall be dependent on the kindness and family feeling of our uncle in Kansas. Oh, I wish we were there already!''

Her hands had twisted her handkerchief into a tight knot. She spread it out on her lap and smoothed it with her fingertips. ''My mistake was to take passage on the *Argo*,'' she continued, more softly. ''I did it in ignorance. I mean no criticism of you, sir, or of your steamboat. But my brother is very young and too easily led. His principles are still unformed. He is prone to mistake bravado for manliness and swagger for gentility. This renders him far too open to undesirable influences and unworthy companions.''

Jason knew well enough where she was going and decided to save her the trials of the journey. ''He has started to gamble, Miss Brigham?''

Her eyes glistened with unshed tears. ''He has. He seems to think that the ability to fling money away recklessly is the mark of a true gentleman. If so, he has already marked himself for life!''

''The tendency is not peculiar to your brother, you know,'' Jason said gently.

''Oh, I know! An old friend of my father wasted two great inheritances at the gaming tables, then shot himself in his garden. But I don't wish Charlie to share that fate!'' She looked up at him for the first time. ''I don't know what I am asking of you,'' she said frankly. ''I haven't thought it out. Your kindness yesterday gave me the boldness to come here like this, but I am afraid I have wasted your time.''

''Yours to command, Miss Brigham,'' said Jason politely, ''but I too am at a loss. I could bar your brother from the tables, of course, but that would not stop him from entering a private game. Has he been losing heavily?''

''Some might think it nothing, but for our means, very heavily. Most of our little inheritance, in fact, and I fear the rest will follow very quickly.''

Jason had been standing all this time; now he began to pace back and forth, while combing his long brown hair with the fingers of one hand. After a minute or so, he came to a halt beside

Elizabeth's chair. "Does he favor a particular game with his patronage?" he asked.

She looked up in sudden hope. "Yes, he prefers faro. He said it was more exciting. Exciting! Do you think you can somehow help?" He was standing very close to her, so close that she seemed to feel the warmth of his body on her cheek. For a moment she felt a mad impulse to fling her arms around his knees and press herself against him, as if she were a supplicant in Bible times and he were a king. The impulse shocked her, but she stayed as she was, head thrown back and eyes lifted in an irresistible plea.

The air of barely subdued mockery had faded from his face, and it came to her that there was a certain nobility in his features. The notion of nobility in a professional gambler should have seemed ridiculous to her, but in his presence it did not.

"I may be able to do something," he said slowly, almost reluctantly, "but on one condition."

"Anything!"

"Don't speak in haste, Miss Brigham. My condition is that no word of this conversation or any that follow between us on this subject, no hint that I have assisted you in any way, be passed to anyone else. I ask nothing less than a vow of secrecy from you."

"I shall keep it to the grave!" She sprang fervently from her chair, stumbled, and for a long moment was leaning with the full length of her body against him. Then he grasped her shoulders and helped her to stand. "I mean what I say," she added through her confusion.

"I'm sure you do. You are pale again. May I

help you to your stateroom? Or would you like another sip of cordial?"

She heard a note of wildness in her laugh. What she wanted was to be alone to think, or not to think. Her skin still burned where he had touched her. She stammered out a refusal and a repetition of her thanks, and fled.

Her stateroom was on the larboard side, exposed to the heat of the afternoon sun. The only ventilation was by way of the louvers above the door and in the shutters on the windows. Light as it was, her gown of black silk was stifling. After unbuttoning it, she lifted it over her head and carefully folded it, then dabbed her temples with a handkerchief soaked in eau de cologne. The knot at the waistband of her crinoline resisted her fingers; she had to tease it with a crochet hook. The corset fastenings were easier to manage.

Free of her usual constrictions, she took a deep breath and walked across the room to the mirror. The corset had made a pattern of heavy creases in her light cotton shift. She tried to erase them by pressing them with her palms, but then her skin protested. She hesitated, then shrugged the shoulder bands of the shift down over her arms and let it fall around her feet.

The sunlight through the shutters cast a reddish glow on everything in the room. How dark her skin seemed against the white of her lace-edged pantelets, and how angry the welts left by her corset! Yet her waist was slender even when free of its stays, and her bosom was high and full even without support. Shyly she touched herself here and there, then turned to observe the effect in the mirror. She had no way of judging her body, no way of knowing how it would be perceived by a man of the world. A man, say, like Jason Lowell.

The genteel teachings of Miss Fanthom's Ladies' Seminary told her to banish such notions forever. But from somewhere—perhaps from Cantal, her black nursemaid—she had inherited a streak of earthly common sense. Were not men and women meant to be attracted to each other? And was not the love of the body part of that greater love?

In New Orleans she had learned to see her chances of marriage as very slim. Her fortune was too small to draw men of the only class proper for her to consider. Whenever she thought of the difficulties of moving to Kansas, she consoled herself with the idea that young women were scarce on the frontier. Perhaps she did not need to resign herself to the single life at the age of twenty-one!

Now a more subversive notion had found a place to root in her mind. If it was proper for men and women to know each other as Adam knew Eve, why was it only proper when marriage vows had been said? Had our First Parents held a wedding ceremony in Eden? Oh, it was a terrible burden to a child to be born out of wedlock, she knew, but she also knew that carnal knowledge did not always result in a child. In fact, on her fourteenth birthday, old Cantal, nearly blind and getting scatty in the head, had muttered some recipes to her for preventing a child. At the time Elizabeth had been frightened nearly out of her wits, but she still recalled what her old nurse had told her.

Slowly she undid the waist of her pantelets, let them fall, and stepped away from them. With grave eyes she studied her reflection as she might have studied a representation of Mother Eve before the Fall. One hand sought the furnace of her being and stoked it into a hot flame.

CHAPTER SIX

Before supper Jason had a word with Gus, who in turn spoke to Rob Maxwell, the floor boss. Maxwell recognized Charlie Brigham from Gus's description.

"Him," he said, making a face. "I had him pegged for trouble. Kids like him always are. They can't help trying to prove something by drinking too much, betting too heavy, and arguing too loud when they lose. Which they generally do, without any help from the other side of the table. I'll tell you, if I had my druthers, I'd keep 'em out altogether. The amount they lose is nothing compared to the trouble they cost us."

"I just might go along with you on that," replied Gus, "but right now we're not talking policy. Do you have it straight what to do, that's the question."

"Oh hell, yes, six ways to Sunday. I'll pass the word to the boys right now. Tell you the truth, I think they'll be glad of it. The way these tables are generally run, they do kinda get bored sometimes.''

When the supper bell sounded, Jason looked around for Elizabeth but didn't see her. All through the soup course he was silent and out of temper. When Captain Clement joshed him about missing his delightful companion, however, he made an effort to be his usual saturnine self. He was not about to let the comings and goings of some half-fledged Miss determine whether he enjoyed his supper or not. No doubt she was in her cabin enjoying a fit of the vapors. She could stay there supperless for all he cared. Her conversation had not sparkled so very much anyway.

Nevertheless, as the desserts were being brought around and she still had not appeared, he instructed the steward to send a boy to her stateroom. The boy returned a few minutes later to say that the young lady wanted tea and toast, nothing more. Jason's lips twitched, and he told the steward to send along an egg beaten in sherry as well. If she meant to let herself sink into a decline, that was her concern, but he wasn't letting it happen on his steamer!

By eight-thirty the Grand Saloon was filled with earnest men intent on their games. The ladies, of course, were in the Ladies' Cabin, reading improving books, embroidering, and discussing the cost of their gowns. At tables to one side some of them played loo and casino, the only card games considered innocent enough for respectable females to play.

Below, on the open main deck, the ragged deck passengers were clustered ten-deep around a furious-paced crap game. The hands watched tolerantly from the sidelines, though they stayed ready to wade in with pick handles at the first sign of a brawl. The Irish and German immigrants disliked each other, and both groups hated the native-born Negroes, who considered themselves superior to any foreigner. A long day of bad liquor and little food added to the strains. Cabin passengers might be given sumptuous meals with the price of their ticket, but the deck passengers were on their own. The natural result was a state of tension in which every quarrel, however private or trivial, threatened to explode into a fullblown riot.

The gentlemen in the Grand Saloon knew nothing of this. If they had known, they would not have cared greatly, so long as nothing disturbed their games. Lionel Hornby had moved from the poker table to *vingt-et-un*. His years with Vanderbilt had taught him to spot an advantage, and his calculations had convinced him that a shrewd player at *vingt-et-un* actually had a slight edge over the dealer. Tonight he was planning to test his mathematics in practice. All he had to do was remember each card as it was played.

Senator Stephenson was invited to join a game of Boston. This was a great favorite of New Orleans aristocrats, so much so that one of the most exclusive men's clubs in town was named after the game. It was also a wonderful device for transferring large sums of money from one player to another. To everyone's surprise, the Senator declined the invitation, though he watched the game for a few minutes before strolling across to the nearest of the faro tables.

Charlie Brigham sensed the Senator's approach, but he was too engrossed to acknowledge it. Twice this evening he had thought that he was about to break his string of bad luck. Early in the game he had put his chips on the eight, then a last-moment hunch told him to copper the bet, to reverse it so that he was betting eight to lose. The next card, a loser, was an eight, but just as he was reaching for his winnings, the dealer drew it off to expose the winner in the turn. It was another eight. A split turn. Instead of doubling his stake, he had halved it, since the bank took half of everything bet on a split card.

A few turns later, he bet the big figure, won, and went paroli, winning on the next two turns as well. Hardly daring to breathe, he left the heap of chips where it was and promised himself that he would leave the game after one more win. But on the next turn the loser was the jack of hearts and the lookout raked in his chips.

Someone had put a glass of wine by his elbow. He drained it, hardly noticing, and continued to study the casekeeper. The beads on the wire frame showed that all of the eights, fives, and jacks had appeared already, three of the queens and tens, but none of the aces. An ace was bound to turn up soon, but would it be as a loser or winner? He counted his remaining chips with fingers that felt as thick as sausages, took a deep breath, and put the whole stack on the ace. Then he stood up, stuck his hands in his trouser pockets, and hoped the Senator was noticing how nonchalant he was.

The next loser was a seven, followed by a winning trey. As the dealer started to slip the trey from the dealing box, Charlie had a sudden premonition that an ace was about to appear. But it was too late to copper his bet. He shut his eyes, then opened them. The loser was the king of clubs. Surely the next card would be an ace. But instead it was a nine. Then, with no transition, the nine was on the winners' pile and there, face-up in the dealing box, was the ace of spades. The last of his chips went the way of all the rest.

The boy swallowed a couple of times and cleared his throat. No one paid any notice. He leaned across to the dealer's assistant. "A marker, please," he said.

The assistant looked up. "Yes, sir. What sum do you have on the field?" He picked up a rectangle of ivory and a pencil and waited for Charlie's answer.

What could he say? A lie would be found out at once. "Uh, nothing," he stammered. "I'm out of chips. That's why I want a marker."

"To play on credit, you mean?" The assistant looked as if no one had ever made such a request before; that was an important part of his method for handling the dozen or so that he heard on an average evening. "I'm sorry, sir, I don't have the authority to give you credit."

"Well, who does?" demanded Charlie.

Another voice cut in. "Any problems here, Mason?" The boy knew before he looked whose voice it must be, and hatred boiled up in him like a sour fluid in his throat.

"Not exactly, Mr. Lowell," the assistant replied. "This gentleman asked to play on credit, and I was explaining why I couldn't let him do that."

"Quite right, sir," Jason said to young Brigham. "This is a cash game unless arrangements are made in advance."

Other players were starting to look at them. Charlie felt his face redden. "Sure, I know that," he said boldly. "I meant to bring more cash, but I must have forgotten and left it in my stateroom. That's why I want credit."

"It might be better if you went to your stateroom then, and got it," said Jason smoothly. The other players, irritated by the delay of the game, guffawed at the boy's chagrin. His face seemed to squeeze itself toward its own center. He glared around at the crowd for a moment, then shouldered his way through and stalked off.

It was nearly eleven when Jason heard an urgent knock on the door to his quarters. He opened it, and Elizabeth Brigham swept by him, then spun to face him from the center of the room.

"What did you do to my brother?" she demanded hotly. "He came to my cabin in tears just now. He hasn't done that since he was nine years old. He said he was going to kill you. He didn't mean it, of course, but what did you do to make him say it?"

"Nothing he wouldn't have done on his own. I merely hastened the process a bit."

"What do you mean? I insist that you tell me!" She took a step forward, as though she meant to assault him.

"I arranged for him to lose his money, that's all." He gestured toward a chamois bag on the lamp stand. "There it is: six hundred dollars. You may take it with you, but I would not let your brother have it if I were you. We should only be obliged to take it away from him again.''

''I don't understand,'' she faltered. ''You . . . you cheated him?''

''I prefer my choice of words. I also declined to let him play on credit, since I had no reason to think he could make good his losses. I think that was the real cause of his anger. I have noticed that men bear their losses much more cheerfully when they are betting with my money.''

''He kept saying that you had shamed him in front of his friends. I didn't know he had any on the boat.''

''On the river one makes friends quickly,'' Jason said in a reedy, preacherish voice, then added in his own voice, ''and loses them pretty fast, too.''

''I suppose he meant that awful Senator Stephenson,'' said Elizabeth thoughtfully. ''I can't believe he means Charlie any good. Why would a man like that patronize a boy like Charlie, unless he thought he had a use for him?''

Since Jason had wondered the same thing, he had no answer to give.

Elizabeth looked around as if she were not quite sure where she was or how she had come there. Then her eyes fell on the chamois moneybag. ''Six hundred dollars,'' she repeated in a voice heavy with sadness and anger. ''He had no such sum of his own. I entrusted him with our joint fortune, all we had. There should have been eight hundred in all. I suppose the rest is gone too. . . . And he came crying to *me* for sympathy, while his hands were still red with guilt! How could he!''

"He probably believed he could win back what he lost last night. Then you'd be none the wiser. It's common enough. I know of a man whose friends gave him a hundred thousand dollars to buy fine breeding stock in Chicago. He lost his own money the first evening, dipped into his friends' funds in the hope of recouping, and lost every penny before his boat reached Memphis."

"What on earth did he do then?"

Jason shrugged. "Wrote a letter of apology and put a bullet through his head. Not that that helped his friends much, but it did spare him a good many painful scenes."

"How terrible! And you get your living off such folly!"

He shrugged again. "Is it folly for a lady to buy a new bonnet when her old one is still good? Of course, it is. And what of the milliner, who does his best to inspire such folly in her, then profits by it? Most men love to gamble. I provide them with a pleasant place to do so, a place where they may be reasonably sure of fair play and good company, and I charge a fee for the service. If I did not give them a place to game, others no doubt would. There they would be almost certain to fall into the hands of sharks who would cheat them blind and pick their bones bares."

"As you just did to Charlie?"

"He was bound to lose." He crossed the room to the sideboard, poured claret into two long-stemmed glasses of Bohemian crystal, and handed her one. "Tonight he learned how quickly and absolutely one may lose. He may also have learned this before the taste for gaming had thoroughly taken hold. I hope so. In any case, even if he succeeds in raising more money, he will not be allowed at the tables on the *Argo*. Your health, Miss Brigham.''

''Thank you.'' She drank deeper than she intended and started to choke, then recovered. To calm the rasp in her throat, she took another sip of the wine. ''I, I think I must apologize to you for bursting in on you like this,'' she said. Her gaze moved about the room, each time sliding quickly past the place where he stood. ''In confiding my worries about Charlie, I had trusted you, you see. And I feared that I had been foolish to do so. After he came to me this evening, so angry with you, I didn't know what to think. I wondered if you were what I took you for. Even to consider that you were not was upsetting to me.''

Her throat was still dry. She sipped again, then realized that her glass was empty. He took it from her and refilled it, then motioned her toward a chair. His legs brushed her gown as he slipped by to sit at the near end of the sofa. His eyes shone with a knowingness that she found hateful. ''And what do you take me for, Miss Brigham?'' he asked.

His tone made the nape of her neck tingle. ''I beg your pardon? Oh, I can hardly say, sir. For a gentleman, of course. For someone who is kind to the helpless, however much he delights to afflict the powerful. For someone—'' She broke off, frightened by her audacity.

''Yes?''

When she finally spoke, it was in a voice so low that he had to lean forward to hear her. ''For someone who was not meant to be so alone as he keeps himself, nor so removed from the bonds of family and society.''

They were both silent for a long moment. Jason was staring down into his wineglass, while she watched the play of expressions on his face. Suddenly his jaw tightened and his brows drew together into a solid line. ''Bonds?'' he said roughly. ''Bonds? Yes, that's the word, I'll vow! Or call it slavery instead; they mean the same. I am a free man, Miss Brigham, and I intend to stay one, whatever I must do. Birth, fortune, fate do not master me, I am *their* master!''

''Hush, sir, for goodness' sake!'' Elizabeth glanced toward the ceiling, as if she expected a lightning bolt to appear on the instant.

''Goodness? What are goodness and badness but the cant put about by those who *have*, to protect themselves against those who *have not*!'' He reached up and plucked a gleaming double eagle from midair. ''I own this gold; therefore I wish you to understand that stealing it would be a hideous crime against man and God! But if I had none?'' A flourish of his hand, and the coin vanished. ''Then if I were true to myself, I would admit that your possession of wealth is a sin against *me*! And there is the *fons et origo* of all morality!''

Elizabeth clapped her hands over her ears and shut her eyes tightly. She had heard of sleight of hand, but she had never seen it, and though she knew that the appearance and disappearance of the coin was a trick, must be a trick, still its effect was magical. Coupled with his strange, almost blasphemous words, it convinced her that she was in the presence of great power. And she was not at all sure that it was power for good.

Closed off as she was, the first she knew of his approach was when his hands clasped her under the arms and lifted her effortlessly from her chair. The palms pressed, lightly but firmly, against the sides of her breasts. She opened her eyes wide, to find his face looming close to hers. His breath was hot on her cheek. She opened her lips to gasp, to protest, and he forced them closed with his own. His tongue, like the Serpent in the Garden, probed insinuatingly, then darted into her.

His arms were tight around her now, pressing her against the full length of his body. Panic clutched at her diaphragm, tightened her throat. As he grazed his lips across her cheek and fastened them on the soft flesh of her neck, just below the ear, one of his strong hands pressed the small of her back, then moved lower, still pressing.

"No! Please!" she gasped. "Please, I beg you!" Her breasts, forced upward by her corset, hurt from the crushing pressure of his embrace. The long muscles of her thighs ached with the effort of resisting his attempt to thrust his leg between them.

Then, so suddenly that she almost collapsed to the floor, he released her and took a step backward. His face was flushed and he was breathing heavily, but his expression was as cool, cynical, and detached as ever. "I beg your pardon, ma'am," he said in a husky voice. "I fear I mistook your reasons for coming to my rooms so late at night. Of course, you came only to recover your money." Striding across the room, he picked up the chamois bag and carried it to the door, where he waited for her.

Elizabeth looked at him in wonder. Then, as the full meaning of his words penetrated her mind, she flamed scarlet. "I withdraw my earlier remark, sir," she said. "You have proved as clearly as anyone could wish that you are no gentleman. Good evening!"

He raised a mocking eyebrow as she stalked across the cabin, accepted the moneybag without looking at him, and left without another word.

Once on the promenade and out of sight of his door, Elizabeth leaned heavily against the railing and took a deep breath. She had not wanted a quarrel, indeed she hadn't, but she had not wanted to be assaulted and insulted either. Should she have tolerated his embraces, in gratitude for the return of the small fortune her brother had lost? But what would that have made her in his eyes and in her own? She had little enough in the world besides her pride, and she could not afford to give that up easily.

"He can be philosophical about good and evil if he chooses," she thought. "He is wealthy and independent. But my virture is no luxury; it is the only garment I have to protect me from the storms and biting winds of poverty and dependence."

As she looked out across the river, tears blurred her vision. Her lips felt bruised, and her breasts still ached. But the worst, the most shameful, was that under the gown of black silk, under the corset and crinoline and camisole and the pantelets trimmed in Belgian lace, she sensed the same moist warmth that she had induced in herself that afternoon.

Even her own body had gone over to the enemy.

CHAPTER SEVEN

The boy Jason and the gambler Curtis traveled the rivers together for almost eight years. Not only did they work the boats on the Ohio and the Mississippi, but those on the smaller rivers, too—the Illinois and Cumberland and Wabash and Tennessee. Wherever the steamboats went, there were men eager for a game and there were other men, like Curtis, ready to give it to them.

Wherever they went, the boy practiced and learned. He repeated every move of the card mechanic's art a thousand times or more, every pass and shuffle and undercut, until his hands knew them as well as a pianist's hands know simple scales. The hardest part was not learning the moves, though; it was performing them casually and faultlessly under the glare of suspicious eyes.

Curtis was a stern instructor with a simple method. Whenever Jason felt ready to demonstrate a technique, Curtis watched him as if he were a wary farmer from Missouri. If he detected the move, he whacked Jason on the palm with his cane. This, he explained, was a good deal less drastic than being gut-shot or having your nose slit. Both were among the likely consequences of being found out in a real game.

The one time Jason saw him really angry was when he came upon the boy, then thirteen or so, entertaining a circle of deck passengers with some simple tricks and flourishes. He ordered him to the cabin they were sharing, pulled down his trousers, and whipped him with his belt for at least two dozen strokes. Jason was astonished, indignant, and terrified, all at once. His father had beaten him regularly, but he had never known Curtis to come so close to being totally out of control. If a man that held in ever let go, what might not happen?

At last Curtis put down the belt and stood up, letting the sniffling child fall to the floor. "Remember this," he said, panting, "and remember it well. Never let civilians see that you can control the cards. They will never forget it, and they will never believe your game is square. If they win, they will walk away with your money and feel very tall. If they lose, however fairly, they will holler 'Cheat!' and try to take back their losses and do what damage they can to your person. Do you hear? Do you understand?"

Jason, huddled on the floor, nodded

"Good. The secret of our profession, the reason we are able to go on, is simple. It's persistence, application, hard work. No one who gambles to enliven his evening can imagine what we go through to sharpen our skills. In his mind, distracting an opponent while he clumsily bottom-deals is the very peak of artfulness. If he knew that I can take any card I choose and move it to any position in the deck I choose, while seeming merely to shuffle . . . But he doesn't, and he won't, because it never occurs to him that someone might spend days perfecting a simple glide. So he looks for clumsy, obvious tricks and overlooks the real gaff. Now get up and wash your face—and hope that none of the cabin passengers saw your little show. If they did, we may have to take a swim.''

Jason's education included a good deal more than mere dexterity with the cards and dice. Most nights Curtis discussed the evening's play with him, explaining the reasons for each of his important decisions. Jason learned strategy and tactics, but more than that, he learned psychology.

"Size up your man properly," Curtis would say, "and he's yours. Everything matters—his age, where he comes from, what he does, how deep his pockets are, and yes, how deep his thirst is, too. You've got to know in advance how he'll treat a good hand and a bad one, whether a big raise will lure him on or scare him out, and most important, whether he'll cut up rough when he finds he's losing. Take that fellow to my right at the poker table this evening: now, what did you make of him?"

And Jason would fumble for recollections of an ordinary man and try to describe his character, then listen as Curtis broke him into his smallest elements, then fitted them into a recognizable portrait. As time passed, Jason himself began to notice more and understand it, until a day came when he was able to warn his mentor that two hayseeds at the faro table were professionals out to snake the game and clean out the dealer. Jason was proud of himself, but Curtis had mixed feelings. "I'm getting old and careless, son," he kept saying. "I should have spotted them myself; their fingernails were too well-kept. I never saw a clodhopper yet with neat nails."

Then there was mathematics. Curtis taught him that chance is not the same as luck. "You're holding two pair," he might say in the middle of a conversation. "What are your chances of filling your hand on the draw?" Or he might set up the case-keeper, the wire-and-bead contraption that showed which cards had already appeared in a game of faro, let Jason have one glimpse of it, and demand the odds of a split coming up in the next three turns. *Vingt-et-un* was even more difficult, because the probability of improving one's hand versus going bust changed with each hand and every card played. But Curtis was merciless.

"If you're in a game," he said, "you don't have the luxury of sitting back and figuring the odds. You've got enough else to think about. So you have to have them at your fingertips, all the time, whatever turn the game may take. The only way I know to get that is the way I got it: drill and practice, practice and drill. You're in a six-man poker game, holding three queens, an ace, and a small card. What are the chances someone else will take the pot?"

Jason's mother had taught him to read as a

matter of religious duty. Curtis taught him that reading could be profitable and enjoyable. Under his guidance, Jason swallowed up Walter Scott and Washington Irving, Cooper and Dickens, and even Fielding, but Smollett he found too remote. Curtis's motto, or rather one of his many mottoes, was, "You can never know too much about the world." New York and Boston might be far away and strange, and London even farther and stranger, but through novels one could become a cosmopolitan. Emerson's *Essays* and Griswold's *Poets* added further polish, though they did not change the lad's underlying view of the world, a view he shared with his teacher.

Once in Missouri they watched the annual migration of the passenger pigeons. Though they were on the extreme edge, still the sky was darkened by the innumerable bodies. When the exhausted birds landed for the night, the villagers went among them with cudgels and knocked them on their heads. They were not worth the waste of powder and shot.

"Most people are born pigeons, fit only to be plucked," said Curtis quietly. "But just remember, if those birds had clubs and the sense to use them, they'd be living off us and not the other way around. People who gamble want something for nothing, and most of them aren't any too choosy about how they get it. Give them a break, and they'll skin you alive. About all we can do is skin them first, then get while the getting's good. And don't forget that there will always be more of them than of us. Don't let them gang up on you, or you're a dead man."

Most of the time Jason passed himself as Curtis's son, but not always. Like a fox, the gambler could catch the scent of danger from far off and act quickly to elude it. Once in Quincy, Illinois, they were watching the arrival of the *Jacob Gelhorn,* which they were planning to take upriver. Curtis studied the passengers who lined the railings of the boiler deck promenade, then said, "You're an immigrant bound for St. Paul. Quick now!"

Jason knew what to do. He edged away from his companion, slipped into a gap between two buildings, and changed into rough clothes. A dozen or so Dutchies were huddled on the wharf, waiting to take deck passage farther north. They took no notice when he hovered near them, nor when he followed them across the boarding stage. Curtis, already aboard, was the only cabin passenger to join the boat at Quincy.

The main deck was crowded with freight and passengers, but Jason found a niche close to the two stairways that curved up to the boiler deck. It was only May, and at nightfall the air grew sharply colder. Most of the miserable deck passengers moved closer to the warmth of the furnaces, heedless of the risk of a boiler explosion. Jason stayed where he was, wrapped himself in a thin quilt, and got a little fitful sleep.

He sat up when he heard a few notes whistled softly. They seemed to come from the air above his head. He strained his eyes, but the darkness was too thick. Cautiously he whistled the continuation of the melody. Something fell heavily on the deck, inches away from him. His searching hands quickly found the leather money pouch and concealed it under his clothes. He listened intently and tried to disregard the pounding pulse in his ear, but all he heard was the rhythmic thud of the pistons and the hiss of steam from the escape pipes.

Blessing the darkness, he stripped to the skin, put on his respectable suit, and donned his immigrant's rags over it. Some Dutchie would be happy to claim his quilt and valise in the morning. The minutes slogged past, and still he listened anxiously.

Suddenly the frail superstructure of the steamboat trembled from a score of pounding hobbed boots. Above him, Jason heard shouts of "He's gone!" and a string of curses in a dozen voices, then from the rear of the boat the sharp *crack!* of a pistol.

"He's making for shore!" "Shoot the whoreson bastard!" *Crack! crack!* After a short silence, "Good work, Tommy! You got the cheating skunk!"

"Well, I guess," said a new voice. "If I didn't account for him, our money did. Dragged him right down, is my notion. Might ha' been smarter to let him get to shore first."

"Don't be a fool, we'd'a been out of range by then."

"That's so," Tommy replied slowly. "Makes shooting him a pretty costly sport though. He didn't anyways leave the money behind, did he?"

"His cabin's as bare as a Chippewa's ass in summertime. Should we search the boat? He couldn't have swum with all his gear."

Jason cowered deeper into his quilt and closed his eyes. The money pouch was next to his skin, under two sets of trousers. Anyone searching him would have to get pretty personal to find it, and he didn't think they would succeed in treating two hundred deck passengers with such disrespect. Of course, if they grew suspicious of him for some reason, they would have him out of his clothes in a moment.

Another voice, surly but free of the muzziness of drink, spoke up. "All right, gents, you've had your fun. Now how about going back to the main cabin? The captain would just as lief you didn't break any more doors down on his steamboat. He asked me to tell you that he knows of some nice deserted islands between here and Dubuque that you might enjoy exploring for a few days if'n you don't put down them chairs and act a little more genteel. Do you take my point, gents?"

Apparently they did. The shouts and bangs died away. And ten or fifteen minutes later the twin whistles of the *Jacob Gelhorn* sounded mournfully into the night. In moments a spark of light appeared ahead as a woodyard operator lit his bonfire to guide the steamer in. The roustabouts clustered in the bow, where they got ready to dash ashore and bring the fresh wood supply aboard. And from his place in the shadows, Jason saw something more ominous: three or four cheroot-smoking gents had come down from the boiler deck and were standing near the landing stage, scrutinizing the rousters.

"Lively, now!" the mate roared, as the boat neared the bank. "Start that gangplank for'rard! God damn you for a lot of white-livered swamp puppies, have you gone to sleep over it! Don't you hear me? 'Vast heaving, I said! Now get ashore and get those logs aboard before I shove 'em up your ass, you poor puny bastard begat of a tired mud turtle and a spavined hearse horse!''

The moment the gangplank touched the bank, the roustabouts dashed ashore. Jason watched and calculated. He figured that each rouster would have to bring four loads of logs aboard to make up a full load. He waited, his nerves stretched so tight they seemed to sing in the breeze and his armpits drenched with acrid sweat. He was surprised that the men by the stage didn't find him by the stench of fear alone. But as he hoped, they were tiring of their vigil. One had turned his back to gaze out into the woods, and two others were talking to each other, hardly noticing the flow of men past them.

A clump of four rousters thudded past, panting under their loads of hardwood logs. This was Jason's moment. As they dumped the wood and started back ashore, he fell in with them, behind the third man. If the last man noticed, he was too tired to care. As he was about to put his foot on the gangplank, the light of the bonfire fell full on his face. The one sentry who was still alert looked at him, and for a moment something like interest appeared in his eyes. Then Jason was past him. He followed the others up the slope, then, out of range of the light, took two steps to one side and disappeared. Five minutes later he watched from between two trees as the *Jacob Gelhorn* continued its voyage upriver.

Dawn found him sitting on a big stump atop the low bluff. His empty belly made the wait seem

long, but before ten o'clock a small stern-wheeler
chuffed up the river and nosed over to the bank.
Curtis was standing in the bow to catch him when
he jumped aboard.

"Did they bother you?" he asked.

"No. You weren't hit? The shots scared me."

The gambler grinned. "They scared *me*. But I
just dived and held my breath as long as I could.
In that light, they must have figured I was down
for good."

The tiny steamer had backed out into midstream
and turned south. Jason looked questioningly at his
friend, who said, "I promised them fifty dollars to
pick you up and take us down to Fulton. You do
have the gold, don't you? I don't feel ready for
another swim yet!"

On April 25, 1846, a force of one thousand six
hundred Mexican cavalry under General Torrejon
surrounded an American reconnoitering party of
sixty-three dragoons north of the Rio Grande near
Matamoros. When the shooting stopped, eleven
Americans lay dead, five more were wounded, and
the rest were captives. Three weeks later, when
the news reached Washington, Congress declared
war on the Republic of Mexico.

Jason heard the news in the lobby of the Planters Hotel in St. Louis. A gray-bearded man was
standing on a table, reading President Polk's message to Congress from the newspaper. "Mexico
has shed American blood upon the American soil,"
he thundered, and added, "By golly, boys, it's not
to be stood for, not for one minute! I fit the

English with Andy Jackson, and damned if I won't fight the Mexicans, too!''

"Go it, Colonel," someone shouted from the crowd. "Show Santy Anny he can't tamper with us wildcats without he gets scratched up some!"

The crowd laughed, but the colonel kept a serious expression. "I will, by golly! I'm calling here and now for the formation of a regiment of Missouri Volunteers, to serve for six months unless the war ends sooner. I know some of you boys, and I know you'll do the right thing. Anybody who wants to sign up can give his name to Homer Burke at that table right over there. Now let's hear it, boys: hurrah for the Republic and the great State of Missouri, and to hell with Mexico!"

The cheers rang through the building and brought the curious off the street and out of the barroom. The colonel, given a fresh audience, started his speech again.

But by then Jason was well on his way, in search of a doctor. During the night Curtis had been overcome by a fit of vomiting and diarrhea, which had not abated by morning. Jason was scared. His partner had never been sick before, not to that degree anyway, and it seemed unnatural to see him so drawn and helpless.

The doctor's face was not reassuring. He studied Curtis, took his pulse, felt the glands of his neck, and peered down his throat. He also looked briefly at the contents of the chamber pot. Then he motioned Jason aside.

"Your friend has cholera," he said bluntly.

"Cholera!"

"Pray God we can keep word of this from

getting out," the doctor continued. "There are plenty of folks in town who remember 1833. There'll be panic if they learn the cholera has returned."

"But Curtis, will he . . . ?" Jason swallowed, unable to finish the question.

"I wouldn't give you a plugged nickel for his chances of seeing tomorrow, son. But I've been wrong before. You'll have to excuse me; there're some people who'd better know about this. You stay with your friend, and don't leave this room, whatever happens, you hear? I'll be back later."

The doctor left, locking the door from outside. Jason turned toward the bed. Curtis was watching him with knowing eyes.

"Last hand, eh, boy?" he gasped. "Feels like I've thrown up all my insides. God, it hurts! I'll be glad when it's over. What did the sawbones say, dysentery?"

"No," said Jason reluctantly. "Cholera."

"Cholera!" His friend burst out laughing, then stopped as a convulsion shook his body. "Cholera, you say? Not a very distinguished or particular sort of sickness, is it? I always liked the notion of being carried off by gout, but I guess we don't get a lot of say about these things, do we?"

"Oh hell, you'll have years and years to work up a good case of gout." Jason looked around desperately, searching for a way to change the direction of the conversation. A bottle on the bureau caught his eye. "How about a glass of rum? It's not port wine, but it might give you gout all the same."

Curtis shook his head slowly. "It's no go, son.

I'm about to cash in my checks, and you know it. Bring me the faro case, will you?''

Jason got the worn mahogany box with the faded painting of a tiger on the top, then helped as Curtis fumbled with the silver latches. ''The lining of the lid,'' the dying man said faintly. ''Pull it out.''

Jason did as he was told. The satin was glued to a thin board, behind which he found a letter on the stationery of an important St. Louis bank and a slip of paper with a woman's name and an address in Vermont.

''My sister,'' Curtis explained. ''She may be dead by now, but she had a mess of kids. Send them half of the money. Better tell them I was in business, or they might be too stubborn in their righteousness to take it. The rest is yours. See George Pfeffer at the bank; he knows about you.''

By now Jason was in tears. ''I don't want your damn money,'' he cried, ''I want you to get well!''

''That's not in the cards, son, deal 'em how you will. And Lord knows you can make 'em do nearly everything but dance a jig. I've gotten a lot of pleasure out of watching you learn, and out of knowing I taught one of the best. I wouldn't have minded staying around to see where you go with it either.''

Another spasm, a longer one, grabbed him. Jason put his arm around his shoulders and held him up, to keep him from choking. When the spasm ended, Curtis's head lolled back on Jason's chest. The doctor found them that way when he returned with the hotel manager and two men carrying a piano crate.

Only the doctor entered the room. The others waited by the door with frightened faces.

The doctor shook Jason's shoulder. "I need your help, boy. We've got to get him in that box right away, you hear? Come on now."

Jason stared uncomprehending toward the door, then down at his friend. Slowly the look of puzzlement was replaced by one of horror. "In that? No, by damn, never! He'll have a decent coffin; I can pay for it. I have money."

"I don't care if you're John Jacob Astor, we've got to get him out of here without folks noticing and starting to talk. He can have a coffin later if you like, but you'll have to lay him out yourself. The undertaker has too much respect for his own skin to go messing with a cholera victim. Now come on, damn you; I'll take his feet."

Sundown found Jason standing by a fresh mound of dirt in the new cemetery on Bellefontaine Bluff, overlooking the Mississippi and the Chain of Rocks. He was getting reacquainted with loneliness. At one point he caught himself thinking that he would have to talk this over with Curtis; then he remembered.

How many times had they traversed the channel down below, on how many steamboats? Once he had thought of going out into the world in search of his destiny. But instead he had become the slave of a schedule nearly as fixed as that of a crack packet boat: Pittsburgh to Louisville to Cairo, St. Louis to New Orleans with stops at Memphis, Vicksburg, and Natchez. There was a difference: the packets emblazoned their names in letters of gold as tall as a man for all to read, while he guarded his identity as closely as the secrets of his calling. Only one man in all the world had known who he was. And now there were none.

He was free. No tie of kin or friendship bound him. No place claimed him as its own. He could stay or go where he wished, and he need ask no man's permission. He could enroll in a college back East or enlist in the army of the Cham of Tartary without anyone taking note of it. He was like a man in the center of a forest, equally distant from everything. It came to him then that complete openness of choice was not very different from no choice at all. But he had no one to tell this to.

The next morning he presented himself at the bank and asked for Mr. Pfeffer. Apparently word of Curtis's death, though not the cause of it, had spread, for Pfeffer was expecting him.

"My sympathies, Mr. Lowell," he began. "Was Mr. Curtis your uncle?"

Jason was prepared. "No, sir, my guardian. He and my mother were old friends."

The banker coughed. The hint that Jason was Curtis's bastard was enough to lead him to change the subject. As Jason had expected it to.

"Your, ah, guardian was an old and valued client of our bank, you know, and entrusted us with all his affairs. Under his latest will, I am to serve as executor unless and until you have come of age. You are not of age, I believe?"

"No, sir. I am nineteen."

"Yes. Well, in brief, half of the money in Mr. Curtis's account is to go to his sister or her offspring. The other half, and the real and personal property, goes to you. The real property doesn't amount to much, a few unimproved lots in different parts of town, and I suppose you've taken charge of the personal property already.''

Jason was very aware of the Jeurgunsen watch in his vest pocket and the abalone-handled dirk suspended just below the nape of his neck. Both had been so much a part of his friend's person that he half-expected strangers on the street to denounce him for possessing them. "Yes, sir, I have. I didn't know what else to do.''

"Quite right. Now, as to the money. A good deal of it is laid out in mortgages and such, so I can't give you an exact figure, but I would expect that your share would amount to about fourteen thousand dollars.''

Only his years of training at the card table kept the lad from opening his eyes wide and pursing his lips to whistle. Fourteen thousand dollars was a fortune! The interest alone would be enough to support him in modest comfort for the rest of his life. Now he understood why Curtis never seemed too flush with money, even though both of them generally won. He had been socking it away in the bank all those years.

"That is your share I'm referring to," Pfeffer repeated. The impassiveness of the boy bothered him. Perhaps he hadn't yet understood his good fortune, or perhaps, despite appearances, he wasn't quite right in the head. "The sister, or her heirs, will also receive a similar sum. Fourteen thousand dollars. Or thereabouts.''

Jason was thinking hard. The moneybelt around his waist held a thousand or so in gold and banknotes—more than enough for the sort of game he favored, which was one that wouldn't attract undue attention. If he carried much more, he would only be tempting the thieves and assassins who preyed on travelers.

He cleared his throat. "You've been investing this money for my guardian? I wonder if you'd do the same for me as well. I wouldn't like the worry of dealing with a fortune like that."

George Pfeffer was relieved. He had been asking himself what he as executor should do if the youngster asked him to hand over the money straightaway. It would have been inconvenient for the bank to realize such a sum at short notice, but beyond that, he felt responsible to the last wishes of an old customer. "Certainly, Mr. Lowell, we'll be happy to."

"And I suppose if I want to draw on it now and then, or add to it, there'd be no difficulty?"

"None at all; I'm at your service any time."

"I may not be in St. Louis," Jason said diffidently.

"We have correspondent banks in every major town. Let me explain . . ."

Twenty minutes later Jason had signed the last document and sprinkled sand on his signature. When he stood up, his legs were strangely tired. For a moment he wondered if the cholera was working secretly in him as well. He would know soon enough if it was.

As Pfeffer shook his hand, he said, "Have you made any plans, Mr. Lowell? I know it's very soon, but . . ."

"Why, yes. I've been thinking of going to Mexico."

"Really!" The banker was impressed. "That shows a proper spirit, sir. I congratulate you. To spring to the defense of our sacred flag and soil in our country's hour of need—why, I'd go myself if I were your age again!"

Jason accepted the compliments gravely, but inwardly he thought the man a fool. Carrying a gun was proper work for mule-skinners and farmboys with calloused hands. And when they weren't fighting, the only thing soldiers wanted as much as a drink and a whore was a chance to lose their pay at cards. Jason meant to give them that chance.

CHAPTER EIGHT

It was the afternoon of Duncan's second day aboard the *Argo*. New Orleans lay five hundred miles behind, and St. Louis was still seven hundred miles distant. He was sitting in his usual spot on the shady side of the boat with his traveling desk open on his lap. For a few moments he chewed on the end of his penholder and gazed across the brown water at the distant bank. Then, dipping the nib in his patent leak-proof inkstand, he began to write.

Sir Charles Lyell, the geologist, informs us that the Gulf of Mexico once extended a thousand miles north of its present bounds, to above where Cairo, Illinois, now stands. All of the land between the Ozarks and the Highlands of Tennessee was deposited, grain upon grain, by the restless River over the course of thousands of years. In New Orleans I was told that the mouth of the River is a clear half-mile farther south than it was a century or so ago. If anyone doubts this, or considers it a 'tall tale,' let him dip a bucketful of water from the Mississippi and allow it to settle for a day or two. The amount of earth he finds on the bottom will persuade him.

Within its bed, now much too wide for it, The River turns restlessly, trying to find a more comfortable position for its repose. The channel meanders from one bank to the other, now casting up a sandbar or towhead, now undermining a handsome bluff whose tall trees attest to its age. Often the River goes twenty miles to cover a journey that, by land, might be accomplished in one, and often too, in floodtime, its fierce current cuts across one of these necks in a single night. The old water-course becomes a 'cut-off,' one of those queer horseshoe-shaped lakes so common in this region.

From above, the *Argo*'s two steam whistles, tuned to a minor third, let off a solemn blast, fell silent, and sounded again. As if in echo, or mockery, a shrill whistle that reminded Duncan of a peanut vendor's wagon sounded twice from upriver. He glanced in that direction. A smaller boat, laden with bales of cotton, was coming downstream. The two pilots, through their signals, had just agreed to pass each other to starboard.

The *Argo*'s pilot was edging closer to the east bank now. The current had undercut the bank along this stretch. Live oak trees, their limbs heavy with Spanish moss, leaned out over the water, ready to fall into its embrace. Duncan had become habituated to the resonant boom of a floating log colliding with the boat's hull. Though farmers and woodsmen came out in rowboats to tow the logs to shore, there were always more of them than the towers could ever snare. The ones that had been in the river for a long time often floated just below the surface, invisible to all but the keenest eye. Or worse, their roots became lodged on the river bottom and they became snags, the most feared enemy of the steamboat. A well-lodged snag could tear the bottom out of the sturdiest boat.

As Duncan gazed at the riverbank drifting by, he was distantly aware that his thoughts were becoming more and more tenuous. What a peculiar world it was, in which a tree from the North Woods of Minnesota might destroy a steamboat in Arkansas and in which that steamboat, sunk to the bottom, might be the foundation of a newborn island on which other trees might grow in time. And how infinitesimal a man's span of years seemed, when measured against the eons it had taken for the Mississippi to build a delta eleven hundred miles long. What meaning could concepts such as honor and duty have against a sweep of canvas so unimaginably broad?

His eyes closed and his head slowly tilted forward. Abruptly he sat straight up, took a deep breath, and frowned in the direction of the horizon. He was young, damn it, and energetic; he had not needed an afternoon nap since the time he still wore a pinafore! Did they put something in the food, or did the very air spread the disease of indolence? No wonder the heavy work was done by African slaves and Irishmen just off the boat; the members of the master race were too busy sleeping off the effects of the climate!

He picked up his pen again.

The grandeur of the River in its normal state has frequently been cited by travelers. Natives of the region respond to such comments with bovine indifference. Yet even their voices become tinged with awe when they speak of the River in flood. Much of the countryside that borders it is at a lesser elevation than the River itself; only the dykes or levees prevent a general inundation. When the water overtops these barriers, as it does three Springs out of five, there is little to impede its advance for miles in either direction. Whole counties disappear beneath the roiling surge. . . .

He paused to admire the sweep of his language and to wonder if a surge could roil. Might not 'ravening billow' be better? The pen hovered indecisively above the questionable words while he gazed into the near distance for inspiration. An approaching passenger caught his eye and nodded a casual greeting; a strongly built young man with a close-cropped brown beard, he was wearing light blue check trousers, a dark coat, and a flowing tie under his soft collar. Duncan had noticed him before and admired his air of ease and self-possession, but he did not want to let conversation break into his writing time. He returned the nod and looked down at the page again.

Gus grinned to himself as he moved away. The Boston feller was certainly keeping his nose to the grindstone. Why was he on the *Argo?* Not to gamble, that was sure; to Gus's knowledge he had not been near the tables, except as a spectator. And he didn't seem to have any friends aboard, though he had sat still a couple of times for some of Senator Stephenson's speechification. If he really was planning to write a book about the Mississippi, why had he chosen to see it from one of the fastest packets afloat? In his place, Gus would have stopped at towns and villages along the way, but maybe authors didn't think like other folk.

He put the puzzle of the young Bostonian aside, to consider the more ominous question of the growing band of toughs on board. More had come aboard at Vicksburg and Greenville. As at Natchez, the big feller called Mangen had rounded them up and given them passage money. By Gus's count there were about forty of them by now, and he wouldn't be surprised if another dozen joined the *Argo* at Memphis. Gus's spy, a sharp young Irishman, was keeping watch over them, but all he had learned so far was that they liked to drink, curse, and fight.

Gus liked to observe people and figure them out. His skill at it was valuable, too, but he thought of that as lagniappe, a little something extra. It was the exercise itself that he was drawn to. His life on the *Argo,* with its constantly changing parade of every variety of humanity, gave him a lot of raw material for this pursuit. The change was as important to him as the variety. He was not forced to become enmeshed in the lives of the people he observed, because in a day or two, or five at the most, they arrived at their destination. Stepping off the boat, they left his life. He preferred it that way.

When he thought about it, which wasn't often, he supposed that his interest in watching people went back to his days growing up in Cincinnati. Pneumonia had taken his mother when he was not quite five. For the next eleven years he had lived with his uncle, Peter Stone, a tanner by trade, who took in his orphaned nephew more out of duty than affection. Stone was a hard man, though not a cruel one. His religious creed was suited to his character, cold and stern, and he practiced it zealously. The only purpose of this world, in his view, was to test the strength of men's souls in a trial whose outcome in any case was foreordained. Obedience, restraint, and self-denial were the outward signs of a strong soul within, and any rebelliousness was necessarily the handiwork of Satan.

The only variation in his behavior was that sometimes he was much stricter. Gus learned at a early age to see the signs and anticipate these periods of repression. It was a matter of a tightening of the muscles around the eyes and a widening of the nostrils, often combined with a slow, steady opening and closing of the hands. The slightest deviation, at those times, meant a severe thrashing and a day in a cold corner without food. Even worse than the punishment itself was his uncle's conclusion, stated loudly and repeatedly, that he had proved himself unworthy and destined for eternal hellfire.

Still, if Stone was strict, he was, by his own light, just. His son Harry was another matter. Harry was nine years older than Gus. Among the members of the church Stone adhered to, he was always spoken of as a model child, obedient, respectful, and devout. Among the children of the neighborhood, he was spoken of in tones of hatred and dread. All the energy he could not express before his elders, he turned on those who were smaller. There wasn't a boy around who hadn't had his ears pulled, his nose twisted, or his balls grabbed by Harry, but never when there was a chance that a grown-up would see.

For years, until Gus became big enough to stand up to him, Harry made his little cousin's life a constant affliction. He soon tired of simple pinches, punches, and kicks. His persecutions grew more elaborate. Once, for example, when Gus was seven or eight, Harry killed a stray cat, cut off its head, and mounted it on a stick near the child's bed. Then he made scratching noises on the wall until Gus woke up and lit his candle. His screams woke the neighborhood, but by the time his uncle reached the room, Harry had tossed the evidence out the window. Gus was whipped for being fanciful, which in his uncle's code was considered closely akin to lying.

Gus soon learned to stay out of reach and to watch his cousin closely for clues to what he was planning to do next. He found that he could look at situations through Harry's eyes and then find ways to frustrate his schemes. Gradually he discovered that he could predict the behavior of others as well, not perfectly, of course, but closely enough to be useful. Any advantage, however small, was a great prize to someone whose position in life rested on such shaky foundations.

At twelve he went to work at the tannery. By his own choice he worked in the tanning yard. He hated the stench and the slime, but the alternative was to be in the office, directly under his cousin. In time he grew to like the work, to take pride in a well-tanned hide, and he rose to underforeman. Then, one day his uncle had a stroke. Unable to speak and barely able to walk, he was forced to let his son take over the business. Gus began making plans to run away, but before he had saved enough to take him to California, a miracle happened . . .

The stranger's salt-and-pepper trousers, dark broad-cloth coat, and high beaver hat made him look like a fashion plate in a magazine. He did not belong in that part of town, yet there he was, standing in the street staring at the premises of Peter Stone & Son, Tanners. Then, tipping his hat back a little and sticking his hands in his pockets, he strolled across and entered the office. Gus went back to riveting a pinhole leak in one of the huge tanning vats and forgot about the dandy until Harry stuck his head out the window and hollered for him to come to the office.

The first thing he noticed about the dandy was his boots. They were knee-high, of a rich leather that took a fine gloss, and they had probably cost as much as Gus made in a month. Then he heard

Harry say, "That's him. Gus, this here's your brother Jason. Seems he ain't drownded after all."

Gus shifted his gaze quickly from the stranger's boots to his cousin's face. He didn't doubt that this was a part of one of Harry's little schemes, but what was it? Where was the hook inside the bait?

There was wariness in the stranger's face, too. "I guess you were too little to remember," he said. "Is Momma . . . ?"

"Dead years ago," said Harry.

"Oh." He was studiously polite, but Gus heard dislike for Harry in his voice and began to warm to him. "Well, cousin, if you don't mind, I'd like to take Gussie for a walk. There's a lot for us to talk about, and I know you must be busy with so much responsibility on your shoulders."

Gussie? Gus didn't recall that anyone had ever called him that, and yet it had a familiar feeling to it. He studied this man who claimed to be his brother more carefully. There was a lot of determination in that face, and some humor, too, in the lines near the eyes and lips. Gus didn't believe it was a jolly sort of humor, though. It was more the humor of a man who is quick to see the foibles of mankind and just as quick to mock them without mercy.

"With your permission," he murmured to Harry, and held the door for Gus. Once they were on the street and away from the tannery, he said, "Are you and your cousin good friends? I see that you're not. That speaks well for your taste."

Gus laughed bitterly.

"Then it wouldn't grieve you to part with him and this place?"

"I'd have run away before now if I'd'a had the tin," Gus replied. He glanced over at the stranger who was his brother. "Am I to part with him then? To go with you?"

"If you're willing. I make my living as a gambler. I am about to move up to a new level of business, and I find I need someone I can trust. Do you believe that blood ties are the strongest?"

Gus took his time replying. "They brought you back here from wherever you were, but they took a powerful long time to do it. You could argue that one how you like, I reckon. As for me, I'll go with you and gladly. I'll show you I'm trustworthy, too, but it's not for the blood tie. It's for the chance of leaving. I'd go with Old Nick himself if he promised me that."

The sound of voices close at hand called Gus back from his memories. He looked around in some confusion. He had been leaning his elbows on the rail of the main deck promenade, mesmerized by the constantly expanding bow wave of the boat. There was no one else for thirty feet in either direction. Yet he *had* heard voices.

"You want to be nicer to me, honey," a man drawled. "It don't pay to be so uppity, indeed it don't. Now how about a little hug?"

Gus suddenly understood. The voice was coming from the stateroom just behind him. The shutters on the French windows were closed, but the louvers allowed the sound to escape. He had no wish to eavesdrop. He was about to walk toward the door to the Grand Saloon when a girl's voice, tremulous with fright but resolute even so, stopped him.

"I didn't invite you here, sir, and I don't want you here. If you're a gentleman, you'll leave now."

"Highty-tighty! Is that how they taught you to talk in that convent school? What do a lot of old maids dressed up like crows know about talking to a man? I ain't asking so much, just a little taste of the dish before it's served up. I want to make sure it's as sweet as I think it is."

"Stop! Take your hands off me, you villain!"

For a moment Gus wondered if he was listening to a rehearsal of a melodrama. But the girl was unmistakably in earnest, and very close to despair. The beginning of a cry for help, smothered by a hand, decided him. He strode rapidly along the promenade, counting windows as he went, then through the Grand Saloon to the corresponding stateroom door. He stopped, suddenly indecisive, wondering if he had counted correctly, if he had any right to interfere. Then, through the open transom, he heard the same voice sobbing and pleading. He tried the handle of the door, but it was locked. A moment later he had his pass key in the lock and was pushing the door open.

The girl was Senator Stephenson's young ward and the man was Luke Shuttlesworth. Gus's lack of surprise told him that he had somehow known who they were all along. The girl was holding the bodice of her afternoon dress up with her hands, and Shuttlesworth had three fresh scratches on his unscarred cheek. Gus stepped inside the stateroom and pushed the door closed behind him. The less publicity the better when a young lady's honor was at stake.

"Who's this boy?" Shuttlesworth demanded. "You're a sly one, ain't you, keeping a little sweetheart on the side, giving it to him and acting Miss Purity with me."

"Oh, sir, whoever you are, will you please go and take this man with you?"

Gus bowed. "Yours to command, ma'am. Well, friend, you heard the lady; let's go."

"And let you come creeping back to suck all the honey from this pretty little flower of mine? I'll see you in hell first." Keeping his eyes locked on Gus's, he reached out his hand, grabbed the shoulder of the girl's gown, and yanked. She shrieked as the cloth ripped and came away in his hand. From the corner of his eye, Gus saw one small, firm breast for a moment; then she whirled and snatched up the coverlet from the bed.

Gus clenched his fists and started toward the scar-faced man, who grinned evilly and pulled a long Bowie knife from under his coat. The edge gleamed in the dimly lit room.

"Now then," Shuttlesworth drawled, "not such a bantam cock as you were, are you? You got two seconds to get out that door before I make a capon of you." He flourished his weapon suggestively.

Gus's eyes darted around the room as he crouched defensively. He thought of himself as being handy with his fives, but going barehanded against a knife was something else. He didn't doubt that his opponent would try to carry out his threat. The thought made his scrotum tighten as if he had been swimming in November.

As Shuttlesworth took a step forward, Gus stepped backward. He considered leaving the stateroom and getting help, but he couldn't leave the girl alone with her attacker. The knife flashed in a sudden thrust. He sidestepped and snatched up the light chair by the desk, swinging it in a low arc that would have cracked Shuttlesworth's right kneecap if he hadn't jumped back.

"Put away the knife and go," Gus panted. "I'll say nothing about your vile behavior."

"Vile behavior, be damned! I use runts like you to pick my teeth with, you pox-rotted pigfucker!" He dodged the chair legs and slashed at Gus's hand. He missed, and Gus stepped back again.

The girl was in the corner of the room behind the bed, as far from the two men as she could get. The coverlet was wrapped about her, and she was holding her hands over her ears. Her wide-set eyes stared almost blindly at the battle.

For the moment, the two combatants were looking each other over, trying to find a weakness in the other's defenses. Suddenly Shuttlesworth lunged forward and thrust with his right hand. Only Gus's familiarity with his brother's sleight of hand permitted him to see that his attacker had tossed the knife to his left hand just before the lunge. The thrust was a feint, meant to bring Gus into the range of the other hand. He ignored the right and slammed the chair against Shuttlesworth's left wrist. For an instant he thought the other man would drop the knife. But then he made another lightning pass, back to his right hand, and backed onto the defensive again.

Gus began to advance, slowly, forcing his opponent back with sharp jabs of the chair. Soon Shuttlesworth would be in a corner, unable to maneuver. He would have to do something before then.

He did. On Gus's next jab, he grasped the stretcher of the chair and wrenched at it. This was exactly the move Gus had hoped for. He released the chair, then, while Shuttlesworth was still off-balance, put every scrap of energy in his coiled-up body into a driving kick aimed at the other man's knee. Had it connected, it would have crippled him for life. As it was, it landed on the meaty part of his thigh. His leg went numb and he toppled over, still clutching the knife. A moment later he felt a boot grinding on his right wrist. He let out a howl and released the knife.

Sunlight flowed into the room for a few seconds as Gus opened the shutters to toss the knife into the river. "You listen to me," he then said to the glowering Shuttlesworth. "If you molest this young lady again, I'll see that you're put off the *Argo* at the nearest canebrake as food for the gators and cottonmouths. You hear me?"

"I've got friends on this boat," Shuttlesworth muttered. "You'll have a job doing it."

Gus quailed a little at the thought of the damage that that gang of desperadoes could do if they went on a rampage, but he kept his concern out of his voice. "Then they can hike the swamps along with you. And in case you think this is a game of brag, my name is Augustus Lowell and I'm part-owner of the *Argo*." This wasn't strictly true, but it sounded firmer than saying his brother owned the boat.

Shuttlesworth seemed impressed with this information. "I thought you were just some meddler," he said slowly, "who'd taken a fancy to the girl I'm engaged to. It's a different matter if you're acting official-like; I wouldn't have drawn the knife if I'd known that. But I still won't have you interfering in my private affairs, boat-owner or not."

"Engaged?" Gus looked over at the corner, but the girl refused to meet his eyes. He wondered if he had been hasty. Then he caught a glimpse of her bare shoulder under the improvised cloak. "I can't say I care for your brand of courtship then. The young lady didn't seem to either, come to that. Maybe you'd best hold back any further little displays of affection while you're aboard this boat. What you do once we reach St. Louis is none of my business."

"What I do is none of your business anytime," Shuttlesworth replied, but the loss of his knife seemed to have cowed him. He got to his feet and looked inclined to outwait Gus, but when Gus stood by the door and gave him a significant look, he shuffled out without further discussion. The expression on his face, however, promised that he would take up the quarrel again.

"Now, Miss Wainwright," Gus said after he shut the door again, "I'll leave you to repair your costume in a moment. I just want to get a couple of things straight first."

"Yes, sir." She took a step forward, keeping her eyes modestly lowered. The color was starting to return to her cheeks; in fact, she seemed on the verge of blushing under his gaze. The maturity of his twenty-one years made him think of her as a child, one to be spoken to in kindly tones and short sentences, but then he recalled that brief glimpse of her uncovered breast. Not quite a child, then, not at all!

Unthinkingly he allowed his eyes to rest on that section of the coverlet that now concealed her upper body. Suddenly she clutched the spread more tightly around her. Her face turned quite red, and she looked at him with defiance in her eyes. "If you have no questions, sir," she said coldly, "I should like my privacy."

Gus couldn't comprehend this abrupt change of mood. How had he offended her? Then the answer came to him, and he felt his own cheeks grow warm. He couldn't meet her eyes, and he didn't know where else to look. "Er, yes, ma'am," he said, gazing up toward the ceiling. "I hope you'll pardon my interest in your private affairs, but I believe the situation excuses it. Is there an engagement between you and that, uh, gentleman?"

She hesitated before answering. "I know that my guardian would like such a match. He has told me so himself. I haven't agreed to it, though, and I, I hope I never shall. I do not greatly fancy Mr. Shuttlesworth as a partner." The shiver that passed through her as she said these last words revealed how greatly they understated her feelings about the scar-faced man.

"Then you needn't have him," said Gus stoutly. "This is the Nineteenth Century, after all. Maidens aren't carried off into forced marriages any more. All you need do is tell your guardian that you don't care for his choice and wish to make your own instead. He may be disappointed, though I can't think why, but he will have to accept your decision.''

''Perhaps.'' She sounded unconvinced. ''I'm sure Uncle Junius has no wish to be cruel to me. If he knew how Mr. Shuttlesworth has behaved, he would be very angry, I know. Perhaps if I explain to him how I feel, he will understand.''

Gus privately thought that Senator Stephenson had about as much understanding as a blown-up pig's bladder. ''Of course,'' he said aloud. ''And if Mr. Shuttlesworth pesters you again, get word to me and I'll have him put off the boat straight away. We have our reputation as a safe, decent boat to maintain.''

He smiled reassuringly, and after a moment she gave him a tremulous smile in return. ''Thank you, sir,'' she said. ''I declare, you've been a perfect gentle knight to me today.''

She took a step in his direction, which he interpreted as a hint for him to leave. Retrieving his hat from the corner where it had rolled, he wished her a good afternoon and retreated to the texas deck. There he relived, blow by blow, his combat with Shuttlesworth and tried hard not to recall the moment when Miss Wainwright's bodice had been ripped away. In spite of his determination, though, the memory haunted him. Was he as bad as that hound Shuttlesworth, then?

CHAPTER NINE

"We are the true democrats, sir. Our way of life, bound as it is to the land, gives us the independence of spirit that those who toil in manufactories for wages can never know. That independence is deeply offensive to the plutocrats of the North, who seek to replace the rule of the people by the rule of capital. Understand that, Mr. Brigham, and you will understand the whole of the present crisis. They mean to fasten the chains of tyranny about our necks, but they know that we are free men and determined to resist, so they disguise their true aim. They claim to be the true friends of the Negro and to abhor an institution that is sanctioned by history, law, and the express word of God Almighty. Well, sir, they lie! If we don't protect our Negroes from them, they will ship them off to the mills to be far worse than slaves. Ask a mill hand in New Hampshire or Rhode Island, a poor laborer who was put out to starve in the last Panic, if he would not gladly trade places with a Negro slave who knows he will receive the kindly care of his master for all of his natural life. Friends of the Negro, sir? Poppycock!''

Senator Junius Stephenson paused long enough to eject a stream of brown tobacco juice and to wipe his lips with a stained handkerchief. Before sitting down, he had moved a brass spittoon closer to his chair, but the state of the carpet indicated that he wasn't very accurate even at short range. His listener, young Brigham, was sitting forward in his chair, drinking in every word, and the Senator knew without looking that several others in the room were listening as well. Some of them would probably repeat his words at the supper table, too. Little by little, through unceasing effort, the tocsin call of danger was reaching the sturdy yeomanry of the South. An inspiring phrase—he made a mental note to use it in his next speech.

Charlie Brigham was not trying to follow the sense of Senator Stephenson's remarks. It was the mellow, rolling sound of them, and the fact that they were being addressed publicly to him, that was intoxicating. He wished he could pull out a plug of tobacco and bite off a chaw, like the Senator, but the one time he had tried it, in his stateroom, he had had to throw up. Why had the Senator stopped talking? Did he expect him to make some remark on his oration? Charlie nervously stroked his upper lip and tried to recall what it had been about. Slavery, of course, but what else?

''Durn right, Senator,'' he said finally. ''They're all right so long as we keep 'em in their place, but give 'em half a chance and they'll be defiling our womenfolk and murdering us in our beds like Nat Turner. Trouble with Yankees is they don't understand niggers the way we do. Up there they think they're always telling jokes and playing banjos like in the coon shows. They just don't realize that they're all born thieves and in heat from the time they're waist-high to a man.'' He sniggered and leaned his head closer. ''Why, last month I was walking down Poydras Street, in the middle of the afternoon, and a little nappy-headed picaninny walked right up to me and put her hand right here! Well, I stepped back in surprise, and she took off in a run. Durn me, if she hadn't got my coin purse out of my pocket while she was rubbing my John Thomas with her other hand! Don't that beat all though?''

Stephenson looked at him oddly. For the first few sentences he had actually entertained the idea that the boy was mocking him. Then he realized that such subtlety was beyond his capabilities. No, Brigham was clearly the stuff of which followers are made. And the Senator knew very well that anyone who was trying to lead a popular movement could not afford to be too choosy about his followers' ideas. As far as he was concerned, they might think what they liked so long as they went where they were led.

Still, there was a danger that the boy's simpleton notions, if overheard, might antagonize some of the more moderate elements who could be won over to a more respectably phrased creed.

''Now, now, son,'' he said in a tone that was both patronizing and good-humored, ''you know that we have nothing to fear from our own Negroes. They know that their lot is the best they can aspire to, and they are content with it. What we should— nay, *must*—fear is those fiends in human guise who go about stirring up animal passions in a few misguided Negroes. Why, sir, roasting over slow coals would be too good for such men! If our way of life, so precious to us, is to survive and thrive, we must sweep them right off the public stage. They deserve no more mercy than the serpent that strikes at your heel, but like the serpent, they are wily, sir, wily!''

Charlie was beginning to understand that his role was to give the Senator an excuse to keep speaking. ''But sir, how can we sweep them from the stage? What can we do?''

''Do? Do! We can defend our rights as free men at every turn! We have the right to determine our own destiny, don't we? Don't we have the right to the quiet enjoyment of our private property? Take away those rights, sir, and you have base tyranny. But that is the plan and program of the abolition-ists and Black Republicans, I assure you. They intend nothing less than the ruination of the South through confiscation, expropriation, and the stir-ring up of race war.''

''Let 'em try it,'' Charlie growled. ''We'll show 'em a thing or two, by golly.''

Stephenson spoke in a deeper, booming voice, like a preacher at a popular funeral. ''They are trying it, Mr. Brigham, at this very time. Their agitators and hired assassins are pouring into the Kansas Territory by the thousands. They are des-perate to keep our people, the real old American stock, from settling lands that were manifestly meant for our use. The children of the men who won our freedom at Yorktown and defended it at New Orleans are to bow the neck to the spawn of the Old World's teeming slums.''

His face swelled and reddened, and he struck the air with his fist. "Well, we won't have it, sir. Kansas belongs to us! We shall defend it to the last drop of blood! Let those who would tamper with our rights beware! We are slow to anger, but when we strike, we strike like the hurricane, leaving only devastation in our path!''

The room burst out in cheers and applause. Here and there a man did not join in the acclaim, but none of them dared to raise an opposing voice. There was Frederick Braugh, for instance, a feed merchant from southeastern Missouri. He had no strong beliefs about slavery one way or the other. He certainly wasn't partial to Negroes. But he was convinced that the cotton economy and the plantation system were ruining the South. More particularly, they were ruining *him,* by driving out the family farmer and small townsman who couldn't compete against slave labor. It made him ill to walk through the main deck of the *Argo* and see all the immigrants—sturdy, hard-working folk, for the most part, and many of them skilled farmers—who were bound for Iowa and Wisconsin and Minnesota. It was the slave system that kept them from stopping in Missouri, where they might prosper and make him prosperous, too.

But Braugh knew what kind of response he would get if he said any of that. Men like Senator Stephenson had it all their own way, persuading some, attracting others with the hope of power and gain, and silencing the rest through intimidation. There were sad times coming for the country, that was clear. In fact, Braugh decided, judging by his newspaper, the sad times had already arrived. He turned the page and raised the paper higher to block the sight of Stephenson and his companion, then tried to concentrate on a discussion of the tariff question.

Charlie had once more naively mistaken the Senator's point. "Kansas, you say, sir?" he said brightly. "Why, that's where I'm going, me and my sister. We've got an uncle there. Dan Church. Maybe you know him—he has a farm just outside a town called Lawrence."

"Lawrence! That's the very den of vipers! Sir, are you aware that Lawrence, Kansas, took its name from one of the most hellish mill towns in the state of Massachusetts? That it was founded by the so-called Emigrant Aid Society for the express purpose of keeping right-minded Southerners out of the Kansas Territory? That, even as we talk, the town is in open rebellion against the duly-constituted territorial government? Do I know the name, sir? I abominate it! It stinks in my nostrils!"

Charlie received the impression that he was, through his uncle, somehow responsible for the crimes of Lawrence. "I'm sorry, Senator Stephenson. I don't know anything about the town, just that that's where we're going to be living now. You don't think much of it, I guess."

Stephenson softened his tone a little. "It is not a place I would want anyone with sound ideas to settle, no. I am confident that before long the treasonous scum who infest it will receive the chastisement they have earned, and history teaches us that punitive campaigns often get out of hand. Consider the glory that was Carthage, sir. Where is it now?''

Charlie confessed that he had no idea.

''Hold on, though,'' the Senator continued, ''it comes to me that someone who was bold and resolute might do a great service to the cause, someone who had an unquestionable reason for living within the camp of the enemy. I must give this more thought, Mr. Brigham. It is no ordinary task I may propose.''

''You just say the word, sir. I'm your man!''

Stephenson looked at him dispassionately, as he might have looked at a new strain of cotton someone was recommending to him. Then he straightened up as he saw Luke Shuttlesworth stalk through the far door, looking ready to scalp someone. ''Ah, you'll have to excuse me, Mr. Brigham,'' he said. ''A little matter of business I must attend to. I hope we can continue our discussion at a later time.''

Charlie sprang up from his chair. ''Sure, Senator, any time. It's a real education for me, hearing you talk.''

Shuttlesworth waited for the young man to leave. Then he pulled a chair over next to Stephenson's. ''I'll pay off the son of a whore, see if I don't,'' he said in a low, rasping voice.

''Who, Brigham? What's he done?''

''Not that little piss-ant. Another one, named Lowell. Not the gambler, his kid brother. I was having a private talk with M'lissy just now and he butted in. I told him to butt out, but he pulled a dirty trick and took away my knife. Threw it in the river, too, damn his black soul. I had that knife six or seven years. Hard to get good steel like that.''

The Senator seemed to be only half-listening. ''What kind of talk were you having with Melissa?'' he asked when Shuttlesworth finished.

''Nothing much, just trying to get her to warm up a little.'' He grinned. ''She's got everything she needs, all right, she just don't know how to use it yet. I figured on giving her a lesson or two.''

''And how did she take to that idea?''

''Well, she put up a little bitty fight at first, but it would have been all right if that dogturd Lowell hadn't butted in like that.''

Stephenson closed his eyes and lightly massaged his forehead. He knew from his reading of history that every great man, every man who succeeded in changing his world, had suffered from the weaknesses and faults of underlings. But to read about a problem was far different from having to cope with it yourself. He needed Shuttlesworth, but unless he handled him very carefully, the scarred man was going to damage his plans more than any enemy could hope to.

''Luke,'' he said, ''Melissa is still very young and inexperienced. You need to remember that. She's not one of your Gallatin Street whores, she's a shy, modest, well-bred young lady. Remember, too, how important she is to us. If you don't behave yourself for a little while longer, all my influence might not be enough to persuade her into this marriage. You don't want her to refuse you, do you?''

"And lose my chance at a sweet little thing like that? Nosirree! But I don't know what's fretting you so, indeed I don't. Persuade her? Why, hell, Senator, she just hasn't had a taste of it yet, that's all. Let me get in the saddle once or twice and I'll have her broken in in no time. Why, she'll come begging for it on her knees! And I wouldn't mind that either, if you get what I mean; I got a little bit of French blood in me on my daddy's side.''

The Senator took a deep breath. Crude as he was, Luke still might be right in his prediction. Plenty of girls who acted like butter wouldn't melt in their mouths turned out to be hot as a two-bit pistol once they got the chance. But was Melissa Wainwright one of them? He realized that he didn't know her well enough to say for sure.

Philo Wainwright had come to New Orleans from Virginia, by way of Cuba, in the 1820s. Starting with a single hundred-foot schooner, he gradually built the most important fleet of boats trading between New Orleans, the West Indies, and South America. Melissa was his only child. Her mother had died bearing a stillborn son when Melissa was six. After that, Wainwright turned the care of the girl over to governesses and a school for young ladies conducted by a teaching order of nuns. He was a good deal more interested in ships than in children, though he did sometimes muse about the pleasure he would have taken in teaching his son the shipping business.

Stephenson was an early secret investor in the Wainwright firm, and over the years he was able to do several important political favors for it. It was natural enough for Wainwright to name him as his daughter's guardian; like most men who write a will, he did not expect it to be put into effect for many years. He considered the designation purely a formality, then forgot it altogether. But one day, when he was standing on the levee listening to a report from one of his captains, a hogshead of molasses fell off a nearby wagon, thundered across the hard-packed dirt, and crushed him flat. Melissa was thirteen at the time.

Stephenson's duties as her guardian were no burden. He continued to keep her in the same convent school, took her for an occasional carriage ride and light meal when he was in town, and generally remembered to send a small gift on her birthday and at Christmas. He had no responsibility for the financial affairs of the estate, which were handled by Wainwright's former banker, Louis Grandcourt.

Grandcourt was part of the old French aristocracy of New Orleans. He was an outspoken royalist, still proclaiming his allegiance to Louis XVIII, the French king who had been kicked out two revolutions before. He frequently told guests at his *hôtel particulier* in the Vieux Carré that the usurper Buonaparte had committed many crimes against France, but the blackest of them had been to give Louisiana to the *sales americains*.

In spite of his dislike for Americans, and especially for American politicians, Grandcourt was cooperative toward Stephenson. He paid Melissa's school fees, dressmaker's bills, and other modest expenses without a murmur. He even suggested that if a suitable companion could be found, the child might enjoy a summer's tour of Europe before entering a proper finishing school in Paris. But the one time Senator Stephenson had suggested an investment for some of the Wainwright fortune, Grandcourt had instantly become icily polite. The management of the estate, he intimated, was already in able hands. The distinguished Senator doubtlessly had more important matters to concern himself with than his ward's dowry.

Stephenson dropped the subject. He did have more important matters on his mind, in fact. It wasn't until a year or two later that he discovered the need for a large sum of money. His own resources were not what they had been. He had speculated in South American bonds, only to see them become worthless when a new regime disavowed them. He had also, in deepest secrecy, bought a share in a plan to smuggle illegal African slaves into the United States. The potential profit was enormous, but unfortunately a British frigate captured the slave ship and he lost every penny.

Once more he paid a visit to Grandcourt's bank, a handsome domed building on Royal Street, to suggest that a loan of a hundred thousand dollars at a nominal rate of interest, secured by his plantations and slaves, would be very welcome. Grandcourt stared at him as if he had just announced that he was the Archduke of Austria.

"*M'sieur le senateur*" is surely aware that his property is already heavily encumbered," he said coldly. "But even if suitable collateral were found, the Wainwright estate has no such sum available on short notice. Much of it is in real estate and ships, of course, and the remainder has been put out at rates of interest that are very far from nominal. I would be traducing my duty as trustee to consider such a proposition.''

''Even if there were intangible benefits to the estate—and to your bank—from accepting it? A great many matters come to the attention of a Senator of the United States in which a suggestion from him carries considerable weight.''

Grandcourt openly showed his distaste for the conversation. ''I am a banker, *m'sieur;* I do not deal in intangible benefits. In any case, I do not conceive that your relationship of trust vis-á-vis Mlle. Wainwright gives you any particular call on the resources of her father's estate. Once she has attained the age of twenty-five, of course, she may lend you the money herself if she chooses.''

''But that's eight years away!''

''This is true. Did you have any other matters to take up with me, *m'sieur le senateur*?''

Stephenson retired defeated from that encounter, but two months later he informed Grandcourt in a curt note that Miss Wainwright was to accompany him on a prolonged visit to St. Louis. The banker was disturbed by the news, but the most he could do about it was refuse to advance the girl's travel expenses. That was not likely to deter someone as resolute as the Senator.

It was around that time that Stephenson began calling for Melissa every Saturday and Sunday afternoon, to take her for a drive through the Garden District or across to Lake Ponchartrain. More often than not, Luke Shuttlesworth was a member of their party too. She didn't seem to take to him, nor could Stephenson blame her much. Luke's idea of the way to make an impression on a girl was to tell one off-color story after another. Most of them Melissa genuinely failed to understand, and those she did understand revolted her.

Even so, the Senator was not prepared for her reaction when he told her that Shuttlesworth was going to St. Louis with them. Up until that point she had been prattling gaily about the delights of the journey, as if St. Louis were Paris, London, and Rome in one. But at the thought of having Luke along, she became very still. He asked her if she objected to his company.

"It's not my place to object, Uncle Junius. He is your friend, after all."

He forced a chuckle. "Not just my friend, no, no. You've made quite a conquest, you know."

"I declare I never meant to, sir, indeed I didn't!" She looked alarmed to the point of bursting into tears.

"Oh, I don't mean to say that you've acted the coquette. You've done nothing the good Sisters could disapprove of. Still," he added with a roguish expression, "my friend Shuttlesworth is quite smitten. Quite smitten!"

"As he is your friend, Uncle, will you tell him please that I am very sorry he is smitten and I wish him not to be?"

His long white hair swayed gracefully as he nodded his head. "Quite right, my dear. A man doesn't feel the same degree of respect for what he gains too easily." He fell silent and gazed into the distance. Then, as if changing the subject, he said, "You know, young Shuttlesworth has his rough edges, but he is a man destined for great things. He will make his mark on this country, and before he is much older, too. I imagine that when that time comes, he'll have girls clamoring for his attention. Unless of course he takes a fancy to someone and marries her before then, hey?''

''Why do you mention marriage to me?'' she asked in dismay. ''I'm not yet of an age even to put my hair up!''

''Oh, of course, of course. I meant nothing particular by it. Still, time and tide stay for no man, hey? You already seem like quite a grown-up young lady to me. And it's none too soon to start thinking about establishing you in your proper sphere of life.''

''If you please, sir, I would rather not think about it just now. I declare, the afternoon has quite flown. I must be back at school before vespers or Sister Thérèse will be very vexed with me.''

After that he didn't venture to raise the subject with her again, though he did tell Luke that he had opened it up. In any case, Melissa was so busy with fittings for her traveling wardrobe that he saw almost nothing of her until the day they were to go aboard the *Argo*. He was spending a good part of every day with her now, but whenever he drifted toward a dangerous topic, she was sure to see a darling cabin on the riverbank or a priceless bonnet on a fellow passenger and rattle on about it until she was breathless. And whenever Luke joined them, she found a reason to retire to her stateroom.

No, he had to admit that his ward was not showing any sign of a partiality for Luke Shuttlesworth. And if the scene that had just taken place was at all like what he imagined from his knowledge of Luke, she was probably even less inclined toward him now. Still, in the long run, her likes and dislikes were unimportant. What mattered was to get her to St. Louis and then on the next stage of her journey without any interference. And that meant keeping her unalarmed for as long as there were so many potential busybodies around.

He aimed another stream of brown juice at the spittoon and cleared his throat. "Now, listen here, Luke," he began, "and mind what I say. Melissa's not used to your ways yet. If you keep sniffing around her like she's a bitch in heat, you'll scare her off for good. Then we'll both of us have trouble. But you'll have twice as much, because I'll sure-to-God visit my troubles on you. Are you following me, son? Any parts you want me to repeat?"

Luke shook his head sullenly. "I hear you all right. But I'm telling you, she wants it as much as any of 'em; she just plain don't know it yet. Once I get her going, she'll be too busy squealing with delight to give trouble to anyone."

He licked his lips loudly. Stephenson noticed with fascinated disgust that his tongue lapped over the tip of his nose. The man's self-assurance was staggering, and so was his faith in the effectiveness of the beast-with-two-backs as a cure for female discontent. But it might be all brag. Stephenson was not willing to gamble on an unseen hand. The stakes were too high.

"You may be right," he said sternly. "When the time comes, you'll have your chance to prove it, too. But not now. You're to keep away from

Melissa for the rest of the trip to St. Louis. I'll tell her that you came to me in a fit of remorse over your drunken misconduct—"

"Drunk! Hell, there ain't the liquor on this whole damn boat could get me drunk!"

The Senator ignored the interruption. His years in Washington had made him an expert at that. "And that you begged me to apologize to her on your behalf. I'll explain that you are too ashamed to face her until time has softened her recollections of the incident and you can hope to receive her forgiveness. In my experience, there's nothing a woman likes better than the chance to forgive a man's misconduct."

Luke growled, and his fists clenched until the knuckles were white. "Forgive me!" he burst out. "Why, hellfire, ain't I the one was made a laughingstock in front of her? Ain't I the one who lost his knife that he'd had for ten years or more? Ain't I the one she been teasing so much I can't hardly bear to walk for the pain of it? No sir, I ain't one to step aside and bide my time while she goes giving it away to some sneak who ain't fit to tote guts to a bear!"

Stephenson's headache was worse. He was strongly tempted to let loose at Shuttlesworth and cut a strip out of his hide, but he wasn't quite sure enough of his control over him. He closed his eyes and took a deep breath, then opened them and said, mildly enough under the circumstances, "You may have reason to be angry; I don't say not. But it's a question of the cause. And for the sake of the cause, you will do as I say. You'll keep clear of her until St. Louis."

He saw the gleam of determination in Shuttlesworth's eye and added, ''You're not to tangle with young Lowell either. Not while we're still on this boat. After that, it's your own affair.''

CHAPTER TEN

"A fine evening, sir!"

Duncan had been standing at the front railing of the boiler deck gallery, leaning against one of the fluted wooden columns that supported the hurricane deck. When he was spoken to, he straightened up and looked around. A dim shaft of light from the Grand Saloon showed him the features of a middle-aged man who had sat at the same table with him at supper.

"So it is," he replied. "The effect of the clouds passing over the face of the moon is remarkable. It makes me wish I had pursued the art of painting, though it would take a master to capture it in any case. Do you know the work of the English painter Turner? He died a few years ago. Now, he might have succeeded with this scene."

"Really? I can't say I know him, but I'll make a note of the name. I have promised myself a complete education in the arts, once I retire from business. Would you like a cigar?''

The two men went through the ritual of biting the tips off their cigars and lighting them evenly. Duncan savored the smoke. The cheroots he had bought in New Orleans were vile, and the selection available in the *Argo*'s bar was not much better. He did not use tobacco very often, but when he did, he preferred to enjoy the experience.

After a stretch of companionable silence, he gave his name to the other man, who, in turn, introduced himself as Lionel Hornby, and added, ''Traveling far, Mr. Sargent?''

''To St. Louis for now, sir; later I may explore the upper river as well.'' Once again he explained about his book.

Hornby's enthusiasm took him by surprise. ''A wonderful notion, sir, wonderful! Why, when I think of the thousands of folks all over old New England, living on hardscrabble farms, always caught between starving and freezing, and all because they aren't acquainted with the advantages of this great territory—then, sir, I become indignant. Write your book, by all means; tell them about the boundless acres of inexhaustibly rich soil, the plentiful game, the cordial welcome their fellow pioneers will give them! In fact, Mr. Sargent, I would have you do more even. Lecture, sir: tour the older sections of our nation and tell the people what you have witnessed. I am convinced that the costs of such an enterprise would be readily defrayed by forward-looking men who want their fellow-countrymen to appreciate the treasure we have here.''

He waved his cigar in the direction of the moon-lit riverscape.

"I'm glad you approve," Duncan said drily. Hornby amused and interested him. "I don't know that I'm much of a talker, though. You sound much better fitted for such a project yourself."

"I? Ah, if only I could. I'd be like a boy let out of school for the holidays. But I'm afraid my responsibilities would never allow it. No, these few days of leisurely travel already stretch the limits of my freedom. I envy you, Mr. Sargent. You have a chance to see something of the world while you are still young, and at the same time you are secure in the knowledge that you are undertaking a useful task."

The praise seemed to embarrass Duncan, who made no reply. A few moments later, the *Argo*'s whistle let out a series of blasts, frightening a flock of waterfowl into flight. Up ahead, on the Arkansas shore, a spark appeared and slowly spread into a blaze. It was time for the boat to take on wood again.

The first day Duncan had been amazed at the frequent wooding stops. Then someone explained that each of the boat's eight cast-iron furnaces consumed as much as ten cords of wood every twenty-four hours. Since even a single cord took up a space eight feet long and four feet wide, the amount the boat could carry was bound to be used up pretty quickly.

"Huh! You call this quickly?" another man added. He had once gone from Natchez to Memphis on a boat that was known up and down the river for its greedy furnaces. Late one afternoon they stopped once again to wood up. The captain didn't see any convenient place to tie up, so he kept the paddlewheels going, to hold the boat against the current. "We took on forty cords or so," the man concluded, "and the captain figured it was time to get going again. But then the mate told him the bad news: we'd used up every scrap of those forty cords already, just staying there in one place!"

The *Argo* slowed and started to angle left toward the woodyard. From the bow, the leadsman's chant rang like a magical spell: "Mark three . . . Mark three . . . quarter less three . . . half twain . . . half twain . . . mark twain. . . ." As if in response, two boys came running forward with a long iron bar that forked at one end. A basket of iron, about a foot wide and eighteen inches deep, swung between the prongs of the fork. It was filled with split pieces of 'fatwood,' Georgia pine full of resinous sap that burned fiercely and brightly. The boys inserted the other end of the bar in a socket set into the forward deck, suspending the basket out over the water, then one of them ran back, to reappear with a flaming splinter and thrust it into the basket.

Flames shot ten feet into the air, lighting a circle that included the bow of the *Argo,* an expanse of muddy river, and a section of the approaching bank. The pungent smell of burning sap spread across the deck. The giant paddlewheels were barely moving now, and two deckhands stood ready to toss a line to the waiting woodyard owner. Soon the boat was tied up, the gangplank was in place, and a solid line of roustabouts and deck passengers was moving between the woodyard and the fuel bunkers. The two boys were still feeding the basket with fatwood. As Duncan watched, one of them reached out with a ladle of pulverized resin and poured it on.

The flames burst out still more fiercely and lit the underside of a low cloud of thick black smoke. Burning tar fell, drop by drop, onto the water and floated away, still burning and smoking, into the darkness. The two lamp-boys, black and greasy from their work, grinned at each other and revealed that under the soot their skin was white. So were many of the roustabouts, but in the weird light of the burning torch, their glistening backs and those of the Negroes among them could not be told apart. Duncan was strongly reminded of the *Inferno* by Dante, but he decided that the allusion was too trite to use in a description of the scene.

Then the brief, frantic activity ended; the gangplank was pulled in, the torch was allowed to gutter out, and the *Argo* was once more moving upriver.

Duncan's cigar had gone out. He studied the end for a moment, then tossed the butt over the side.

"Have another, Mr. Sargent." Hornby proffered his sealskin cigar case.

Duncan had forgotten the other man was there. He would have loved another of those fine cigars, but etiquette forced him to decline.

"A very romantic scene we just watched, wasn't it," said Hornby, putting away the cigar case. "Picturesque and full of interest. Damn foolery, of course; another ten years and that sort of thing will be only a memory.''

''What do you mean, sir?''

He snorted in contempt. ''Wood-fired boilers, stopping for fuel every few hours . . . and the engines! Do you hear that noise, sir? Do you know what it is?''

Duncan listened and heard a steady hissing. ''I'm not sure; isn't it the escape pipes?''

''Right you are! The steam expands once only, then it is vented up those pipes. Half the energy those boilers produce goes right up the pipes with it. Idiocy!''

The man seemed deeply offended by the inefficiency of the engines, Duncan thought. Perhaps he was a mad inventor whose patent double-acting whorstle gear had been rejected by the steamboat constructors. ''You think the mechanics can be improved, then?'' he said cautiously.

''Oh, that, yes. Nothing to it: switch to coal-firing and recirculate the steam to preheat the boiler water. A boat like this could ship enough coal to take her halfway from New Orleans to St. Louis, if the engines were improved a little.''

''Then why does no one change?''

Hornby made an impatient movement of his shoulder. ''They've fired with wood since the first steamboat on this river forty years ago. Besides, the coal is up along the Ohio and the trees are right here. For now, anyway.''

He fell silent. The two men listened to the thump of the wheels, the chuff-chuff of the engines, and the hiss of the escape pipes. Somewhere, far off, an owl hooted.

"It doesn't much matter," Hornby said abruptly. "They say that great elephants with long fur roamed this countryside a long time ago. By the time you're my age, Mr. Duncan, boats like this one will seem just as much like fairy-tales as those hairy elephants. You find that amusing, maybe, but I know what I'm talking about."

"Pardon me, sir, but just what *are* you talking about?"

"Railroads, my boy; steam cars. My line of business. One company has already bridged the Mississippi, up by Rock Island, and others will follow. Once the east-west system is finished, in five or ten years, we'll have to start filling in the north-south links, sure as tomorrow's dawn."

"But surely the river traffic is too well entrenched to be in serious danger?"

"Hmph. I'll let you be the judge, son. Take this journey we're on now. New Orleans to St. Louis is roughly twelve hundred fifty miles by river, and a real spanker of a steamboat like this one will average ten or twelve miles an hour. A fast railroad train might average as much as forty miles an hour."

"Well," said Duncan, "that is an improvement, but—"

"I'm not finished, son. I said the distance is twelve hundred fifty miles by river. But you've seen how the Mississippi twists around on itself. By *land* it's no more than seven hundred miles from New Orleans to St. Louis. So now we are talking about eighteen hours traveling as against five full days! And no worries about snags or boiler explosions or sandbars when you're riding the steam cars. They run in any weather, don't care if the river's high or low or frozen solid, and in time they will offer as much comfort as one of these floating palaces.''

Duncan laughed. ''You're a powerful advocate, Mr. Hornby!''

''That's my occupation, Mr. Sargent. But I'll let you in on a secret: I couldn't be one-tenth as powerful if I weren't speaking from firmly held conviction. No sir, the Mississippi steamboat is doomed. It may last out my lifetime, but not yours.''

Duncan reached out to touch the fretwork bracket at the top of the column he was leaning against. ''It's a pity,'' he said. ''They're very graceful.''

''Oh, yes. And I dare say King Arthur's knights were a pretty sight riding across a field in their shining armor. But give me a Sharps repeating rifle and a box of shells and I warrant I could stand off the lot of them. The world changes, Mr. Sargent; nothing's more certain than that.''

He tossed his own cigar into the river. ''I guess there's time for a few hands of cards before turning in. Will you join me, sir?''

Duncan considered the invitation for a moment, then said, ''No, thank you. I think I'll enjoy the moonlight for a while longer—before it, too, is improved out of existence.''

''Evening, gents. Is this place free?''

Jason looked up from shuffling to nod a welcome to the new player. One of Gus's live ones, the railroad man from Chicago. He had the look of a man who liked an exciting game and didn't mind paying for it. Jason appreciated that. There was nothing duller than playing cards with someone who was overly cautious. Not that tonight's players suffered from too much caution. On Jason's right was Captain Bolling, the big landowner from Texas, and on his left was a short fellow in butternut-dyed homespun who had come aboard at Greenville, bound for Memphis, and who had been winning pretty steadily all evening. The railroad man, Hornby, was next to him, and to his left was the man with a scarred cheek who was a crony of Senator Stephenson. The last seat, between the scarred man and Captain Bolling, was filled by a Vicksburg lawyer named Ginther. He was running about even as far as Jason could tell, and he had started yawning about ten minutes earlier, so it looked likely to become a five-handed game again pretty soon.

Jason finished dealing and picked up his hand. Nothing there: the queen, ten, and three smaller diamonds. Interesting that all five were the same suit; some players back East were pressing to have that accepted as a winning hand, along with five cards in numerical order. They didn't have much hope of success, though, until they agreed on the value of the two new hands. Any idiot could see that four of a kind beat three of a kind, but understanding the probability of holding five of a single suit was beyond most poker players.

"I'll open with a V," said Hornby, pushing a half-eagle into the center. No one seemed very pleased with his cards, though no one was displeased enough to fold his hand before the draw. Jason managed to improve his hand to the extent of a pair of tens, but when a betting war broke out between Bolling and the fellow in homespun, he tossed it in. From the sidelines he watched the stakes grow to over four hundred dollars before Homespun took it with three jacks. The Texan, who had been backing three eights, was not pleased.

Homespun won the next hand, his own deal, as well, though the pot was a good deal less impressive. The cards were not cooperating. The court cards seemed to have gone into hiding, and even a small pair was starting to look like a sure winner. After two more boring hands, Counselor Ginther wished a good night to all and went off to his bunk. A couple of minutes later someone slipped into the vacant chair. To Jason's irritation, the new player was Charlie Brigham.

Where had he gotten the money to join the play? After Jason had taken the trouble to win it all from him, had his sister handed it back? Maybe the fact that it hadn't been fair play offended her prissy conscience, the same way a friendly hug did. Jason had meant no more than that, or if he had, it was only because he expected her to be as interested in a little fun as he was. And then to have her pull back and give him a look as though he had tried to take her by force! He had never needed to force a woman in his life, and he did not believe he would enjoy doing so. It was easy enough to find willing partners. If Mistress Elizabeth Brigham was not one, why then, to the devil with her! And with her brat brother as well, who had just put a couple of hundred in coins and notes on the table.

"I poque ten dollars," said Hornby. The others quickly chipped in. Jason had not yet looked at his cards, but he tossed an eagle on the table anyway, only to have Homespun make a twenty-dollar raise. Jason shuffled his hand, for luck, and fanned it out, to find a pair of sixes. The way the cards had been falling, that was good enough to pay thirty for a chance at the draw. When the betting came around, he added two more gold pieces to the growing pile.

Everyone took three cards except Homespun, who took two, and Brigham, who took none. When Jason picked his up, he found an eight, another six, and another eight. The way the others were sitting just a tad straighter in their seats, he wasn't the only one to improve his hand. Hornby opened again, for twenty this time, and was immediately raised twenty by Scarface. The brat swallowed a couple of times, looking as though his Adam's apple would slice right through his collar and cravat.

"I'll go you forty more," he said. His voice cracked in mid-sentence, soaring into a treble range.

Bolling gave him a sharp sidelong glance, but pushed his four double eagles in without comment. Jason did the same, but not very happily. Sixes over eights did not strike him as a very remarkable hand. Homespun apparently liked his even less, for he threw it in without comment. That brought the betting back to the opener, Hornby. He fingered a stack of gold thoughtfully, counted out the sixty he owed the pot, and added forty more. Scarface immediately folded.

If he hadn't regarded his presence as a nuisance, Jason would have felt a pang of sympathy for young Brigham. He was playing out of his depth. He didn't have the money or the experience to go against a player like Hornby or Bolling, not to mention Jason Lowell. Over half his table stake was already in the pot; if he threw in his cards, he lost it for sure, but if he stayed in he might lose the rest as well.

"Get along, youngster," Captain Bolling muttered. "In or out."

Brigham flushed and threw two twenties on the table. "I'll see you," he said, paused to gather his nerve, and added defiantly, "and go you fifty more."

Bolling folded, and earned a look of hatred from Charlie Brigham. It was to Jason now. What was the state of the game? Hornby had drawn three, holding a pair. His betting indicated that he had improved it to two pair or perhaps a weak full house. Brigham was harder to figure; inexperienced players usually were. He had stood pat, but his betting before the draw didn't suggest someone holding strong cards, not at all. Jason's hunch was that he had found three of a kind or two pair after the deal and decided just before the draw to try a bluff. If so, he had picked the wrong table to do it at.

"I'll buy a sight," Jason said.

"So will I," Hornby added.

There was an odd pause, in which all six players looked at the stacks of coins and bills in the center of the green felt. Then Brigham, glaring defiance, showed his hand: two kings, two tens, and an ace. Apparently he hadn't had the heart to discard a useless ace for the chance to better his cards.

"Full," Jason said, spreading his cards. "Sixes and eights." Brigham hunched up his shoulders as if expecting a blow; but the blow had already fallen.

Hornby, on the other hand, was smiling. "Nines over fives," he said. "My hand, I guess."

Brigham sat out the next hand, which became another duel between Bolling and the fellow in homespun. Homespun took the pot once more. Jason didn't like the way Bolling kept wiping his palms on his thighs. There was more tension in the gesture than was warranted by the amounts the Texan was losing.

When they anted for Homespun's deal, young Brigham chipped in his five bucks with all the rest. He had two or three hundred more in front of him now. Jason wondered if anyone else had noticed Scarface passing it to him. The boy's sister had almost fainted on learning that he had dropped six hundred at faro; what would she do when she found out that he was borrowing as much to play poker? There was another question too: what was Scarface's interest in the boy? He must know that he had no means to pay it back. Did he have an eye for the sister and hope to get to her through the boy? Some hope, thought Jason sardonically.

The level of betting and the odds against improving his no-account hand led Jason to fold right off. Brigham had done the same; perhaps he was learning. Most of the betting was between Hornby and Bolling, but Scarface and Homespun, who had dealt the hand, were along for the ride. By the draw, a good six hundred was on the table already. Hornby and Scarface took two cards, Bolling took one, and the dealer stood pat. Once again it was the Chicagoan and the Texan who led the betting, raising each other back and forth in jumps that climbed to a hundred and then two hundred dollars. Scarface abandoned ship early on, and in their concentration on each other, the two duelists hardly noticed that the silent farmer was staying with them step by step.

Finally the two bettors were exhausted. "A full house," Hornby said. "Queens and sevens."

"Hah!" replied Bolling. "I'm holding aces over tens." He reached both arms out to pull in his winnings.

"Just hold on, gents, if you don't mind," said Homespun. One by one he placed his cards on the table. There were four fives among them. A respectful silence greeted them. The clink of gold as the farmer stacked his newly won fortune was the only sound.

Bolling's voice, tight and thin, broke into the silence. "The cards fell mighty convenient for you, sir," he said. Jason saw that the veins in his forehead were standing out like cords. "Mighty convenient indeed."

Homespun stopped with a stack of double eagles in his palm. "So they did," he drawled. "What of it?"

The Texan leaned back in his chair, swept the skirts of his coat aside, and placed his thumbs in the pockets of his vest. On the stage his pose would have indicated a careless indifference, but Jason knew better. He looked up, caught the eye of a passing steward, and made an inconspicuous gesture.

"What of it, sir?" the Texan repeated. "Nothing, sir. I merely remark on it. I make no personal allusions, sir, if I note that it is damn queer how you dealt yourself such convenient cards.''

Homespun pushed his chair back from the table. So did the other players, who wanted to be out of the way of whatever happened. "You better explain yourself a little clearer, mister, or I might be inclined to get riled over your words.''

"I think my meaning is clear enough, sir. I care nothing for whether you get riled or not, nor do I care to remain in a game where you may be dealing. It's no place for honest gentlemen.''

This was too much for the farmer. He sprang to his feet and leaned across the table in reaching for the Texan's throat. The Texan's right hand slipped with practiced ease into his vest pocket and reappeared with a tiny single-shot pistol. He was bringing it to bear on his assailant's forehead and pulling back the hammer when suddenly it was plucked from his grasp. Strong hands held him in his seat. Across the table two grim-faced stewards were holding Homespun as well. The flurry of activity ended before anyone in the rest of the gaming room noticed it.

"Let me loose, you dirty polecats! I'll tear his heart out with my teeth!''

"Captain Bolling," Jason said, in a quiet voice that cut through the Texan's ravings. "The use of firearms is not allowed on the *Argo*. Maybe this escaped your notice. If you and this gentleman"—he nodded toward Homespun, who was standing quietly between the stewards—"have a quarrel, you are welcome to disembark and settle it in your own fashion. But not on this boat. Do I make myself plain?''

Bolling had transferred part of his rage to Jason, but he nodded reluctantly.

"Good. Let me also say that I have seen nothing to make me believe that this evening's play wasn't on the square. Since you made no accusations, no apologies are called for, but I tell you that to forestall any further unpleasantness." He glanced around the table. "Well, gentlemen, shall we go on with our game?"

But Hornby was the only one who wanted to continue. Scarface and young Brigham walked away together in the direction of the bar, while Bolling, still furious, retired to his stateroom, and the quiet farmer packed his winnings—two or three thousand dollars, by Jason's reckoning—into a large leather wallet that was strapped to his waist. "Thanks for the game, gents," he said with a nod, and taking a nearby armchair, he tilted his hat over his eyes and went to sleep.

Hornby met Jason's gaze and they both started to laugh. "Do you play backgammon, sir?" Hornby asked. "The cards have not been treating me kindly this evening. Maybe the dice will be more obliging."

CHAPTER ELEVEN

When Jason returned to his rooms, he found his brother sprawled on one of the chairs. His boots were off and his eyes were closed, but at the sound of the latch he opened one eye and muttered something incoherent. Then he struggled into an upright position and pressed his index fingers against the sides of his nose.

"What's the hour?" he said in a muffled voice.

"Gone midnight. Have you been here long?"

"Nope. Matter of thirty minutes or so. Something queer's going on; thought you should know right off."

Jason poured himself three fingers of German hock and added soda water from a syphon, then waved the glass toward Gus in an invitation to continue.

"I told you I'd set a Paddy to keep watch on that gang of bravos? He's had piss-all to tell me about them so far, but tonight he saw someone sniffing around some of the deck cargo."

"Pilferers," Jason said indifferently. "Common as mud-turtles."

"Maybe, but this pilferer was very particular in his interest. You remember in New Orleans, watching a lot of big wooden crates come aboard? The fellow in charge of them was Luke Shuttlesworth."

Jason looked up with new interest. "The one with a big scar on his cheek? I was at the poker table with him this evening."

"Uh-huh. It was those crates someone was prowling around, trying to get a look into. And there's more. One of the toughs seemed to have an eye out for the same crates. He tried to tangle with the prowler, but he got away. My man, O'Donnell, says he thinks the prowler ran up the stairway to the boiler deck."

"Really?" This was interesting news. Deck passengers were not allowed up on the boiler or hurricane decks, and the crew enforced the restriction harshly. The implication was that the prowler might well be a crewman or a cabin passenger. "When was all this?"

"Eleven or so."

"Damn. Our game had already broken up by then. Not that I can think of any reason for Shuttlesworth to be prying at his own merchandise. Have you checked the bills of lading?"

Gus grinned complacently. "Did it two hours out of New Orleans. Agricultural equipment, no saying what kind. To be transshipped at St. Louis to a boat bound for St. Joe."

"Ten crates of agricultural equipment?" Jason said skeptically. "Tell me, what do you think Captain Clement would do if he were told that part

of his cargo was dangerously inflammable and not
properly marked?''

"Do? My God, he'd be down there in a minute
with a prybar and a lantern!''

"That was my reckoning, too. Of course, he'll
be in his bed by this hour, but I don't see how we
can let a rumor of that sort go unchecked until
morning. Think of the peril to the passengers.
You can handle a prybar, can't you? I'm a dab
hand with a dark lantern. We'll pick up a couple
of deckhands to keep the curious at a distance.''
He smiled, and for a moment Gus felt a long-
buried memory stir, of the time when Jason was a
boy and the world had not yet sundered their little
family. What would have become of them if they
had been able to stay together? Gus would have
had a big brother to take his part, which would
have spared him a lot of misery. Would they still
be in some little Ohio river town? It didn't seem
likely. Gus thought of himself as an average sort
of fellow, but he had no doubt that Jason was
always meant for big things. How many sons of
bankrupt storekeepers owned their own three-
hundred foot steamboat at the age of thirty?

"Are you asleep again?'' Jason demanded. Gus
blinked and pushed himself to his feet.

The only light on the main deck was the flickering reflection from the open doors of the furnaces.
The stokers, barefoot and naked to the waist, heaved
the split logs to the hungry flames in a steady
rhythm. The second engineer, nearly as black and
dirty as his work gang, strolled up and down
inspecting his gauges or leaned against a scantling
and chewed his thumbnail morosely. Deck passen-

gers slumped wherever they had found an out-of-the-way space for themselves and their miserable belongings. The wisest of them were at the stern of the boat, as far away as possible from the boilers.

The dim beam of Jason's bull's-eye lantern darted over the stacked bales, barrels, and crates. "There," said Gus. "Looks like someone tried to get that one open already, unless it fell off a wagon. Shall I have a go at it?"

He forced the flattened end of the prybar under the lid of the wooden crate and pulled. Nothing happened. Taking off his coat and rolling up his shirtsleeves, he spat on his palms, took a firmer grip of the shaft of the prybar, and tried again. His mouth was drawn downwards in a grimace and the cords of his forearms stood out in relief. With a screech like a scalded witch the nails pulled slowly from the wood, and the lid was up. Jason leaned over and focused his lantern on the opening.

"Well, well," he said. "All right, little brother, you can close it up again."

Gus opened his mouth to protest or to question him. Then he shut the crate again, pushed the lid down, and banged the nails home; Jason would tell him about it when he was damn good and ready to.

Ten minutes later they were back in his rooms on the texas deck. Jason was mixing another hock and soda for himself. Gus poured a shot of Tennessee whiskey and knocked it back. "Well?" he demanded, emboldened by the booze.

Jason was in one of his infuriating moods. "Not so well," he replied. "Then again . . . Have you

ever heard tell of agricultural equipment manufac-
tured by Sharp's Repeating Arms?''

"Rifles! Is that what we're carrying?''

"About two hundred stand of them, by my
reckoning.''

"But . . .'' Gus poured himself another shot. "I
don't follow. Isn't Shuttlesworth a friend of Senator Stephenson? And he's about as pro-slavery as
anybody. I thought it was the Free Soilers who had
the Sharp's rifles.''

"So they say. But maybe the Senator has decided the other side shouldn't have all the fun.
Whatever the reason, that box I looked in was full
of repeating rifles, and I'll wager the *Argo* against
a capsized skiff that the others are as well. Hell, it
wouldn't surprise me to find a brass cannon down
there, the way they're whooping it up in Kansas.''

Gus gave him a worried look. "What are you
going to do now?''

"Do?'' He sipped from his glass, rolled the
liquid around on his tongue, and swallowed.
"Nothing. It's no business of mine. This steamer
is my business, not what a bunch of farmers get up
to off in the wilderness somewhere. Still, I reckon
we ought to let that fellow know that someone's
been having a gander at his playthings. Look him
up in the morning, will you?''

"What fellow? Shuttlesworth?''

"Um-hum, it's his cargo.''

Stammering a little from embarrassment, Gus
explained why he would rather not have any conversation with the scarred man. At first Jason
seemed absent-minded, but as his brother started
to describe the fight, he listened sharply. When he

heard the ruse that finished it, he snorted with glee.

"And all over that little girl?" he said when Gus fell silent. "She didn't look worth much of a fight to me, but maybe you know better."

Gus turned away, biting back whatever reply had tried to force its way out. After a moment he said, "Anyway, you can see why he might not take kindly to any messages from me. And between his riffraff and his rifles, he's got the makings of a small army on board. You don't want to forget that."

"I haven't. But I told you before, it's none of my business. Or yours. I don't give a good goddamn if a man's a pro-slavery planter from the Ouachita or an abolitionist editor from the Wabash as long as he likes to gamble and doesn't kick up a row when he loses. All that politics is mostly a matter of whose ox is gored anyway. Give that editor five hundred acres on the Yazoo and a hundred prime field hands, and you'll hear the words and chorus change soon enough. One side talks about the dignity of man, and the other talks about the sacred right of property, but look at Kansas. What does it all come down to? The Free Soilers don't think their farms can stand the competition from big slave plantations, so they're against slavery. And the planters don't want any free states handy for their slaves to run away to, so they want Kansas a slave state. But when you put it like that, it sounds a little raw, so they dress it up in fancy words before they blow each other to Hell."

He took a long drink. "Look at that," he chuckled. "They've even got me speechifying. It's easy enough work, I guess, if you know how to make it pay. I'll wager our pal Senator Stephenson does. Does that filly you're so smitten with possess a fortune?"

Gus resented the question, or its possible implications, but he said grudgingly, "The only child of the late Philo Wainwright. The Wainwright Line, warehousing, real estate, banking. . . ."

Jason let out a low whistle. "And all controlled by her guardian until she's twenty-one, I reckon."

"Or until she marries."

Jason gave his brother a sharp look, but he could not see any sign that the comment had been more than an additional piece of information. In the few years they had been together, he felt that he had gotten to know Gus better than anyone else on earth, but there were still pockets of privacy that he had never made any attempt to explore. And who knew better than a professional gambler that money in large sums made men act in the most unpredictable ways? Could his brother turn into an unscrupulous fortune-hunter? He had to admit to himself that he didn't know the answer.

"Well," Jason said with a yawn, "I don't imagine the Senator is any too eager for that to happen. He's probably brought her along on this trip to take her out of reach of some young buck in New Orleans. I saw a play like that in St. Louis a couple of years back. It all ended happily, of course. For the lovers, I mean; the old guardian was left sitting by the fireside grumbling. I'd pay a goodly amount to see that windbag Stephenson in a like situation, but men like him don't allow themselves to become figures of fun. They don't care to be crossed either. I'd bear that in mind before you go on exchanging meaningful glances with Miss Wainwright.''

''I didn't do any such thing! I went to her assistance, that's all! There is nothing between us at all!''

Jason looked at him sardonically, but made no reply. After kicking off his boots, he picked up the accounting of the evening's play. ''What's going on at Joe Baring's roulette table?'' he demanded. ''The take's been down every night this trip.''

''A couple of runs of luck, that's all. Baring's straight as a die—one of our dice, I mean. I won't vouch for anyone else's. I heard a strange tale the other night, about runs of luck. A fellow was playing roulette last month in a hell on Carondelet Street, playing the field, four bits or a buck at a time, staying about even. Then suddenly he pulls out a double eagle and puts it on red. Red hit, and he left his winnings on the field. Red hit again, and again, and again, and each time he left it all there. By now there was a big crowd watching, yelling at him to quit, but he just sat there with his sombrero over his eyes, saying nothing. Well, when red came up twelve times in a row, there was about a hundred thousand dollars sitting there, and the house called the game. Couldn't cover his bet. Still he just sat there. Then somebody shook his shoulder and he just fell right over. He was stone dead, had been since who knows when, maybe the fourth roll. The house tried to take back his winnings, but a bunch of his friends said they'd bust up the place unless the money went to his family. Isn't that something, though? Just think, red came up twelve times in a row. What do you suppose the odds are against something like that?''

"A little over two thousand to one," Jason replied automatically. "But I hate to tell you this, little brother: that tale has a long white beard to it. The first time I heard it, an old gent swore he'd been there, in a gambling house in Marseilles, the night it happened. He got into quite a dispute with the first mate off an English ship, whose best friend had helped to rescue the widow's winnings from a brothel in Valparaiso.''

Gus was crestfallen but not yet vanquished. "It could happen, though, couldn't it? The fellow who told me said a good friend of his had been there.''

Jason yawned again. "A run like that? Sure, it could happen, about once every two thousand sets of twelve rolls. But now throw in the odds against someone cashing in his chips—without cashing his chips!—at just the start of one of those runs and nobody noticing he was dead. Too unlikely for me to worry about, though I admit it makes a good story. Now, about the faro receipts . . .''

The next morning was mostly cloudy and warm. The *Argo* was half an hour north of Memphis when Charlie found his sister. She was sitting on the gallery, in a little nook just ahead of the starboard wheelhousing, watching the passing shore. A stray beam of sunlight found the Chickasaw

Bluffs and made them glow in the grayed-out land-
scape like a brightly painted backdrop in the theater.
Someone on the rim, a boy perhaps, waved to the
steamboat as it puffed upriver.

The rumble of the paddlewheel hid the sound of
Charlie's footsteps. When he touched Elizabeth's
shoulder, she stiffened in alarm and looked up.
For a moment her face brightened, then she recognized the expression her brother wore.

"What are you doing here?" he demanded. "I
thought you'd be in your cabin. I've been looking
all over this durn steamboat for you."

She glanced at the novel, open but forgotten on
her lap. "I couldn't know you would want me,
could I, Charlie? I like it here. I can read and think
undisturbed. I don't mean that you're disturbing
me, love; indeed I don't."

"I should think not, and I do want you. I want
to talk to you. I didn't know I'd have to spend the
morning just finding you. Fine thing, hiding yourself off like this."

"I wasn't hiding from you," Elizabeth said
mildly. "I thought you would be fully taken up
with your new friends. You have been passing so
much time with them these past days."

"Durn right I have! And it's a good thing, too,
that *one* of us is paying attention and thinking
about our future and getting ahead and all that. I'm
not complaining, exactly, but it's hard that I should
have to do it all by myself. If you'd put your mind
to it, Lizzie, you could be a deal of help to me."

"With your friends? But you told them you
didn't even know me. You disowned me."

"Why do you always bring up things and throw

them in my face? It's not very fair or well-bred of you, Lizzie. I hate to say it, but there's a common, ungrateful streak in you sometimes, though I do my best to overlook it.'' He sprawled on the bench near her with his ankles crossed, his hands stuffed in his trouser pockets, and his shoulders hunched toward his ears. He had the look of a man doing his best to seem unconcerned while, in fact, expecting a blow.

Elizabeth's face flamed, and she seemed on the point of making an angry reply. Then her hand touched the onyx brooch pinned to her bodice. The mourning jewelry reminded her of her loss—hers *and* Charlie's—and of the many reasons she ought to tolerate his bad temper. When all was said and done, he was still a boy, and an orphan. If she did not understand his reaction to the sudden changes in his life, if she sometimes wished that he were kinder, more thoughtful, toward her, she was still the elder. She had a duty to fulfill as best she could, that of a parent.

''I only meant, Charlie dear, that I don't know how to help you with your new friends when they don't know of our close connection.'' She took a deep breath and fixed the image of her father, kindly but stern, in her mind. ''Nor do I know what kind of help you want from me. What are you doing of such importance, besides drinking and gambling?''

''Who told you I drink and gamble!''

She turned, fixing her gray eyes on his. ''Will you tell me that you don't, Charlie? *Can* you tell me that?''

He met her gaze for as long as he could. Then

he looked out at the river and muttered what sounded like a curse. "Well, what if I do! I'm not a child to be spoken to like that. A gentleman is expected to share a convivial glass and an evening of play with his friends. I can't expect a girl to understand that sort of thing, so you'll just have to take my word for it. You won't doubt my word, I suppose? You haven't sunk that low?"

He glared a challenge at her, but once again it was he who looked away. "Anyhow," he mumbled, "if I do play cards a little, it's in a good cause. I'm not doing it for fun, you know. I have to do it, to keep in with these fellows. My whole future— *our* future—can be made on this trip. I may be someone important, really important, even famous, before very long, Lizzie, and I promise I won't forget you when the time comes. But I have a right to expect you to help me now. You will, won't you? You'd better, that's all!"

She ignored the belligerence in his last words and responded to the undertone of pleading. "Of course, I'll help you, Charlie, in any way that's fitting. Haven't I always, ever since you were little enough for me to carry in my arms?"

"Never mind all that," he said hurriedly. "I don't need anyone to carry me, thanks! I'm a man now, aiming to do a man's job of work. I can't let anyone think I'm just a no-account boy. But it's hard to have to do it all myself."

She rested her hand lightly on his forearm. "Tell me what you want of me. If I can, I'll do it."

Her compliance seemed to stun him for a moment. When he did speak, his manner suggested, or tried to suggest, that he was merely passing the time of day. "It beats me why people put up with being cheated all the time. I like an exciting game of cards, I admit that. Not that that's the reason I play—like I told you, it's something I have to do for the sake of my position. Still, it galls me to think that I lose because the game isn't square."

"Do you lose, dear?" Elizabeth asked softly. She held her breath, hoping against her better sense that Charlie would be frank with her.

"Oh, a little," he said hurriedly, "not much. And I wouldn't lose anything, I'd win, if the games weren't crooked. People respect winners. But I come out looking like a fool kid through no fault of my own."

"Why do you think the games are crooked? I have heard people say that on the *Argo* the play is honest." This was equivocation of the worst sort, because she knew very well that her brother had been cheated two nights before at faro. Still, she *had* heard people say that the games were generally run honestly, so her reply was not really a lie. Not really.

He sniffed derisively. "Sure, they say that. Why not? But I know the games are rigged, because I've figured out a system. If they were honest, I'd be winning. And let me tell you, that would do a lot for my reputation with some very important men, men whose names will be in the history books a hundred years from now."

Elizabeth was tempted to ask if mention in history books was a guarantee of virtue, but she restrained herself. Instead, she said, "That may be, but I still don't know what you want of me."

"Well . . . If that fancy-Dan you're so friendly

with passed the word, I'd get honest play. Then I'd start winning instead of losing. You can see what a difference that would make.''

She turned and stared at him with just enough disbelief to keep her from giving way to indignation. "Can you be referring to Mr. Lowell?''

Charlie was devoting all his attention to gnawing a bit of loose skin from his left thumb. But he stopped long enough to nod.

"The last time—'' She realized that her voice was rising and stopped, to start again in a more discreet range. "The last time you mentioned Mr. Lowell to me, it was to warn me against being seen in his company. You told me that I had, in your presence, been called vile names because I went in to supper with that gentleman. Now, if I understand you, you are asking me to intercede with Mr. Lowell on your behalf. Is that right?''

"Now, you got no call to take that tone—''

"Is that what you are asking?''

"Well . . . Sure it is. So what?'' The band of freckles across his nose stood out sharply against a face pale with fright, but his chin jutted determination to carry his point.

Elizabeth was just as determined. "Do you know the name they give to men who use women to gain their ends? Do you?''

"Lizzie—''

"I don't know if there's a special name for men who make use of their own sisters in that fashion,'' she continued, riding over his protest. "Perhaps you could ask your friends. They seem well acquainted with vile and wicked names. Perhaps they could tell me what to call you.''

"Durn it, Lizzie, you got your dander up over nothing! What did I say, anyway?" His face began to crumple and his eyes glistened. The change took ten years off his age.

She tried to hold on to her conviction and her anger. "You asked for my help, which I agreed to give you. Then you made a proposal that no honorable man would have even conceived of, much less spoken aloud to a lady!" She blinked rapidly, trying to hold back her own tears. Her throat ached with the effort. Was it possible that she was being unjust? He looked like such a child—perhaps he hadn't understood what he was asking of her. Or perhaps she had read into it more than he had meant. Was she the one with the dishonorable thoughts, then? Was her indignation aimed at the wrong target?

"What proposal?" Charlie cried. "I didn't say anything bad!" But in his eyes, for just an instant, she saw a sneaking satisfaction that he had communicated his meaning without being forced to be plain. And she knew that he shunned plainness, not for her sake, but to protect his self-esteem against the knowledge of his own actions. The vision of such a many-leveled maze of dishonesty took her breath from her.

"All I meant," he went on, with a mixture of boldness and shame, "was that, since you're on speaking terms with Lowell, you could let him know how upset you are at the way his men are cheating your brother. I reckon he doesn't even know about it himself. You'd be doing him a favor by bringing it up." He smirked at the cleverness of this point, then pressed the argument home.

"It's not like I'm asking for any special privileges, you know. I just want a fair chance, that's all. With my system, I'm bound to win if I get it. It's not even the money. It's the principle I care about."

Elizabeth stared out over the water. The sky was gray to the horizon and the darkened bluffs loomed ominously over the flimsy craft. "Very well," she said quietly. "When next I see Mr. Lowell, I shall mention your concern to him."

"Mention my concern! You got to pitch it hotter than that, Lizzie, or it'll leak from every seam! I got to start winning, I tell you! If I don't, I'll know he's still cheating me, and I can't say what might not happen. There's more than one man on this steamer who respects my opinions, you know. If I get too riled, they might get riled, too. There could be a ruction. Now, I don't want that, and I know you don't, and it's my belief that Lowell don't either. So if you tell him just how important it is for me to start winning, and tell him strong, I reckon he'll see the point of it. Don't you think so?"

She studied her brother's face. It was receding and becoming less familiar by the moment, as if the face of another, a stranger, was taking over its features. An eddy of breeze touched her, and she shivered.

"I said I shall speak to him, and I shall."

"This afternoon?"

She nodded slowly.

"Good girl! I knew I could count on you if I put it to you right. I better go now—there's somebody I got to talk to. You'll see, Lizzie—before I'm done, I'll have big men bowing and trying to make my acquaintance. Won't I just give it to them, too!'' He hurried off in a self-generated cloud of glory. Behind him, his sister's head was bowed, but her eyes were dry now. Once again her fingers found the onyx brooch and touched it in a momentary gesture of mourning. Then she closed her novel and stood. Resolution was written in the line of her back as she stepped toward her stateroom.

CHAPTER TWELVE

Steamboat *Argo*
En route St Louis
5 May 1856

Dear Tuttle,
Yrs of 12 April found me in N.O. I grieve to hear of yr misfortune & assure you that the *Argo* can always use a man with your hands. I enclose passage to St Louis where you will find us every 12 or so days—

Jason put down his pen and wiped his fingertips on a handkerchief while Daniel, his steward, went to see who had tapped at the door. A moment later Daniel returned, followed by Elizabeth Brigham.

What the devil did she want this time, Jason wondered as he stood and inclined his head politely. Something to do with that worthless cub of a brother, no doubt. "Good afternoon," he murmured.

She saw the unfinished letter on the desk and hesitated. "I'm interrupting you, sir. I am sorry. Perhaps I may return at a more convenient time?"

"It's no interruption, Miss Brigham. It's a pleasure to see you again." This was more than a mere formula. He noted appreciatively that she was no longer wearing strict mourning. True, her gown was of a shade of gray deep enough to soothe the feelings of a Quakeress. But he was sure no Quakeress had ever worn a gown so fashionably, or revealingly, cut, however doleful its color. Her neck was very graceful, and her shoulders were fine and white as fresh milk. A cameo on a simple chain rested just between the twin swellings of her breasts, whose upper slopes were only partially hidden. Her hair was drawn back and fastened with a simple clasp of silver, from which it cascaded over her left shoulder.

She stirred restlessly under his gaze, and he lowered his eyes. "Will you take tea or coffee?" he said. "I generally find champagne refreshing on a warm afternoon, but it's not to everyone's taste."

"Well, I . . ."

"Champagne, then." He nodded to Daniel, who disappeared. "Please sit down, ma'am, and tell me how I may serve you."

This time she was careful to take a chair that was separated from the divan by a low table. She seemed to be having difficulty finding words, and her confusion deepened when, after a loud *pop!* from the next room, the steward reappeared with two beakers of cool sparkling wine.

"Leave the bottle, Daniel. Your health, ma'am."

"Thank you, sir." The bubbles tickled her nose and the roof of her mouth. The wine was very cold; it must have been waiting on ice. Ice that had been cut from a lake in the far north the previous winter, then stored in layers of sawdust, becoming steadily more valuable as it inevitably melted. What could the sort of sum her brother wanted mean to a man who kept iced champagne ready to his whim? "You are right," she said, "it is very refreshing. You are positive that I am not intruding?"

"Not at all. One advantage of my profession is that I am not obliged to keep regular hours." He smiled, showing a row of even white teeth. The word 'vulpine' came to her mind, though she was not entirely sure of its meaning. "Tell me," he continued, "how are you enjoying your voyage so far? I believe you told me this is your first journey up the river."

"Indeed it is, and it is wonderful." A delicate pink suffused her cheeks as she spoke of her pleasure, and her manner became more animated, less cautious. Really, thought Jason, she was remarkably pretty at times. What a shame that he did not seem to arouse the same excitement in her as a picturesque bit of scenery!

Elizabeth was describing a little dell, set into a gap in the bluffs north of Memphis, that had caught her eye. "You'll think me quite fanciful," she concluded, "but I was reminded of Scott's *Lady of the Lake*. Of course, the trees and bushes of Scotland must be very different from those of Tennessee, but the spirit of the place, the wildness and solitude—those struck me as the same."

Both amused and touched by her earnest air,

Jason said, "The day may be coming when this countryside, too, has its poet. Painters it has already. Have you seen Banvard's panorama of the Mississippi from the mouth of the Missouri to New Orleans? It's said to be the largest painting in the world, some three miles long. Accurate enough, too, though the river has changed some since he executed it."

"Yes, my father took me several years ago when it was exhibited in New Orleans." The memory brought with it a score of others, happy moments with her father that were all now colored with grief as well. She hardly noticed that Jason had refilled her glass with champagne. After an inward silence, she went on, "But grand as the panorama was, it hardly prepared me for the reality. What artist could capture the scenes that open up on every hand, the changing light, the sparkle of the water, and the ever-varied colors of the shore?"

Jason had never thought of the Mississippi as sparkling—generally it appeared to him only a few steps removed from a mudflat—but he made allowances for the effect of the sort of literature young ladies were taught to read.

"And the people," she continued. "I believe there is every variety of humanity to be met upon the river, from the primeval savage to the nobility of Europe. What an education you must have had, Mr. Lowell, in the ways of mankind!" She forgot for the moment that Jason was a professional gambler; if she had remembered, it might have suggested to her that his education, however thorough, might also be rather narrow. Jason would not have agreed; in his view, the stress and greed of the gaming table produced the clearest possible portrait of what she called the ways of mankind. And an uninspiring picture it was, too.

"Yes," he said, with the faintest hint of mockery in his voice, "traveling the river can be an enlightening experience. And it offers such chances to meet people, as you say. For instance, I don't know that you and I would have been likely to become acquainted back in New Orleans, and I'm certain that I should not be entertaining you privately in my rooms. But on the river some of those niceties can be left behind."

The effect of his words was to make Elizabeth acutely self-conscious. What on earth had she been thinking of, to come here like this? She knew perfectly well how others would interpret her action if they knew of it. Jason Lowell might talk of niceties as if they didn't matter, but he was a man, and one whose occupation gave him a raffish name to start with. For her, however, the niceties mattered very much. A girl's reputation was a blossom that, once plucked, withered and died. And when it was gone, every man treated her as easy prey. Unless she had the protection of a man, a father or brother, she might as well go hang herself straight away.

Most galling, it was reputation itself that mattered, not character. If she were said to visit a man's rooms, then she would be branded a harlot, however pure her motives or actions. As long as she kept knowledge of them from the world, though, she might commit whatever sins of the flesh she chose and still be thought respectable. How unfair it was, and how hypocritical! She sensed in herself an urge to defy convention as a protest against its sanctimonious reproofs, and at the same time, a contradictory urge to retreat timidly to the safety of conventional behavior. Either way, she sacrificed herself to those same conventions. But what if she embraced the hypocrisy of the system? Did just as she pleased, but preserved appearances? Something in her rebelled against such falseness, but wasn't that really the only sensible path? Her thoughts whirled past, pausing only long enough to call attention to themselves before they danced away again.

She tried to concentrate. Why had she come here? Because Charlie had asked, had begged her to? She could have refused, or she could have put forward her brother's case in a more public place, one that wasn't open to misinterpretation. If she felt obliged to speak privately, she could have come here directly from her painful conversation with Charlie and still dressed in proper mourning. There had not been any need, had there, to go to her cabin, dress her hair, and don a more attractive gown. There had not been any need to accept the offer of a glass of champagne at four in the afternoon or to show off her sensitivity and taste by prattling of Walter Scott. She could have declined refreshment, stated her business, and returned to the Ladies' Cabin or her nook on the promenade, instead of lolling at her ease and quaffing chilled wine.

She became aware that he was refilling her glass. She also became aware that he was looking more at her bare shoulders than at the glass. Well, hadn't that been her purpose in putting on this gown, to attract his notice when so many other matters were clamoring for it? It was doing so, that was clear. She felt her chest growing warm under his gaze, and knew that he must notice the flush of color and put his own interpretation on it. Could he know that, under the thin silk of her gown, the skin around her nipples was tightening and becoming hard? It was a most peculiar sensation, made even more intense by the friction of the cloth. Hardly aware of what she was doing, she shifted her shoulders back slightly to increase the pressure. She saw his eyes widen, and the thought that he was looking and admiring made her pulse quicken.

She recalled the story her schoolmate Mary Lou had told her when they were both no more than fifteen. One evening, as Mary Lou was getting ready for her bath, she realized that a man was watching from a window across the courtyard.

"Did you close the shutters?" Elizabeth asked.

"And acknowledge that he had seen me in my drawers? I couldn't! What if I had met him on the street the next day? I couldn't have held my head up!"

"But what did you do then?"

"I pretended I hadn't seen him, of course," Mary Lou answered, then added with a giggle, "and took just about the longest bath of my life!"

At the time her friend's behavior had seemed utterly incomprehensible. Now she believed she was beginning to understand her.

There was a hollow, gnawing sensation below her rib cage. Somehow she was convinced that champagne would ease it. And she was right, she found, though the effect was only temporary. An-

other swallow helped a good deal, but acted oddly
on her head.

"Are you well, Miss Brigham? You look pale."

She swallowed, put her hand to her forehead. "I
feel rather faint," she said with surprise. "The
closeness of the room, the champagne . . ."

She struggled to her feet and stood swaying,
unwilling to take the risk of a step. Her forehead,
her whole face, was burning now. "I'm sorry,
I . . ."

He hurried to her side and put a strong arm
around her waist. "Let me help you. You ought to
rest." He led her, half-carrying her, across the
room to a half-open door. Through it she saw a
large bed. Her breath came more shallowly and
quickly. She saw something else as well. Elizabeth
was inexperienced, but she was not naive; she had
taken care of a younger brother. She knew what
the largeness below his waistband signified. Thrilled
with a sense that she was tempting forces more
powerful than she knew, she allowed her arm to
brush accidentally against it. His hand tightened
on her waist.

"You may rest here," he said. He cleared his
throat before adding, "I'll see that no one disturbs
you." He lowered her to the bed and leaned over,
so close that his long hair brushed her naked
shoulder. She closed her eyes and held her breath,
and felt one of his hands under her knees while the
other rested on her back. Was this how it began?
Her imagination, working on skimpy information,
failed her. Then, with a smooth motion, he lifted
her legs onto the bed and lowered her head to the

pillow. A rustling noise, and something soft touched her arms. She sighed and took another deep breath.

Then the door closed. The room was silent.

For a long moment she waited. Then the quality of the silence struck her. She opened her eyes and sat up. Even a moment of dizziness couldn't hide the truth from her: he had left her alone! How could he! To awaken such feelings in her, then go away—what sort of man was he! She pushed off the light coverlet and swung her legs around to stand up. Then she imagined facing him, and her courage drained away like water poured on sand.

What was he thinking of her brazen behavior? She had made it as plain as she knew how that she was prepared to be seduced, and he, like a true gentleman, had pretended not to see. What could she possibly say to him? Could she even dare to look him in the eye? She might leave the room and walk past him without speaking, but that would be distinctly odd, almost unbalanced. It might even suggest that she was reproaching him, when it was her own unmaidenly impulses that were at fault. And she hadn't even mentioned Charlie's plight yet, though that was her ostensible reason for coming.

Damn Charlie, and damn Jason Lowell, and damn his damned champagne! Her head ached and her thoughts were a jumble.

The door opened quietly, and Jason's head peered around the jamb. Concern had taken the place of his usual impassive expression, and it deepened as he saw her.

"Are you sure you should be up? You weren't resting long." He advanced into the room, holding out a small bottle. "I found some smelling salts. I don't know if you require them. You are looking better," he added doubtfully.

"Thank you, I am quite well." His solicitude only magnified her sense of shame. She clambered to her feet, took one step, and slumped forward into his arms. It felt very natural to be held by him. She rested her aching head on his chest and listened to the rhythm of his heart. Its tempo was picking up, and his arms were holding her more closely. She shifted her weight, to bring her body into closer contact with his, and put her arms around his waist. Propriety, shame, brazenness—these suddenly became very distant abstractions. What mattered now was taking this state of closeness and carrying it to its farthest reach.

With gentle but inexorable force, he tilted her head back and stared into her eyes. For a moment the change of scale made him look a stranger, and she caught her breath in fear. Then his mouth came down to cover hers and she took comfort in his fierceness, meeting it with her own. One of his hands was at the buttons of her gown, unfastening them with easy skill, but she pushed her awareness of it away. Nothing mattered but the pervading warmth of his embrace.

For a while, how long she did not know, she gave her mind over completely to the touch of his lips and the explorations of his hands. Suddenly he released her and took a step back. She trembled, fearing another incomprehensible rejection. Then she understood. A bubble of laughter, the stronger for the fear it replaced, forced its way from her throat. He had undone her gown and slipped it from her shoulders, but her stays had baffled him!

Holding his eyes in a challenging look, she shrugged off the gown and unlaced the corset, then let it and her shift slip to the floor together. Never since she became a woman had any man seen her unclothed; yet somehow it was easy to stand there, shoulders back, head proudly erect, and hair flowing unchecked down her back. Just as she had seen her firm breasts, slender waist, and generous hips reflected in the mirror of her stateroom, now she saw them reflected in his face. Then she had doubted their effect, but now her doubts were ended.

"You are very lovely," he said in a low voice.

It came to her that modesty had been invented by men to keep women from discovering their power over them. But men had power of their own, she found, when he reached out and placed the tips of his fingers on her shoulders. Slowly, delicately, he traced the contours of her body. Her nipples became as small and hard as pebbles as he passed, and the muscles of her stomach rippled uncontrollably. She was afraid to move, terrified of remaining still. His hands were below her waist, gliding over the smooth skin of her hips, then reaching back to cup her and pull her toward him with bruising force.

"No!" she gasped, and pushed him back.

His eyes grew cold and narrow. He released her and stepped away, but before he could say anything, she reached for the buttons of his shirt. Then he understood. Moments later his coat and shirt were a crumpled pile in the corner of the room and he was unbuttoning his breeches. Elizabeth gasped again, and tried to look away. The experience of bathing a baby brother had done nothing to prepare her for the sight of an aroused, rampant male adult. She swallowed tightly at the thought of that entering her body, and felt a tiny focus of nausea gather just below her breastbone. When he reached for her, she closed her eyes, as much to hide the threatening sight as to concentrate on his caresses.

Once again he lifted her onto the bed, but this time she had no doubts about his intention. She lay back, allowing his hands the freedom to explore the secrets of her body. Gradually her fear dissolved into passion. She opened her eyes to watch the play of muscles in his broad chest. The difference from her own body fascinated her. She reached out, very tentatively, and placed her palm on his rudimentary nipple. The gesture seemed both to acknowledge and to overcome the gulf between them, and he responded in kind, dipping his head to fasten his lips on her breast. The sensation shot through her like a flame through dry grass. A low moan escaped her, and he moved his lips and tongue, teasing her almost into incoherence. Her hips began to move in slow, tight circles.

By now his fingers had found the nexus of her desire and started to stroke with mounting urgency. She barely noticed. Each separate sensation was stirred into the fire, losing its identity to become only part of the whole. If she was aware of anything, it was the convulsive movements of the muscles of her stomach and the continuous stream of little cries, which seemed to come from somewhere, or someone, far beyond her. She certainly did not know that she was squeezing the emblem of his arousal in her sweat-dampened hand.

Even so, she recognized the moment when he lifted himself away from her and reached down to part her knees. She recognized it and was instantly chilled by terror. All that had happened until now had happened to someone else, but this was about to happen to *her*. She stiffened and tried to fight off the stranger who was looming over her, who was about to pierce and destroy her with his throbbing red spear. But once again her own body proved to be the enemy. Against her will, her thighs spread wide and her hips tilted upward to meet the thrust.

The instant of pain was lengthened and strengthened by her dread of it and by the helplessness of being pinned down by a stronger body. She cried out in earnest now as she moved her head feverishly from side to side and tried to elude the terrible weapon that was rifling her body or, failing that, to block it out of her mind. But gradually she began to know the awful attraction in her pain, and with that knowledge the attraction grew while the pain faded. Once again her hips began to move with novice eagerness, trying to locate and become part of the rhythm of the ancient dance.

He sensed the change in her and changed in turn. She had no idea what he was doing, but its effect was to awaken in her an urgency to meet his own. Her arms went around him—stroking, clutching, scratching at the bare skin of his back, pulling him still closer, still deeper. The warmth in her belly was contracting, contracting to a single white-hot point. Just when she knew she could not stand any more, she flung her legs about his waist and pulled the entire lower part of her body off the bed. The point of heat exploded and sent a wave of sensation through every nerve. But still its center held, convulsively filling her and withdrawing, though, like a beach after high tide, each successive wave reached a lower peak.

Then it was done.

Slowly her breathing returned to its normal pace as the perspiration on her forehead and cheeks dried, and her thoughts became her own once more. She was a woman in truth now. She had tasted of the fruit of the tree, and she could never again be what she had been before. And she did feel like a different person, although she could not say what the difference was, just as the pleasure she had felt with him was indefinably different from pleasures she had given herself.

But what of him? Why was he so still and heavy? She opened her eyes and gave a low, throaty laugh. Men were such children: he had fallen asleep. Seeing him like that, with his face in complete repose, she thought he even looked like a child, though not a very happy one. Slowly, carefully, she rearranged her body to support him more comfortably, and then she closed her eyes again.

Jason drifted back to consciousness convinced that he was back in California and that Benita was still alive. Those days were five years in the past, but they were never far from him.

He found the army of General Winfield Scott

assembling in New Orleans. Scott himself was still in Washington, and the mostly volunteer troops had a lot of time to waste. Soon the encampments were surrounded by gamblers and whores, like flies around a week-dead carcass. Jason did well and sent sums back to the bank in St. Louis regularly. When the expeditionary force sailed, a little gold in the palm of an ill-paid second mate gained him a berth with the officers, who liked a game of cards as well as their men.

From Tampico to Vera Cruz, and then three hundred miles across tropical forests and high plateaus, the American troops marched and cursed and swatted mosquitoes and fought battles and died of smallpox—and gambled. Some gained a taste for the Mexican game of *monte,* not knowing or caring that a gang of sharps had had thousands of decks of marked *monte* cards printed. Most stayed with their old favorites, with poker, craps, and faro.

Jason's faro spread was particularly popular. One reason was that no one had ever detected him cheating. The men knew that faro games were usually crooked, but an unskilled crook was insulting their wits as well as stealing their gold. Another reason was that, although Jason almost always finished the evening ahead, he was never greedy. Some of the men had even won substantial sums from him, though they generally lost them again before long. That was all right; the excitement of playing was worth the price.

After the battle of Chapultepec and the capture of Mexico City, the more cautious dealers who had stayed at home during the fighting took the next boat they could find to Mexico. Soon the halls of Montezuma looked more like a waterfront dive. Every cantina had its resident card mechanic. In a couple of months Jason grew tired of the scene. After sending a last remittance off to St. Louis, he packed the faro spread in its battered mahogany box and drifted westward toward the Pacific. He had been two weeks in the tiny port of Manzanillo when a sailor off a coastal schooner told him that gold had been discovered in California. The fever struck him, as it would so many thousands of others, but it was three more weeks before another ship appeared at the entrance of the bay. Jason located her captain in the town square and learned that the *Martha Colburn* was bound north, to the old provincial capital of Monterey, and had room for a paying passenger who didn't mind sleeping on deck. He and Jason quickly agreed on a price and went on board together.

Captain Beech, like the ship's owners back in Massachusetts, may have thought she was bound for Monterey, but once there he learned that every kind of cargo was bringing record prices farther north, in San Francisco, the port nearest the gold camps. His sense of duty told him to continue northward another day's sail for the sake of greater profits. He didn't anticipate the effect of gold fever. Once through the Golden Gate, no appeal or threat could have kept the crew aboard the *Martha Colburn,* which joined the growing fleet of deserted vessels tied up along the Embarcadero. Even the mate took off for the hills, leaving Captain Beech to write a letter of explanation to Boston.

San Francisco was still near the start of its

transformation from sleepy port to boom town, but already the bars and streets were crowded beyond capacity. On every hand tales were told of men stumbling over nuggets the size of a baby's head or panning dust worth a year's wages in a morning. Some of the tales were true, too. With hard work and a little luck a man could become rich in California. Whether he could stay rich for long was another question. After a couple of months in the goldfields he wanted some fun, and he was ready to pay well for it. Why not? There was always more gold to be found back in the hills.

Jason Lowell had no intention of standing in a cold rushing creek, wet to the waist, peering at pans full of sand for a trace of 'color.' There were easier ways to find gold. He spent his first evening in San Francisco looking over the gambling houses that were springing up around Portsmouth Square, the central plaza of the town back in Mexican days. Then he found the owner of the oldest and largest of them, El Dorado, and offered him fifty dollars a day for the right to run a faro bank. This, he knew, was almost half the rent for the entire casino, but he calculated on making money even so.

El Dorado was a hastily built structure about seventy feet long that had been knocked together of rough boards. A row of pillars down the center supported the roof, from which hung a half dozen blazing chandeliers. The walls were concealed behind mirrors, paintings, and tapestries that did their best to give an air of luxury to the crude room. The bar took up one side, and from the far wall jutted a little balcony usually occupied by a German band. The rest of the space was given over entirely to gaming tables, each with its packed crowd of bettors.

Faro, as Jason expected, was a favorite of the miners, along with *monte,* chuck-a-luck, and *vingt-et-un.* Poker was too slow and dull for them, and too unprofitable for the house, but from the moment he laid out his spread, he had men three-deep putting their money down. He cheated, of course—faro was intrinsically such a fair game that he had to cheat to stay ahead—but, as in Mexico, he was never greedy or obvious. He despised thimble-riggers and broad-tossers with their three shells or three court cards, because the player had no chance at all. To his mind, their games were only one step away from taking money at gun point, but at the faro table one could win, and even win big. All Jason did was make certain that the players as a group consistently lost. He had his rent to pay.

That turned out to be easy. At the end of his first month in San Francisco, he had almost five hundred ounces of gold, worth about eight thousand dollars, to his credit at the bank, and the boom was only beginning. True, expenses were high—coffee was five dollars a pound, whiskey thirty dollars a bottle, and it was said that one miner had given half an ounce of gold dust for a single apple—but the profits were even higher. When two other dealers asked Jason to go in with them on opening their own house, he refused; he was making all the money he wanted from a single faro table.

And then there was Benita. Women of any sort were so scarce in San Francisco that when one walked down the street, men lined the sidewalks to watch. That gave Chambers, El Dorado's owner, the brilliant notion of bringing in a girl as a drawing card for the casino. Somewhere down the peninsula he found Benita, whose father had come to California as a Mexican soldier and stayed behind to raise corn on a little patch of land overlooking the bay. Benita's broad cheeks and thick black hair revealed the Indian in her ancestry, but her long, finely sculpted nose and sensuous mouth would have looked appropriate in a portrait of a Castilian grandee's lady.

She was a bewildered fifteen-year-old when she first stepped into the gambling house. It was natural to turn to Jason as a friend; aside from her, he was the youngest person there, and he spoke Spanish, her first language, with a familiar accent. Natural, too, for Chambers to take advantage of the friendship by making Jason a sort of chaperone for her. He placed her table a few feet from Jason's faro spread, in easy view, and let the rest happen informally. As it did.

Benita's job was simple, even for a young, inexperienced country girl. She sat behind her table and sold cups of tea and coffee, pieces of cake, and chocolates at absurdly high prices. That was all, but it proved to be one of the most popular features of El Dorado. Hard-bitten miners in dirty flannel shirts and shapeless hats waited in line to buy a cup of tea, in the hope that she would give them a smile as well. That was all they asked for, because everyone knew instinctively that Benita was a modest, respectable girl. Anyone trying to speak to her roughly or make an improper suggestion would have been shown his error by the other customers, for whom her innocence was an essential part of her charm. California was soon filled with men who thought of her as their little sister.

Somewhere within Jason Lowell, the gifted and successful gambler, there waited a twenty-one year old boy whose growing years had never known affection from others of his own generation. To Benita he was a hero, an idol, a knight-protector, as well as a reservoir of wisdom about the wider world. Every day around noon he called for her at the house of an elderly widow and walked her to Portsmouth Square, and every night at around two he walked her back to her lodgings. During the hours in between, he was seldom more than ten feet away from her. On Sundays, her day off, they took longer walks, climbing one of the hills that surrounded the town or exploring the teeming waterfront. Once Jason hired a buggy and took her to visit her father, who could not understand what she was doing in the city but understood the small bag of gold and silver she gave him.

Of course, Jason fell in love. He put up no fight; he knew it was happening, and he encouraged it. If he was beginning late in comparison with other men, he compensated for it with the strength of his passion. He murmured her name as he went to sleep, in hopes of dreaming about her, and tried to decide if there was greater misery in being apart from her or being in sight of her but separated by their occupations. His appetite began to decline. The crisis came when, after months of mounting agony, he found that he could not concentrate on his dealing. His faro table was the only one in California that was showing a loss.

Something had to be done. Trembling with fear that his gross desires would make her turn away from him, he asked Benita to marry him. She gave him one of her most brilliant smiles and burst into tears. After a while she explained that she had been sure his feelings were brotherly and had blamed herself for allowing more romantic notions to intrude. Now everything would be as it should be.

Chambers was the first person they told, and the last. Once he calmed down, he explained in simple terms the place that Benita held in the hearts of her customers. For her to marry at all would be a heavy blow to them. But if she were to marry a gambler, an unpopular sort of fellow at the best of times, her new husband could expect to find himself dancing from the nearest tree limb before he had time to consummate the marriage. That was no way to end a wedding day.

"We'll leave," Jason declared resolutely. "We'll go back East." Benita looked troubled by the idea of going so far from the only home she knew, but she was eager to be guided by her husband-to-be.

"That's a rough trip for a lady, however you do it," Chambers observed. He didn't want to lose either of them, and he was fond of them besides.

"We'll make it all right. The first ship I hear of returning East, we'll be on. Until then, I reckon we'd better keep this to ourselves. It's nothing to be ashamed of,"—he gave Benita's shoulders a squeeze—"but we don't want to cause a ruckus for you and the house."

Two weeks passed, then three. Ships were arriving at San Francisco every day, but none could hold a crew long enough to leave. Jason was beginning to consider risking the Overland Trail; it seemed to be the only way to get out of California.

Early one Thursday morning, the proprietor of a boarding house off Washington Street stoked the stove up to cook breakfast. The shoddily built chimney overheated and set fire to the house. Sea breezes, funneled by the hills, quickly spread the flames. By the time the fire was under control, six blocks lay in ashes. By the standards of the day, it was a minor incident. Other fires that year had come close to destroying the entire city. But on one of those blocks was the house where Benita lodged. When Jason went to meet her, to walk her to work, he found nothing left of it but a chimney making a despairing gesture to heaven. He identified her body by a ring he had given her. It was fused to her finger.

Two days later he hired a horse and rode south, away from the gaming tables and gold camps, to the dense forests on the seaward slope of the coastal range. He was gone for several weeks, and when he returned, men said that he had changed. He was becoming a youthful version of the typical gold camp faro dealer: cadaverously thin, clad completely in black, and self-contained to the point of bringing his kinship with the human race into question. Those who played at his spread did not win as often as they had before, nor were they reconciled to their losses by a smile, a friendly word, or a joke. Some decided to frequent another table, but for every one who did, there were two coming in from the hills with a poke of dust, a powerful thirst, and a lust to buck the tiger.

One day Jason told Chambers that he was leaving San Francisco. The owner of El Dorado was not surprised; he had expected it for months. What he didn't expect was the young gambler's announcement that he was sailing at the end of the week for China. "I promised myself once to see the world," he explained. "There's a lot still to go."

The clipper Jason boarded was sailing in ballast to Canton, where she would pick up a cargo of tea for the English market. He stayed in Canton for a couple of months, then moved on by restless stages to Singapore, Calcutta, and Bombay. He was seeing the world, but he was not convinced that he was any closer to finding his destiny. That it was awaiting him, he knew; but where?

From India it was a natural step to go to England, a country where, because of its familiarities, he felt even more a stranger than he had in the Orient. One evening he was taking a hand in a high-stakes game of whist, when he found a peculiar sentence running through his mind. "The earth is round," it said, "and the origin and goal are one." After a long walk through the chilly, damp streets, he returned to his hotel and packed his trunk. The next morning he was on the boat train to Liverpool with reservations on a fast Cunard packet to New York. Three weeks later he was in the offices of the best boatyard on the Ohio River, describing what he wanted the steamboat *Argo* to be. And a week after that, he walked into a tanning yard in Cincinnati, looking for the brother whose very existence he had forgotten for years on end.

He had recovered his origin; now it only remained to find out in what way it was his goal.

CHAPTER THIRTEEN

At supper that evening, Count de la Fevre noticed the change in Elizabeth's and Jason's behavior toward each other. Being a man of wide experience in the world, he made a very shrewd guess about its significance. He had thought that something of the sort was going forward, but *morbleu*, these Americans were so uncultivated and slow! With each mile the steamer sailed away from New Orleans, he felt the fog of Calvinism and Anglo-Saxon hypocrisy growing thicker. Even the cuisine, never very good, was deteriorating noticeably.

Many of the Americans were very good fellows, of course, and some of them were surprisingly cultured as well, but their twin—and contradictory—fetishes of democracy and slavery made even the clearest conversational path thick with hidden snares. His title offended some who, in the next breath, announced that the planter aristocracy of the South was chosen by God and Nature to rule over their ignorant but contented slaves. How this differed from his remote ancestors ruling over their peasants, he could not tell. But he hesitated to ask. Possibly the comparison would have reminded some of his acquaintances that those peasants had shown their lack of contentment in a very direct and bloody way. Even implying such a parallel would be thought only a short step away from preaching abolitionism and servile war.

Never mind; he would be discreet and patient with them. He would concentrate on admiring the remarkable, if uncultivated, beauty of the scenery and the women. Young Mlle. Brigham, for instance, whose beauty was unfolding like a blossom suddenly exposed to warm sunlight. How had he ever thought her rather plain? Perhaps it was simply that mourning did not become her well.

Her appearance at breakfast the next morning caused him to reconsider. The blossom had been touched by frost. The animation he had found so attractive was gone, replaced by a morbid sensitivity to the words and even the glances of others. She ate hurriedly, keeping her eyes on her plate throughout, and was the first to flee the table. As for her paramour, or former paramour, or whatever the devil he might be, he too was silent, but aggressively so. His face challenged the company to address so much as a 'Good morning' to him. No one took the dare, though de la Fevre, from curiosity as much as politeness, caught his eye and bowed. Lowell returned a ferocious frown and a chilly inclination of the head.

Merde, thought the Count, these Americans are as quick to quarrel as they are slow to court! And he went off in search of Elizabeth. He was interested in discovering if the attentions of a sympathetic listener might restore the bloom to her face.

Elizabeth was not in the public rooms of the steamer. She was in her cabin, face down on the bunk, wishing that she could sleep. Unconsciousness seemed the only escape from the repeated rehearsal of her encounter with Jason the night before. By now, each recollected moment was so encrusted with imagined alternatives that she was no longer sure what had really happened, what each of them had really said.

They had made love a second time, more slowly. Before he was spent, both of them were bathed in sweat and whimpering on a peak of tension where ecstasy and agony could hardly be told apart. Afterward, suddenly shy, she covered herself with the sheet and looked away when he got up to sponge himself off. To her intense relief, he had the intuition to leave her alone to cleanse and reclothe herself. When she appeared in the other room, he took her hand and placed a courtly kiss on the inner side of her wrist. She felt the thrill of it to the very center of her being.

Supper was a great trial. She had to remind herself constantly not to break into laughter, and she was sure that everyone noticed the silly smile that came to her face each time she thought of Jason. He was no help either; his arm must have accidentally touched hers two dozen times or more in the course of the meal. And to endure the sympathetic amusement in the eyes of the French count and the concern in the glances of the captain's wife was equally a trial. She would have fled in confusion if it had not meant leaving Jason.

Leaving the dining saloon for a stroll on the promenade, they passed the table where Charlie was sitting. To one who knew him as well as she, his face portrayed an amalgam of emotions. There was anger, and a touch of shame, and self-concern, but dominating these was the nasty gloating of a child who, out of boredom, has just broken a playmate's toy and realizes that no punishment can make it work again.

Had he known that would happen? It seemed likely. But had he also known that, in taking a decisive step toward womanhood, she was leaving her girlhood—*and him*—behind? Her father and brother had been her whole world, and when her father died, Charlie had become everything. Now he was—not nothing, certainly—but a great deal less than he had been. And the place he had lost, he could never regain, because it was no longer there.

In the darkness of the promenade, she dabbed at the corners of her eyes. Charlie's was not the only loss, though it was by far the greater. And still she had not carried out her promise to him. Delay would not make it easier. She turned to face Jason.

"Another fine night," he said before she could speak. "I know moonlight on the river is no novelty to you, raised in New Orleans as you were, but I never tire of it." He laughed, and added, "The reason may be that my trade keeps me from seeing it too often. I should go soon, just to see that everything is as it should be. I don't think I'll play this evening, though. You've ruined my concentration.''

He started to lean toward her, as if to kiss her, then straightened up as he heard footsteps approaching.

Clutching her courage to her, she said, ''I meant to ask you about that. The play. My brother—''

Jason made a low noise of exasperation. For a moment she wavered, but then she continued. ''My brother spoke to me today. He continues to gamble—how I don't know—and to lose. He is sure that he is being cozened.''

''On the *Argo*? Bunk! He plays poorly, that's all.''

''I'm sure you're right, but . . . Didn't you tell me that your men had bilked him of all his money?''

''At your request, ma'am, and on that particular evening, yes.'' His voice was grim.

''Oh, I know, but couldn't they be doing it still? A misunderstanding? He seemed so certain.''

''No. I tell you, he is an unschooled, unskilled, ignorant, foolhardy gambler who might as well throw his money over the side as put it on the table—not that it is his money he loses. Judging by his play, he should still be on his nurse's leading-strings with a sugar-tit in his mouth, not thrusting himself among serious men. I may make a good living out of such stupidity, but I am not obliged to like it or to call it anything but what it is.''

The passion in his voice told Elizabeth that she would be wise to speak of something else. It was precisely the new weakness of her connection with her brother, the conviction that she was in a larger sense forsaking him, that kept her from abandoning him in this smaller way. "Perhaps, but he was so sure. He said that if the play were fair, his system—"

"Tcha! His system!" Contempt dripped from the words.

"Are there no systems to win at cards?"

"Of honest systems, one only: buy the gambling rooms! The others are complete bubbles. The laws of chance cannot be repealed, only circumvented. What your brother is saying, or what you are saying for him, is the cry of every weakbrain who hopes to break the house. 'If I lose, they are cheats!' The only refutation is to arrange for them to win, and then they give the credit to their precious system. I tell you this: if there were a system of the kind they brag of, I would sell this steamboat and open a grocery store! So far I have not seen the need for such a step."

Something broke through his elaborately ironical manner and caused his voice to crack. He fell silent, and turned away to stare at the Missouri shore. She knew better than to break in on his thoughts, whatever they were.

When he spoke again, it was as though he had stepped behind a wall of thick glass. "Is that what you are requesting, ma'am, that I tell my employees to arrange for your brother to win?"

"No, I—" But she couldn't finish. She knew that that was exactly what Charlie, speaking through her, was asking.

He saw the knowledge in her face and retreated farther behind his barrier. "May I inquire, then, what you believe to be a suitable sum? Under the circumstances?"

Baffled and hurt, she simply looked at him.

"The money he wins," Jason elaborated, "must come from somewhere. In this case, from my pocket. If I am to pay your, ah, brother, I must know the price you set on your favors. I do not want to insult you by paying too little."

The darkness hid the flood of color to her face. Charlie had understood the implied bargain he was proposing, and so had she. But she had forgotten it after her unimagined closeness with Jason. That had been a gift, freely offered, and somehow she had hoped that the favor she was asking would be the same. To hear him state so plainly that she had sold herself to him made her understand for the first time that she had done precisely that. All her rationalizations and justifications fell away, leaving her to face unsupported the fact that she had become a harlot.

For a moment she thought of denying, of trying to explain, of calling back her monstrous request. But she could not. To speak, even to stay within range of his accusing eyes, was more than her overmastered self could do. She ran.

The entire conversation was seared into her memory like a brand of shame. But the worst moment came much later that evening, when someone tapped on her stateroom door. Sure that it was Jason, come to apologize, she ran over to open it, rehearsing her own apologies as she went.

Charlie stood there, a half-drunken grin spread across his face. He jostled past her and sprawled in the armchair. "What did I tell you?" he demanded. "Didn't I tell you I'd win if I got fair play?"

She shut the door and leaned her forehead against

it. She couldn't look at him just yet. "You won tonight?"

"You durn right I did! I won nearly a thousand frogskins at faro! I said I would, didn't I? Why, even after I pay Luke what I owe him, I'll be 'way ahead, and tomorrow night I mean to do even better. And you thought I couldn't look after you! There's more to me than you give me credit for, Lizzie. You're starting to find that out, I bet."

She assented silently. "Who is Luke? Have you been gambling with borrowed money?"

"A friend of mine, that's all. And it wasn't gambling, not with my new system. Do you want to hear how it works? See, with faro you can—"

"No, I don't. And I don't want you to gamble again while we are on this boat. You won a great deal tonight, and you must be content with it."

"What? Liz, don't be stupid! I can make a fortune now, it's a sure thing!"

"If it is, we both know why. I mean it, Charlie: you're not to play again on the *Argo*." She confronted him silently. If he was really unaware of the sordid bargain they had made, if he really believed in his 'system,' he would certainly continue to protest.

But he didn't. His eyes slid away, and he said, "I don't know what's gotten into you these days." His tone said that he didn't care if she believed him or not. He pushed himself to his feet and crossed to the door, then turned. "You stand in my way whenever you can, don't you? It's mean and ill-natured of you, Lizzie, that's all. You'd like to keep me a child all my life, but it won't do. It just won't do."

She had done her crying earlier. Now she flung herself on the bed and stared emptily at the ceiling. She should feel pride, she supposed. Not many girls succeeded in selling their virtue for a thousand dollars. In a way, Jason Lowell's most cutting insult to her was also a great compliment. It was also a battlement even stronger than his new opinion of her; that she could argue with, but a thousand dollars was too solid to be melted away by words. Whatever might have been, whatever she had dreamed, had vanished as quickly and surely as a lost bet or a maidenhead. With that as her only consolation, she prepared herself for a restless night.

Morning brought a new ordeal: sitting next to him at breakfast. They spoke only once, at the entrance to the dining saloon.

"My brother tells me he won a great deal of money last night."

"So I understand. Was that not your wish, ma'am?"

"No! I never wished for any of this!" She forced back a sob. "You wrong me, sir, indeed you do!"

"If I do," he said coldly, "I apologize. I doubt that your brother's luck will continue, however, so I advise you to make the best of what you already have. Good morning."

After that exchange she was scarcely able to choke down a few bites of food. She knew she must look a fright, but she didn't care. She just wished the Count would stop looking at her as if she were the wronged heroine of a melodrama. It was enough that she felt that way herself.

*   *   *

Pilot Bowles leaned over and shot a stream of tobacco juice into the darkness. An instant later the splash told him that it had found the spittoon. He leaned back on his high leather bench and peered out into the night. The flagpole in the bow made a black, straight line against the starry sky. In a moment the *Argo* would be far enough through the bend for him to pick up the dead cottonwood on the far point and swing to larboard until the flagpole lined up with it. That course would take him on a slant across the river, following the wayward channel and avoiding the shoal that had built up over the previous two years or so.

As he made the adjustment to the wheel, he also reminded himself to tell Theo Bain, his relief pilot, about the new sawyer he had spotted three miles upriver from Cape Girardeau. Sawyers were the most wily hazards on the river. Like snags, they were huge trees whose roots had become fixed on the river bottom, but unlike snags, they did not stay rigidly in place. Instead, they were forced underwater, and out of sight, by the current, only to float back up according to some occult rhythm. A stretch of water that looked clear and safe could suddenly part to reveal a sawyer aimed like a spear at the vitals of the boat. Even an alert pilot might lose his boat that way.

The silhouette of a low hill appeared against the sky to the northwest. Bowles held his course for another half minute, then swung a point to starboard until the rounded top separated into two. The lower one, with the trees, was his mark. Setting the flagpole just to larboard of it, he prepared to take the *Argo* between a small wooded island and the bank of the river. During low water, this cut-off was dry land, but the present level of the river allowed him to save about a mile of travel and even more in fuel. In his view, the difference between a good pilot and a great pilot was the ability to make use of every cut-off the mazy river offered.

The channel was narrow, yielding only a few dozen feet of clearance on either side, but Bowles was unconcerned. He sometimes said that he would take a steamboat anywhere that gave him six inches to each side and six inches of water under the keel, and those who knew him did not think he was bragging. He was halfway through the cut-off and about to make a cunning turn to starboard when suddenly the walls of trees on either side were illuminated by a flash of light. An instant later he heard and felt the muffled *crump!* of an explosion somewhere on the boat.

Without even thinking he rang for slow ahead. The greatest danger on a river steamer was fire. The upper works were built as lightly as possible, of thin wood well daubed with paint. It was a perfect recipe for a bonfire; all that it lacked was the forced draft that their forward speed would provide. Judging by the shouts and screams now coming from the lower decks, the passengers saw the danger as well. Whether they could be gotten to do anything useful to avert it was another question.

As the *Argo* began to lose headway, Bowles traced his way through a maze of conditional statements—what to do if the boat was afire, or sinking, or essentially undamaged, and how the configuration of river and land affected those decisions. In his mind was a detailed map, complete with depths of water, for the next mile or two ahead, but first he had to know what the boat's condition was.

Captain Clement, fighting his way through the terrified crowd on the main staircase, was wondering the same thing. Whatever had happened, it had not been a boiler explosion. That would have broken the boat in half and sent a good many of them on their last flight before reaching heaven. He knew; he had been less than a mile away when the boilers of the old *John W. Lockard* had let go back in '46. One of the bodies had landed in the river just off the stern of his boat.

"Make way, damn your eyes, or I'll scatter your feeble brains to the winds with my bare fist! Move, you pox-ridden pigs' asses!"

Captain Clement looked in the direction of the familiar bellow and saw the second mate, Anaximander Russell, enforcing his commands with his bull strength. He cupped his hands and called out. Russell turned and moved toward him, scattering the mob like a fox in a flock of chickens.

"What's our situation?" Clement shouted.

Russell waited until he was close enough to answer quietly. "I've got ten men on the donkey pump. They're keeping the fire from spreading so far. But whatever happened must have blown a hole in the hull. We're taking on water too fast for the pumps to handle."

"I see." Poor old *Argo*, he thought; the river that had claimed so many of her sisters was reaching for her. "Send a man to the pilothouse right away. He is to tell Pilot Bowles that we are in a sinking condition. He must use his best judgment to ensure the safety of the passengers. And tell the engineer to give the same message over the speaking-tube. He won't be understood in this uproar, but we must try."

"Aye, sir."

"Then pass out batons to every man you don't need on the pumps. If we don't keep this mob in order, they'll be the death of all of us!" As if in illustration of his prophecy, a short man in homespuns climbed the railing of the boiler deck promenade, gave a shrill cry, and fell, arms windmilling, into the river. The captain shuddered, imagining that he could feel the thump as the great paddlewheel mangled the unfortunate.

Pilot Bowles also heard the man's cry, but he had no attention to spare for one man. The message from Mate Russell was confirmed by the way the wheel answered to him: the *Argo* was sinking. He considered his choices. The island to starboard was little more than a greatly enlarged sandbar. The water shelved very gradually; if he tried to put the boat aground there, he might find himself sitting twenty yards or more from dry land. Inevitably some of the passengers would panic and drown crossing the gap.

The channel and the current stayed closer to the Missouri shore. If he drove in that direction, he might even manage to get close enough to drop the landing stages and let everyone walk ashore in dry shoes. But the cost could be the loss of the boat itself. Unless he put her aground very soon, she would sink in the channel. With some luck, her engines might be salvaged, come low water. The rest would be good for nothing but kindling.

There was a chance, a slim one. On the trip downriver he had noted a towhead some thirty feet offshore. If he could reach it in time, and if the depth between towhead and bank was just right, he might beach the *Argo*'s bow out of the direct force of the current, save the passengers, and save the boat. All he needed was more steam and a lot of good luck. Altering the course with a touch as delicate as a watchmaker's, he rang for more speed on both paddlewheels and spat once more into the darkness at his feet.

Jason was deciding whether to fold a pair of nines when he felt the floor shake. The stack of gold ten-dollar pieces in front of his left-hand neighbor toppled over. One of the coins rolled across the table and was caught dexterously and flipped back to its owner. Jason's first thought was that the boat had struck a snag. Then, from the commotion rising from the lower deck, he caught a single word of terror: 'Fire!'

Men were coming to their feet all over the room. In a few moments they would begin to surge toward the doors, each of them feeding and being fed by the other's panic. He beckoned to the head steward, who hurried over.

"Put two or three of your best men in the strongroom," he said in a low voice. "*Armed.* This could be a try at distracting our attention. Send three or four others to check every stateroom and make sure no one is asleep. Cabin passengers to assemble here at once. And *nobody runs*! Get me? I'll make life hell for any man I see moving faster than a walk. Once you've seen to that, find out what happened and let me know, if you can.''

The steward hurried off and Jason stepped up onto his chair. "Gentlemen!" he shouted over the rising tumult. Those within twenty feet or so turned to look, and gradually the noise died down. "Gentlemen, it seems that something untoward has happened—what, I don't yet know. When I do, I'll tell you. Meanwhile, the best thing we can do is resume our seats and retain our composure. The only thing I can add to that is that—the next round is on the house.''

Ironic cheers greeted this announcement, but most of the men did sit down. Even the arrival of a cluster of women, many of them visibly terrified, did not quite renew the danger of panic, though it did heighten the noise level.

Gus was striding purposefully across the room. Jason took his arm and led him away from the table and its eager ears. "Well?"

"An explosion, somewhere among the cargo. Cap'n says the fire is in check, but we're taking on water fast. Must have blown a hole in the hull. We're in a cut-off—looks like Bowles is aiming to set everyone ashore by running aground.''

"Damnation and hellfire!''

"Could be worse; we could have had a boiler blow the bows off her out in the middle of the river. Anything you want me to do?''

"Yes. Make sure the strongroom is secured, then find out what caused the explosion. I'd better make an announcement; the crowd is getting restless again.'' Once more he stood on the chair and explained that, although there was no danger, the captain was planning to put everyone ashore for their own safety. As he spoke, he looked over the room. In a far corner, near the door to the Ladies' Saloon, Elizabeth was standing with her arm through that of her brother. He could not really make out her face, but he thought there was defiance in her stance. To hell with her then, and more especially to hell with her brother.

He repeated his assurance that no one was in any danger. Just as he finished, the bow of the *Argo* struck the mudbank at eight miles an hour. Racked planks twisted against each other with the howl of a flight of banshees as the boat shuddered to a stop. Screams and curses contrasted strangely with the genteel tinkle of shattered glass. Jason was catapulted from his improvised rostrum and landed on his belly in the middle of the poker table. He struggled to his feet in time to see a shower of flaming oil stream down from the nearest chandelier and ignite the Turkey carpet in a score of places. Instantly each patch of fire had one or more stamping on it, ignoring the damage to their shoes and legs. Several stewards came running with buckets of sand.

"Check every room," Jason shouted to them. "We'll handle this."

He stayed until the flames were out, then made his way out onto the promenade. The thickly wooded bank was so close that he thought he might jump ashore if he chose. The deck had an unsettling tilt to it, the bow wedged firmly in the mud and the stern slowly sinking, but he had to say that Bowles had chosen his spot perfectly.

Already the larboard stage was in place and a line of passengers were filing across to dry land. What was to be done with them now?

That question had occurred to the pilot, too. Once he finished raking himself over the coals for not knowing how steep that mudbank was, and once he was sure that the boat would not slide backward off the bank and sink after all, he let off a blast of the *Argo*'s steam whistle. Off to the right, where the cut-off rejoined the main channel, a spot of brightness appeared. Good; the woodyard owner was awake, then. He reached up and gave half a dozen short tugs on the whistle lanyard. He calculated that would bring the man to see what was going on, and half an hour later he had the satisfaction of seeing a candle-lantern come bobbing through the woods.

Toward dawn, Jason stumbled to his cabin and lay down on the sofa. All the passengers were safely ashore with their luggage. The members of the crew were hard at work, keeping one furnace going to power the bilge pumps, shifting cargo forward to lighten the stress on the boat's damaged fabric, running a crazy web of lines from the boat to the sturdiest trees along the bank. By Captain Clement's estimate, his men needed two weeks to finish the makeshift repairs that would allow them to steam the remaining ninety miles or so to St. Louis. How long the boatyard would want to return the *Argo* to first-class shape, he couldn't venture to say, nor how much the repairs might cost. Like Gus, he finished his report with the thought that it could have been much worse. Jason had to bite back his retort, that it needn't have happened at all.

The cabin door opened. Jason raised his head. It was his brother. "Did I wake you? Sorry, I figured you ought to hear this as soon as possible."

Jason swung his feet down and used the momentum to bring himself to a sitting position. "I wasn't sleeping. What is it?"

Gus looked over his shoulder. "Come in, man." A young fellow in canvas pants, tattered frieze jacket, and sturdy brogues shuffled through the door, clutching his cap in both hands. "I told you I'd set a man to watch those rowdies," Gus continued. "This is him. Go ahead, O'Donnell, tell him what you told me."

"That I will, Your Honor." He nodded an awkward greeting to Jason. "I hope I find you well, sir. As I was saying to Mister Lowell, I was hanging about near the cargo when I saw him again. 'All right, then,' says I to meself, 'this time I'll get the look of you,' and it's up I creep until I'm no more than the distance from me to you from him. Dark as the halls of Hell it was, but I'd know him again anywhere."

"Who is he talking about?" asked Jason irritably.

"The prowler from the other night. Go on, O'Donnell."

"Yes, sir. He was bending over something, I couldn't see what. Then, bedad, if he doesn't strike a match and touch it to a fuse, then run like the devil. 'Holy Mary,' I says to meself, 'we're all dead men,' and off I go in the other direction, nor get more than halfway down the length of the boat when I hear the blast and fall to my knees shaking with fear.''

"*A bomb?*" Jason exclaimed. "Who, by God!''

"A young gentleman it was, in a fine suit of clothes, with whiskers to the sides of his face as thick as a rosebush and his chin as smooth as a baby's bottom.''

Jason looked questioningly at his brother, who said, "Only one man it could be. Name of Duncan Sargent, claimed to be writing a book. Always scribbling in a ledger.''

"I recall him. But *why*? Is he a lunatic, to do such a thing? He could have drowned us all, or burnt us to a cinder!''

Gus gave him a portentous look. "The bomb was put in the midst of that cargo we looked into the other night. Did a pretty thorough job of work on it, too. And Sargent is a Massachusetts man. First he found out what the cargo was, then he made sure it wouldn't be much use to anybody.''

"A Free Soiler, by God! Where is he? I'll strangle him with his own guts!''

"Halfway to St. Louis by now, I expect. I took a gander at his cabin after I heard O'Donnell's story. He must have cleared out pretty damn fast—I found a blotted letter under the bunk. Hard to make out, but it said something about meeting in Lawrence.''

"Kansas again? Why can't they keep their damned quarrels to themselves! I don't give a damn if they ram their bombs up each other's asses, but they've no call to try to sink my steamer!'' He stood up, brushed his hair back with both hands, and stretched. "God, what a night! I'll tell you this, Gus. I'm not going to lie down under this. That bastard is going to be sorry he ever heard of the *Argo* or Jason Lowell!"

CHAPTER FOURTEEN

"Mr. Lowell! Mr. Lowell!" The clerk hurried across the lobby with a folded paper in his hand. "Message for you, Mr. Lowell. Gen'm'n said be sure to catch you when you came in."

Jason muttered an acknowledgment, stuffed the paper in his coat pocket, and started up the stairs to his room. He had reached St. Louis just before dawn, after a night in which the slightest noise brought him bolt upright with sweat pouring down his sides. The Planters Hotel had held his rooms for him, but he had had just enough time to wash and change clothes. He wanted a talk with George Pfeffer as soon as the bank opened, then it was down to the boatyard with Captain Clement's letter describing the *Argo*'s condition. Siegel, the master boatwright, had bargained like an old clothes man, but in the end Jason got his promise to do the needed repairs for a price Jason could afford and to put them ahead of two less urgent projects in the yard. Now all Jason wanted was a few hours of undisturbed sleep.

As he was taking off his coat, he recalled the message. He fished it out and read it. Gus wanted to see him on *matters of the greatest import* and was coming to his rooms at three o'clock. A glance at his pocket watch confirmed his guess: it was nearly three already. He was half-tempted to pretend not to hear Gus's knock, but he knew his brother was no alarmist. If he said a matter was important, it most likely was. Jason shrugged his coat back on, opened the window a little more, and poured himself a glass of claret.

Without warning, the door opened and Gus thrust his head in. "You're here," he said in a conspiratorial voice. "Thank God." He withdrew, to reappear a moment later escorting a pretty—and frightened—young girl, who jumped at the sound of the door latch. Jason recognized her at once as the Wainwright girl whom Gus had been talking about a few days earlier. What the devil was she doing here, though?

Gus introduced them, and the girl gave a shy curtsy. Jason replied with a courtly bow and a covert glare at his brother, who cleared his throat loudly. The girl jumped a second time; her nerves must be wound tight as the strings of a pianoforte. "Will you take a chair, Miss Wainwright?" Jason said soothingly.

"Thank you, sir, you're very kind."

Once they were seated, he looked at Gus and raised one eyebrow. Gus cleared his throat again. "I, ah, met Miss Wainwright this morning. At a shop."

And not by accident either, thought Jason. His brother had an unsuspected streak of slyness in him, it seemed.

"She was in a very nervous state, and when she told me the reason, I could understand completely. It's an odd and alarming situation, and as it concerns you, I thought you ought to hear her account yourself."

What had gotten into Gus, to make him speak like a book? Any other time, he would have called it a queer kettle of fish or some even more pungent name. In Jason's experience, high-flown language generally meant one of two things: a courtship or a duel. It wasn't hard to guess which was in the offing here.

He nodded gravely. "Please go ahead, Miss Wainwright."

"Oh thank you, sir. Your brother told me how kind you are, but I declare I didn't know what to expect, and then to be coming to a gentleman's rooms at a hotel, too! I can hardly catch my breath, I'm so flustered."

"A glass of wine might calm you."

She looked as though he had offered her an opium pipe. "Oh no, I couldn't, thank you. If only I knew where to begin."

"The marriage?" Gus prompted.

"Mercy, yes! I've been trying not to think of it, but I suppose I have to." She leaned forward and lowered her voice. "This morning I heard my Uncle Junius talking to his friend Mr. Shuttlesworth. Of course, he's not really my uncle, he's my guardian, but I can't hardly call him 'Senator' all the time, can I? Anyway, they must have thought I was asleep. Uncle Junius said because of the wreck, they'd have to hurry up the marriage, and his friend said that was fine with him. He used coarse language that I won't soil my lips by repeating. Then I almost screamed when it came to me: they were talking about marrying *me* to that Luke Shuttlesworth!''

''The match isn't to your liking?'' Jason said dryly.

''*Liking!* It makes my flesh creep to have him anywhere close to me! And Uncle Junius knows it, too; I told him so. But he doesn't care one bit for my happiness; he only wants to get hold of my daddy's money. He even said as much to that awful Luke Shuttlesworth!'' She stopped to sniffle a few times. Gus offered her his handkerchief, but after looking suspiciously at it, she found one in her reticule.

''If my daddy were alive, he'd take a horsewhip to the two of them,'' she declared. ''But what am I to do, a thousand miles from home, a poor, unprotected young girl?''

''Not poor,'' said Jason.

''And not unprotected,'' added his brother in a ringing voice, then glowered at Jason, who pretended not to see.

''Oh, you're both so kind; it's a mercy I met you. I don't know how to thank you.''

''Please don't try, Miss Wainwright. Perhaps you can enlighten me, though: why does Senator Stephenson need to marry you to his friend? Doesn't he control your inheritance already? If he is as unscrupulous as you say, that ought to be enough.''

''*If!*'' Gus muttered indignantly.

"That's just it. He never got along with Uncle Louis at the bank, and now I think of it, I'll bet he brought me up all this way to keep Uncle Louis from finding out what was going on."

"Uncle Louis?" asked Jason aside.

"Grandcourt," Gus replied. "Trustee of the estate."

"Then, when I got up and went out there, the two of them were all sugary-sweet to me, so I thought I was going to be sick. After that Shuttlesworth left, Uncle Junius told me he was going to make a princess of me, and he went on about how much that terrible Luke was in love with me and what a wonderful match it would be, until I about died. Then he said we were leaving St. Louis and going out to Kansas Territory, just he and I and that Luke man. I said I'd rather stay in St. Louis, but he pretended he didn't hear, same as he did when I told him I didn't much want to be a princess."

"So what did you say?" Jason was becoming interested in spite of himself.

"I reckoned I'd better be just as clever as I knew how, so I said he'd won me over to the marriage, but I'd always dreamed of a June wedding and wouldn't have it any other way. And then I said it wouldn't be proper for a young lady to travel alone with two gentlemen, and he would have to find a respectable female companion to go to Kansas with us." She sat back and smiled, inviting Jason's compliments for her craftiness.

He stared. "I don't understand: why did you agree? You don't really mean to marry the man, do you?"

"I'll die first, indeed I will! But . . ." The color mounted in her face, but she forced herself to continue. "After what I heard this morning, I wouldn't put it past Uncle Junius to leave me alone with that Shuttlesworth long enough to make it so that I'd have to marry him. It's a hard thing to say, but I heard the way they talked about me. So I realized if I said I wouldn't have him, something might happen to me right away. But if I pretended to go along, and got some kind woman with good morals to stay near me, maybe Uncle Junius wouldn't see any need to make sure of me that way. I know June's just three weeks from now, but I had to say something I thought he might believe, and that was the only thing I could think of."

She studied Jason's face, as if searching for approval. His expression was as unreadable as if he were in a poker game for high stakes. Just as the silence began to stretch to the edge of awkwardness, she burst out, "Oh, it's a hard thing to be a girl and all alone in the world! Who can I turn to for advice and help? And so far from home, too—it's a crying shame. If my dear daddy is looking down from heaven and sees what's going on, he must be weeping with rage. I declare, if I didn't think I could count on your brother, sir, I would fling myself from a high window!"

Gus was patting her hand, as if to say, "There, there." He avoided Jason's look of sardonic inquiry.

"Hmph. Please excuse an indelicate question, Miss Wainwright, but what is your age?"

"I am seventeen. I'll be eighteen, come July."

Jason's dominant reaction to Melissa Wainwright's

predicament was impatience. The *Argo*, into which he had invested practically all his savings and all his feelings, had just been damaged by a bomb. She might well have sunk. What was Gus thinking of, bringing the girl to him at such a time? Did he hope to distract him? Was he going to be burdened with the responsibility for every waif and stray in St. Louis and points south? He hadn't much taken to either the Senator or his henchman Shuttlesworth, but what did that signify? He wasn't obliged to interfere in the private affairs of every man he failed to take a shine to; the idea was ridiculous.

"Well." His unwillingness to involve himself was starting to register. The girl's lower lip quivered, and a frown was gathering on Gus's face. "You have my sympathy, of course. But with the greatest respect, Miss Wainwright, all this is none of my business. It's between you, your guardian, and your trustee. I don't see why you think it concerns me at all, as a matter of fact."

"But—"

"Damn it, Jason—"

The two stopped in confusion. Each seemed reluctant to continue, until Gus said, "You'd best tell him what you told me. Maybe that will change his mind."

Melissa stirred uneasily. "I'll have you thinking I'm a terrible eavesdropper, Mr. Lowell, but there was more to the conversation between Uncle Junius and Mr. Shuttlesworth this morning. I couldn't make out exactly what they were talking about, but there was some cargo on your boat that was very important to them, that got ruined in that explosion."

She paused and looked at Jason, who nodded his understanding.

"Whatever it was, they think you and your brother are responsible, and they're terribly wroth against the two of you. That Shuttlesworth already had a grudge against your brother, for something else." Her cheeks turned pink at the recollection. "They were making awful threats, and what made it worse was the *way* they were talking. They were going on just the way they'd talk about planting a field of cotton or slaughtering a hog, not shouting or carrying on. Somehow that made it seem a whole lot more serious."

Jason was mystified. "Why do they hold us responsible? Because the *Argo* is mine?"

"No, they had someone watching their goods. He told them he saw you two meddling with the cargo a couple of nights ago. They figure since you're the only ones to know what it was, you must have been the ones who destroyed it. Uncle Junius said something I didn't understand at all. He said that with your name, it's no wonder you're a ruffian for the Immigrant Aid Society. What does your name have to do with it, and what is this Society he means?"

Jason brushed the questions aside and swallowed back a mouthful of curses unfit for a young lady's ears. The Senator's reasoning was tolerably clear. Even the rumor that Jason was an offspring of the Boston Lowells fit in perfectly, though how even an old bag of wind like Stephenson could think that Jason would endanger his own steamboat was baffling. If he were an agent of the Abolitionists, he would have watched the crates of rifles to their warehouse in St. Louis, then blown that up. And of course, the midnight inspection of the crates had been noticed, though it seemed that the earlier prowler had slipped by the Senator's watchdog unseen.

". . . Why you've got to get out of town right away."

Jason blinked. "I'm sorry, what was that?"

"They mean to teach you a lesson," she repeated. "Not Uncle Junius himself, of course, but some men who are followers of his. It was just terrible, the things they said they would do to you. I had to hold my hands over my ears. That's when I knew that I just had to warn you. It would have been unchristian of me not to, after the things I heard."

"Yes, I see." Inwardly he shrugged. Threats were a constant feature of his life. Scarcely a day had passed since he was fifteen when some rival dealer or sore loser didn't swear to hang him by his thumbs or feed his balls to the alligators. Most of the time the threats seemed to serve as a substitute for violence, not a preface to it. The important thing was to take as little notice as possible. If you let people get the idea that you could be cowed by words, they would stomp you into the mud in nothing flat, but if you put up a bold face, they were likely to step carefully around you.

Somewhere outside, a clock chimed four. The girl turned pale. "Mercy! So late already? Uncle Junius will miss me if I don't get back right away. If he suspects anything, I don't even want to think what he might do!" Gus sprang to his feet as she stood up. Jason was a little slower.

"I hope I'll see you gentlemen again real soon,"

she continued. "You *will* take care now, won't you? No," she added to Gus, "I'll see myself home, thank you, sir. I wouldn't want anyone to catch sight of us together, would you?" With another little curtsy to each of them, she was gone.

"Whew," said Jason, pouring two glasses of whiskey. "I never knew being nursemaid was such hard work. You seem to take to it pretty well, though, little brother. What do you make of her story?"

"I think she's right," Gus replied glumly. "We ought to get out of town for a while. Stephenson must have forty men in that gang of his. Those aren't the sort of odds I like."

"What of it? If he means to meddle in the situation in the Kansas Territory, his men won't be much use to him here in St. Louis, will they? All we have to do is stay out of the way until they leave town."

"And if some of them stay behind? He's a big man in certain circles, you know. Suppose he asks his friends here to deal with you? We'd be better off some place where we knew what side people were on."

"What side are *we* on? I don't recollect joining anyone's side but my own. Look here, Augustus my lad, you're no good at being devious. What are you after?"

Gus looked away in embarrassment at being found out so easily, but after a moment he said, "I think we should go out to Kansas. I know," he continued over Jason's sarcastic laughter, "I know. That's where Stephenson and Shuttlesworth and the whole gang are headed, too. But it's a big territory. We could stay out of their way, *and* keep track of what they're up to.''

''I don't care what they're up to, though. It doesn't concern me.''

''Not even if the Senator spreads the word that Jason Lowell of the *Argo* is a secret Abolitionist agent? How do you think your Mississippi planters will take the news? What kind of welcome will we get in Natchez next time we dock?'' He saw that this point impressed Jason. Quickly he reached for another argument. ''The only way you can stop that is by exposing the real Abolitionist, that fellow Sargent. You swore you'd get him for trying to blow up the boat. Well, where you do reckon he is? In Lawrence, K.T., that's where, or he will be in a couple of days. And that's where we ought to head, too.''

''Hmm.'' Jason took another sip of the fiery liquor and rolled it around in his mouth. ''Well, son, there's more between your ears than wet sawdust, but I swear I hear a couple of bees buzzing around in there, too. Just what sort of arrangement did you make with that filly this morning?''

''I didn't,'' replied Gus heatedly, ''and I think you should refer to Miss Wainwright in more carefully chosen terms! She's as nice and proper a young lady as any you'll find, and very brave, too.''

''I beg your pardon, and hers as well. Once more: did you arrange any appointment, rendezvous, or what not with that very brave, nice, and proper young lady I had the honor of entertaining this morning?''

"Well . . . not exactly, no. I did give her to understand that I meant to be in Lawrence or thereabouts and would consider myself at her service in any need."

"Three flashes with a lantern and a ladder under the window?"

"Joke if you like, but she's in a terrible predicament, and I'm the only friend she has within a thousand miles. If I don't help her, who will?"

The almost painful earnestness of his brother's face reminded Jason that for all the maturity of his judgment, Gus was still in the process of emerging from boyhood. If he felt an impulse to imitate the knights of King Arthur's court, he was hardly the first, and even if it led him to make a fool of himself or to step heedlessly into danger, the impulse deserved a degree of respect. There was nothing mean or petty about it.

"I didn't intend to make light of her predicament," Jason said in a gentler tone, "or to mock you for wanting to help. But are you really serious about going three hundred miles out of your way—and into the middle of a small war—on such an errand? She must mean more to you than you're telling."

"I—" Gus stammered. "That's not the point. What about Sargent? And what about that gang that's after us?"

"A pox on both their houses! Come on, little brother, you're running from shadows. I'll tell you, let's have a wager: we'll stop by the bar and pay our respects to the Professor over one of his Tom and Jerry cocktails, then have supper at Maudie's. If the Senator's toughs give us any trouble, we'll talk about Kansas again. If not, you'll drop the idea. Is it a bet? Yea or nay?''

Gus's face was troubled. ''A walk of a few blocks won't prove anything, though. They might not know where to find us.''

''In St. Louis?'' Jason scoffed. ''Horsefeathers! If they don't have the sense to check the Planters first, they're about as much danger to us as the risk of being bitten on the ass by a rabid monkey! Come on, do we have a bet?''

''Well . . . all right.'' He stuck out his hand.

Downstairs, at the bar, Gus noticed that Jason was carrying a silver-mounted walking stick of some dark Oriental wood. He reached over to examine it, and suddenly found his wrist imprisoned in a painful grip. He looked up in astonishment.

''Sorry,'' Jason said, releasing him. ''It's a favorite of mine. I don't use it very often, for fear of breaking it.''

''That must be why I never saw it before.''

''I suppose.'' He seemed to think the subject was closed. He did not offer Gus a closer look at the stick. ''Are you ready for our evening stroll?''

Gus moved his shoulders around to loosen them. ''Ready as I'll ever be.''

The lobby was redolent with the aroma of the Planters' specialties, fried chicken and candied sweet potatoes. For a moment Gus was inclined to suggest that they have supper in the hotel. But, of course, food wasn't the chief reason to go over to Maudie's. It was Jason's way of making a point.

As the two brothers started across the street a block from the hotel, someone jostled Gus roughly. He spun around. ''Here, what do you think—''

He fell silent and stepped back. The jostler was no one he knew, but his type was familiar: unshaven, with small eyes like a wild boar, a body shaped like a keg, and a rank smell that would have put a billy goat to shame. "You better look better where you're going," he said in a backwoods drawl. "I 'spect you'd like to say you're sorry, right?"

From the shadows, another of the type drifted over. "These dudes bothering you any, Bobby? Dressed like a whore's fancy man, ain't they? I reckon they think that gives them a right to walk all over honest working men like you and me."

He reached out a huge, filthy hand and took the lapel of Gus's coat between thumb and forefinger. "My, my," he said as he rubbed it, "that's a fine piece of goods. I don't believe any man'd wear something so fine—you must be one of them ladies I heard about that dress up in men's clothes! My, yes, Bobby, just you look at how soft that cheek is!"

As he brought his hand up toward Gus's face, Gus slapped it down. He knew, even as he acted, that he had fallen into a trap.

"Ignore them," Jason said stonily. "Come on. We have affairs to attend to." But over his shoulder Gus saw that their path was blocked by a line of three more men who waited like buzzards on a tree limb.

Jason turned to face the newcomers. His posture, with one hand on his hip and the other on the head of his walking stick, was nonchalant, like a man in a tailor's style-book. His opponents were not deceived. They spread out a little as they came toward him. When he raised the stick to point at the one in the center, all three flinched. "You, sir. I'll thank you to step aside. You may not have noticed that you are in my way."

"Talks just like a book," one of them laughed.

"Or a preacher," added another. "Bet he fights like a preacher, too. Or an old granny. Hey—you a granny?"

"Shit no," the third one said. "I know what he is. He's a goddamn nigger-stealer. I swore I'd kill the first one that ever I met, and damn me if I don't. I'm gonna wrap that cane around his neck, just for starters."

He grabbed the walking stick by the lower end. If he was surprised that Jason allowed him to, he was more surprised that it came away so easily that he nearly fell backward. But he had not captured all of the stick. Jason was still holding the upper seven inches, from which a two-foot long, needle-pointed blade projected. The three edges of the triangular blade gleamed evilly in the waning light.

"The warriors of the Orient," Jason said conversationally, "believe that it is terribly bad luck to sheathe a bare blade without blooding it first. I never cared to risk it myself." As he spoke, he darted the point toward the left eye of the one who had grabbed for the stick. He gave a hoarse cry and, dodging, fell to one knee. The one on the left took advantage of the diversion to run in toward Jason. An instant later he howled with agony as the pointed toe of Jason's boot found his groin. The rapier whipped around, narrowly missing the third thug.

Jason reckoned that he was doing pretty well, narrowing the odds from 3-to-1 to 2-to-1 so quickly. But even as he watched his opponents prowl back and forth, searching for a way past the bite of his blade, he was less concerned about the outcome of the fight than about the danger to his hands. They were his living. He would as soon use one of them to hit a man in the jaw as a ship's captain would use his chronometer to drive nails. The sword-stick was one answer to the problem. Another, which they had had only a tiny taste of, was the style of boxing he had picked up in Canton and Singapore, a style that used the feet even more effectively than the French *savate*.

The one who had grabbed the sword-stick's sheath was still holding it. He came forward in a crouch, waving it as if to parry the blade. Jason kept the man's attention focused on the point until he was about four feet away. Then, with a motion so fluid that like running water it was almost invisible, he pivoted onto the ball of his right foot and lashed out with the left. The blow landed with devastating force just over the thug's breastbone. He reeled backwards, but even before he fell to the dust, Jason had spun around and aimed a second kick at the neck of the remaining tough, who dodged, stared at him as if he were insane, and backed slowly away.

Jason risked a quick glance over his shoulder. Gus had dealt with one of his assailants, who was on one knee in the street, puking his guts out, but now he was in trouble himself. The second man had one fist twisted into his shirtfront and was drawing the other back to smash in his face. Gus's right arm dangled uselessly; with his left, he pounded at the other's ribs, but to no effect that Jason could see.

After making sure that the rest of the thugs were out of the action, Jason lunged forward and put his rapier entirely through the meaty part of Gus's attacker's arm. The man jerked back in surprise and pain, and thus damaged his arm still more, then let go of Gus, who slumped to the ground. For a long moment the man stared in disbelief at the spreading stain of crimson on his filthy shirt; then with a wild cry he went running off down the street. Now that the action was over, a curious crowd started to gather. Jason found the sheath of his sword-stick, then helped his brother to his feet. Gus was very pale and his eyes were very wide.

"Can you walk?" said Jason quietly. "We should get back to the hotel before they bring up the reserve troops."

Gus nodded and swallowed. As they made their way through the crowd, he started to speak, but Jason just shook his head.

Back at the hotel, Gus accepted a shot of whiskey. The glass pinged against his front teeth. Suddenly he started to laugh helplessly. "Violence," he choked out. "Haven't you told me a hundred times that violence is stupid?"

"I hope so. It's the last refuge of the incompetent. Look at what just happened—Stephenson and his gang just turned a neutral into an enemy. Do you call that wisdom?"

"Do you call laying out four bravos unviolent? I'd like to hear their opinions on the matter!"

Jason shrugged, as if the question did not much

interest him. "I could easily have killed two of them, and I chose not to. I used no more force than I had to to convince them not to use violence on me."

"I'm not ungrateful, you know, just surprised. I never knew how dangerous you can be."

"I wasn't always a ship-owner with troops of stewards on call in case of trouble. I had hoped that I'd left the need for those skills behind, but I guess not. Well, little brother, it appears to me that you've won the wager. They'll be after our heads all the harder now."

Gus looked up, eyes narrowed. "You mean you agree we should go to Kansas?"

"I agree we should get out of St. Louis for a little while. I can't think of any place I'm less inclined to go than Kansas, but since you feel so strongly about it—someone has to watch over you, I guess."

For a moment Gus felt wounded by what could have been a slight, but then he heard the affectionate joking in Jason's voice and grinned back. "I'd better pack," he said happily.

"Not so fast. Dumb as they are, that gang will have thought to watch the hotel and the riverfront. We'll have to throw them off the track."

"How?"

"We'll wait until after dark, then ride west to Washington. We should be there by mid-morning. Then we wait for the next steamboat going up the Missouri, and hope it isn't the one that Stephenson and his bunch are on!"

CHAPTER FIFTEEN

Everything was different about the second stage of Charlie's and Elizabeth's journey to Kansas Territory. Their steamboat, the *Isaac Adams*, was short, low, and grimy, with a single paddlewheel at the back, and the stateroom they were obliged to share was just big enough for a set of bunk beds, a wardrobe, and room to squeeze between. The river, too, was narrower and more convoluted than the Mississippi. On both sides, raw banks and leaning trees bore witness to the river's endless battle with the land, and a look at the brown, turbid water suggested that the river was winning.

Charlie was upset that there was no organized gambling aboard. He had convinced himself, after his one night of winning, that he was a gifted player. He grumbled and growled until a pock-marked man with dirty linen, dirty nails, and a very wide smile tossed three cards down on the table and offered to bet that Charlie couldn't find the lady. A few minutes later the boy was $120 poorer, but still sure of his talent for cards; the game, he decided, was rigged against him.

Elizabeth was almost glad to see him lose. The money had come to him already tainted, and he was better rid of it. Once he had lost it all, he would have to stop gambling and trying to cut a figure among a very questionable set of men. She certainly did not intend to give him more, and she doubted that Lawrence was the sort of town where all-night gambling hells flourished, even if he found the money to play.

The boat's whistle gave a shrill, nerve-jolting blast to announce its arrival in another town. Elizabeth made an impatient gesture that drew stares from her nearest neighbors. The air in the Ladies' Cabin was dusty and stale, and flavored with the scents of bodies too long between baths and meat too long without curing. The sunbeams that found their way through the narrow transom windows were so full of dust motes that they seemed to be solid columns of white. It came to Elizabeth that if she sat there another minute, she was likely to start throwing a fit. Closing the book she had not looked at in half an hour, she rose and stepped out onto the open gallery.

The *Isaac Adams* was veering to the left, toward a little huddle of buildings that overlooked a ramshackle dock. All the dogs of the town barked frantically, all of them aroused to an unbearable pitch by the boat's whistle and each other's baying. In the distance a child screeched excitedly. A dozen or more figures were sauntering down the dusty track to the dock now. Most of them, she realized, had no particular aim in meeting the boat, only a vague hope that something of interest might happen.

"What a hole!" Charlie was standing beside her. "You don't think Lawrence is like that, do you? I'd go off my head in a week if I had to live in a place like that."

"I don't know what Lawrence is like. But since it is to be our new home, we must take it as we find it and make the best of it, Charlie. I hope you don't mean to start off in a dissatisfied state of mind. If you do, you will injure no one but yourself."

"Hang it, Lizzie; quit preaching at me, will you? You can think of Kansas as your new home if you're minded to, but as far as I'm concerned, it's just a place I have to pass through on my way to the top. A way station, you might say. And I don't mean to like it any better than I have to, so we better just agree to disagree right now."

Elizabeth was taken aback. Though the familiar whine was still in her brother's voice, she heard a new note as well, a note of separation from her. A kind of dizziness struck her at the thought that he might cast her off one day soon. She took his arm and held it despairingly.

"Say, Liz," he continued, unaware of her feeling of forlornness, "look there on the dock. It's that durn gambler and his kid brother. What do you suppose they're following me for? I can't tell them nothing, nor I wouldn't if I could!"

Elizabeth looked, without following his words. She expected to see the pock-marked *monte* dealer who had trimmed Charlie earlier, if she had any actual expectations at all. Instead, she saw a pair

of sturdy shoulders clad in superfine English broad-
cloth, long brown hair flowing softly from under a
slouch hat of beaver felt, and trousers stuffed non-
chalantly into riding boots that dazzled even under
a thin coating of white dust. She did not have to
wait for him to turn to recognize him; she knew
the lines of that body better than she did her own.
But why was he here, after the way they had
parted, before the accident? Had he had a change
of heart and followed her?

He turned to glance up at the approaching
steamer. She shrank back behind Charlie's shoulder.
Absurd though it was, she felt as if she were the
one who was pursuing him, and she dreaded to see
his disgust at her brazenness. She could not possibly avoid him on such a small boat, but how could
she bring herself to face him? She felt all her
resolve, all her hard-won resignation, draining away,
leaving her once more directly confronting her loss
and the blame she bore for it. In a moment she
would no longer be able to hold in her tears, but
she could stand no more humiliation. Swallowing
hard, she walked quickly to the tiny stateroom,
closed the door, and slid softly to the floor. Charlie did not notice her leave.

Down on the dock, Jason was trying to keep the
scorn from showing on his face. Of course, a
Missouri riverboat was not to be compared with a
Mississippi packet like the *Argo*. The two rivers,
the nature of the cargos, the number and sort of
passengers—all were too different. But the *Isaac
Adams* was not merely graceless in her lines and
cursed with that ridiculous stern wheel like an
overgrown chuck-a-luck cage—she also looked

grimy and uncared-for. A boat with peeling paint was odds-on to have inedible food and flea-filled mattresses as well, and the journey upriver to Kansas City would take two days or more. For a moment Jason considered scuttling the trip and riding back to St. Louis, but he had already given Gus his word. Keeping that was more important than a few discomforts.

Unloading the bales, bags, and boxes bound for the village took three or four minutes, and taking on a fresh wood supply consumed another five. As the last split logs were being carried up the gangway, the mate looked at Gus's and Jason's carpetbags and said, "You gents coming along? You'd best jump lively if you are. Cap'n Ralston ain't what you'd call a patient man at the best of times."

As if to illustrate his point, a puff of steam announced that the gangway was about to be lifted. Jason and Gus hurried across, followed closely by the mate. Another shrill blast from the whistle, and the steamboat turned her bow into the current. "Lots of folks aboard this trip," the mate continued. "All the staterooms are filled up, 'cept the bridal suite. There's an extra charge for that one, a dollar apiece over the fare."

"Lead on," said Jason, and flipped him a twenty-dollar coin. The mate tried his teeth on it, grinned, and took them up to a cabin that was rather smaller than the tiniest stateroom on the *Argo*. The berths were against opposite walls rather than stacked one atop the other, but it was not clear how that qualified the room as the bridal suite. A wardrobe, a three-legged table, and two shabby armchairs completed the furnishings. Gus, whose experience with the world was limited, looked around in dismay, but Jason said, "Thanks, friend. Is the bar open yet?"

"Sun's up, ain't it?" the mate replied cheerfully, and left them in their palatial accommodations.

Jason slapped his brother on the back. "Come on. You'll feel better after a couple of drams of Old Monongahela."

The bar was at the front of the Grand Saloon, which obviously doubled as the dining room. Quite a few passengers seemed to feel a need for a short snort before dinner. It was a while before Jason got the drinks, and several minutes more until he noticed Charlie Brigham glowering from the other end of the bar. He stopped with the glass partway to his lips, then continued the motion so naturally that no observer would have detected the hesitation.

Of course, he should not have been surprised. Had he recalled, when Gus proposed his plan, that Elizabeth was on her way to Kansas, too? Was that the reason he had fallen in with it so easily? In any case, boats making the difficult passage up the Missouri were not that frequent at that time of year. This must have been the first to leave St. Louis after the *Henry Clay* arrived with *Argo*'s rescued passengers aboard. It made good sense that the two Brighams had taken passage on her. A coincidence, no more—but a damnable one all the same!

He had been far too harsh, he knew that. The insults he hurled at her had served to hide, even from himself, the pain of his own wounds. Now, at this distance, the disguise no longer worked. Somehow, without meaning to, he had let himself hope that Elizabeth was drawn to him by more than his seductive wiles and her own self-interest. The discovery that she was acting, not even on her own behalf, but for the sake of her worthless cub of a brother, had stirred up an anger he still didn't understand. He had better try, though—because he was about to be plunged into the situation once again.

"Pretty thoughtful, aren't you?" The 'highly rectified' corn liquor had cheered Gus up considerably. He was again thinking of the journey—even the part that involved the *Isaac Adams*—as an adventure, or even a quest. A few discomforts simply made the quest more noble and the ultimate reward sweeter. "Say, look down there—isn't that that sprat from the *Argo*? Sure it is. Looks pretty grumpy, too. Maybe drink doesn't agree with him. You know, I had a suspicion a couple of days back that you had an eye for the sister, the way you put her at your table and all. I could see you found her handsome. Not to my taste, though. That jaw—a woman with a jaw like that likely has too much of a will of her own. I figure a woman ought to look up to her man, without a whole lot of questions and arguments."

Jason had been letting his brother rattle on without paying much attention, but now he looked over. "What if the man is lacking in qualities for the woman to look up to?"

"That's easy," Gus laughed. "He finds a woman with lower standards, that's all."

Jason's reply was lost in the din of a brass handbell, which set off a rush for the dinner tables. There were only two, stretching the length of the hall. By the time Gus and Jason found chairs, most of their fellow-diners were busy on their third course, slices of unidentifiable meat in thick brown gravy, accompanied by boiled potatoes and mashed turnips. The all-night ride had given Gus an appetite that dulled his sense of taste, but Jason only sampled the food. His weariness turned it to ashes in his mouth. After a few minutes, he pushed his chair back, muttered an excuse to Gus, and walked out onto the open promenade at the front of the deck. The fresh breeze seemed to cleanse his lungs and his mind at once.

He was going to have to apologize, that was clear. However disappointed he had been by her mixed motives, he had not had the right to be so cold, so cutting. Nor had he been very smart to do so. What a tigress she had turned out to be, once one got past the intitial shyness! He felt a stirring in his loins as he recalled their two encounters that afternoon. Her passion had not been feigned, he was sure, and he knew his own had been equally real. Nor was it a light thing for a well brought-up girl to give up her virginity. When she came to marry, she would have to hide her lack of innocence from her husband-to-be, or he would certainly cast her off.

Jason became aware that he was grinding his teeth over the thought of some Kansas clodhopper winning the sole right to till the field he had just opened to the plow. She was worth more than any ten farmers! Not that most people would see that. Like her intelligence, her beauty was visible only at certain times and from certain angles. And her loyalty—well, that was visible enough, for all that it was given to someone so undeserving of it. And no one could doubt that there was backbone under that soft exterior. Even Gus had seen it, though he had never spoken to her.

No, he would certainly apologize. He had looked for her during the meal, but she had apparently chosen to stay in her cabin. A wise decision—even the little he had eaten was waging war on his stomach. He must see if there was a bottle or two of drinkable wine on the boat. Once he had made his apologies, Elizabeth might like to share one with him, in his stateroom. And afterward, who could tell?

"I beg your pardon, sir. Do I have the honor of addressing Mr. Lowell?"

The voice was unfamiliar. Jason turned slowly, relaxed but ready for instant action. The speaker was a man of forty or so who looked as though he had spent a good many years staring out over sun-drenched spaces. His clothes were unremarkable, but his boots were very expensive and well cared for.

"That's right, sir. I believe you have the advantage of me."

"Robert Laird, sir, at your service." He offered his hand. "I took passage from Memphis to St. Louis on your fine steamboat last fall, and you were pointed out to me. I took the liberty of approaching you because I am about to join some other gentlemen in a friendly game of cards. We would esteem it a privilege if you would play a hand or two."

The other four players were already at the table. Jason acknowledged Laird's introductions and sat down. "Are you a Tennesseean by birth, Mr. Laird?" he asked idly. One of the best ways to take the measure of his opponents was to get them talking, preferably about themselves.

Laird was pleased by his interest. "That's right, I hail from about twenty miles west of Nashville. But I consider myself a Kansan now. I'll never stop loving the place of my birth, o'course, but the first time I saw the grasslands on the banks of the Kaw, I knew I'd found home. Finest pastureland in the world, sir. First visit out this way?"

"Yes." He paused to look at his cards; nothing of note. "A friend in St. Louis offered me a parcel of land as settlement of a debt, and I thought I'd take a look at it before I agree." He let them suppose that it was a gambling debt; the story gave him a credible reason for the journey.

"A V," Laird said, tossing his five dollars onto the table. "Sound idea," he continued to Jason. "It's like anywhere else, I reckon: there's better and worse spots. Whereabouts is this land?"

"It's on the California Road, a little west of a place called Lawrence."

A silence fell over the table. The other players studied Jason as if they didn't expect the chance to do so again. Finally, Laird said, "There's a deal of trouble down that way, you know. The town's a nest of Abolitionists and traitors, and there's more than a few hotheads about ready to burn it to the ground."

"I heard something about that." He smiled. "Maybe that's why my friend is so ready to part with his land."

No one returned his smile.

The man across the table, a burly fellow with half his teeth gone, said, "How do you stand on the goose question, Mr. Lowell?"

Jason knew what this bizarre phrase meant: did he support the extension of slavery to Kansas and the other territories? The truth was that he didn't give a damn, but he knew that the truth would not satisfy those on either side. "Why, sir, I'm as sound on the goose as any reasonable man must be. The economy and way of life of the entire South depends on it. Without Kansas, that way of life will be in grave danger."

His questioner brought his right hand above the table again, empty, and Jason relaxed his hidden grasp on the edge of the top. He had been ready, the moment a bowie knife or pistol appeared, to turn over the table as a shield, but his answer had passed muster.

"Is the betting to me?" he continued easily. "I'll fold."

For a wonder, the 'friendly game' was just that, a slow-paced game for fairly small stakes and accompanied by desultory conversation. Though he took a pot or two, Jason was bored to distraction. When one of the players mentioned Senator Stephenson, though, he began to take an interest.

"I reckon he'll be President one of these days," said a drummer for a St. Louis farm-implement firm. "Maybe four years along."

"Naw, those Yankees'd never put up with him. He's a man of vision and principle, and there's nothing they hate worse." This was from Jason's former questioner.

"Well, it's a crying shame, that's all," the

drummer continued. "A man like that oughta be President, and if he can't be in the United States, it says a lot about the state of the country. We're at the mercy of people who put their partisan, sectional interests above constitutional principles. That's what the Senator says, and danged if I don't agree right down the line."

"Does he say what to do about it?" asked Jason.

"Well, sir, not in so many words, no, but didn't our forefathers know what to do when the tyrant's boot was on their necks? There'll be deeds done soon as great as any done in those days, mark my words. The tree of liberty must be watered with the blood of patriots. The Senator said that, too."

"Seems to do a powerful lot of talking," grumbled a grizzled former muleskinner who now owned his own freight business. "Not the only one, either. I'll take two cards."

The drummer was stung by his tone. "He's not all talk, not by a long chalk. No sir! Before the month is out, the whole world will know of the Cavalier Legion and its brave commander!"

"What is it, a minstrel show?"

But the drummer, looking upset with himself, refused to say any more. After another hand, Jason thanked the other players and retired to his state-room for a nap. As he dozed off, he decided to search out Elizabeth and give her a warning. Her intended destination was sounding more and more unhealthy.

He did not see her at supper or in the Grand Saloon during the evening, though her brother was there, holding his liquor badly and bragging incoherently. Jason even braved the hard looks of the old hens in the Ladies' Cabin, but with no success. Was she sick in her room? The usual deadly diseases were going around; she could well have caught one of them. The brother didn't look worried, but then, would he? The degree of concern he felt took Jason by surprise. He tried to tell himself that his earlier bad behavior had put him in Elizabeth's debt, that all he wanted was to tender his apology and even the account. But he had to admit that that didn't explain the way he had held his breath on entering the Ladies' Cabin in hopes of catching sight of her, or the sharpness of his disappointment when she wasn't there.

When Gus came to their stateroom late that evening, he looked worried. "Have you been listening to the talk?" he demanded. "Sounds like a damned civil war they're having out there—killing people from ambush, burning down farmhouses, marching here and there. What's going on?"

"As you said," Jason replied dryly. "A civil war. The whole country is like a pair of pincers, and Kansas is the tip, where all the pressure is felt. Are you still keen to go?"

"I *have* to go, I'm pledged to. But I think we ought to split up. Stephenson and Miss Wainwright are on their way to Leavenworth, up near the fort. That's solid pro-slavery territory, where the Senator will pull a lot of weight. I've got to be there, near her, but in case anything happens, I'd like to know I can find you in one of the Free Soil towns. They'd as soon plant Stephenson head-down as do him a favor."

Jason rubbed his eyebrow in silence, then said,

"You'll be on your own, no one to cover your back. Is that smart?"

"I don't like it much, but it makes sense. Besides, you may not realize how well-known you are. There must be two dozen men on this boat who recognized you. If Stephenson hits town and hears that Jason Lowell is around, there'll be hell to pay for sure. The only one who'd be likely to know me is Luke Shuttlesworth, and I plan on keeping out of his way."

Once more Jason thought in silence. What were Gus's real reasons for advancing such a plan? His explanation was not very strong—what if he ran across any of the five men who had attacked them the night before? They would certainly know him again!

Perhaps it was a matter of proving himself. After all, he was twenty-one years old. No one would hold that he was too young to leave the shelter of his big brother's wing, though that certainly wasn't the way Jason himself saw their relationship. And there was the girl—he was a good deal more taken with her than he was letting on, that was sure. Would he make such a journey, into known danger, out of pure gallantry?

Maybe he wanted to be away from Jason's side because he already knew that he might decide to act in ways that Jason was bound to oppose. The careful assessment of odds in which Jason had so thoroughly drilled himself might seem too cold-blooded and unchivalrous to a young man with romantic ideas.

Jason felt a pang at the thought of Gus putting himself in danger when he was too far away to help.

He had not really noted the slow growth of closeness between them, or if he occasionally glimpsed it, he took it too much for granted. It seemed to him something that had always been there and would always continue to be there. That was foolish of him. The time came for every fledgling to leave the nest—but it was not an easy moment.

Gus was watching him uneasily, as if he could follow the succession of thoughts in Jason's mind. Perhaps he could at that. Jason let out a long breath and said, "I don't like it; it sounds too risky." His brother's face fell, then tightened with determination. "Still," Jason continued, "this is your game, and I'll play by your rules. But not unless you let me help you plan. You'll need a new name and home state if you're going to Leavenworth. Have you given your name to anybody on this steamboat?"

Gus shook his head. In the next few minutes the two brothers decided that he was Gus Cooke and from one of the little towns on the Kentucky side of the Ohio River. "You know those places, your accent will pass, and you're not apt to run into any natives of Milton, Kentucky, in Leavenworth, Kansas," Jason concluded with a short laugh. "You should keep yourself to yourself anyway; put yourself in the mind of a man on the run from the law. Kansas Territory has a good many of them already, so folks won't think your reserve is peculiar."

"What about you? Where will I find you, and under what name?"

"Oh, I'll keep my name, since you tell me I'm so well-known. As for where I'll be, I still mean to track down that polecat who tried to blow up the

Argo. Since Lawrence is the biggest Free-Soil town, I reckon I'll start there.'' Gus gave him a sharp look, but did not comment. ''How long do you figure to stay around Leavenworth?''

''No more than a week, probably only a day or two.''

''I'll stay put in Lawrence, then. I wonder if any of those Free-Soil Yankees are gambling men. I'll have a dull time of it if they're not!''

CHAPTER SIXTEEN

Ich kam von Alabama
Mein banjo auf dem knie . . .

Elizabeth leaned over the railing, smiling with delight at hearing the familiar words and melody so strangely altered. Down below, on the main deck, the little group of German immigrants noticed her listening and returned her smile. They had crossed the wide ocean, come to a foreign land where the language and customs were new to them, and yet they seemed so happy, while she, who had come a mere thousand miles, was already so homesick she thought she would die. The worst of it was that the home she so longed for did not even exist any more, could never exist again. Her daddy was dead, and her brother grew farther apart from her every day.

"You have a charming smile, Miss Brigham. May I hope to see it again?"

Her hands clenched the railing. She had put off this moment for as long as she could. She had stayed in her cabin, avoided the ghastly meals, lived on bread, cheese, and fruit—all to hold it off. Yet she had known it had to come, known it from the moment Charlie pointed out that familiar figure on the wharf. She was no better prepared to deal with it now than she had been then. Inhaling deeply, she looked around.

"Good morning, Mr. Lowell." Her tone left him no room to mock her. Though her cheeks were burning, she let no sign of self-consciousness soften her expression.

"I was afraid you were ill, not seeing you these past two days. I'm delighted to see you looking so well."

He must know perfectly well that she had been avoiding him, which made his expressed concern for her health another of his subtle but deadly insults. But there was nothing in the words she could object to. "Thank you, sir. A minor indisposition. How is your beautiful boat? That was a shocking night for all of us."

His face turned grim. "The damage can be repaired. I hope to have the *Argo* in service again by the first of July. In the meantime, I have to go to Kansas to look over some land."

"Really? Where?"

Her first impulse when she heard that he was also going to Lawrence was to wonder if he was following her. For a minute or so she allowed the idea to thrill her, then her sturdy good sense took over. Was it likely that a man like Jason Lowell would traipse across the whole state of Missouri in pursuit of a girl he had practically called a whore?

"We're going to Lawrence ourselves," she said calmly. "Our uncle lives near there. He wrote that we should leave the boat at Kansas City and hire a carriage in Westport, just south of there."

"I was told the same. Would you object to our keeping company?"

Elizabeth looked away to hide the latest wave of blushes. He was being either very obtuse or deliberately provocative. He must know that 'keeping company' was an expression for courting. To use it in that way, to her, was cruel! But once again she could not openly object to his words.

"The roads are free to all, I imagine." His face, and her own conscience, told her that she had been much too harsh. In remorse she leaned in the other direction. "Your presence will be very welcome, Mr. Lowell."

"Thank you," he said gravely. If he meant to say more, a long scream from the boat's whistle changed his mind. Ahead, on a bluff overlooking the river, they could see rooftops silhouetted against a sky of summer blue. Lower down, on the levee, half a dozen mule-drawn freight wagons waited for the *Isaac Adams* to tie up.

"That is Kansas City," said Jason. "Please excuse me for a moment; I have to fetch my portmanteau."

The bridal suite was only a few steps away, but the walk gave him time enough to reproach himself several times. He had intended to apologize, to make up their differences, and instead he had stumbled from one gaffe to another. She had noticed, too, though her kindness hadn't let her properly rebuke him. Was he doomed to do and say the wrong thing with her at every turn? It seemed so, but the next few days would show the truth.

Gus was waiting in the room. Jason checked that the clasps on his bag were locked, then turned. "I'll be at the local hotel in Lawrence until I hear from you. Don't come on deck with me; better we're not seen together."

Gus swallowed, opened his mouth to speak, and closed it again. Jason reached over and took him by the shoulders.

"Mind you take care of yourself, little brother, and I'll see you again in a week or less." A brief, awkward hug, and he was out the door.

Elizabeth was standing on the main deck near the gangway. Her brother, standing next to her, acknowledged Jason's greeting with a mutter and a sullen look. Elizabeth gave him a nod and a quick smile, then returned to watching the groups of men who clustered on the levee to inspect each passenger disembarking from the *Isaac Adams*. Elizabeth seemed caught between fascination and disgust.

Even Jason, who had seen a good deal of the world, admitted that they were picturesque. Most of them wore long, mud-covered boots pulled up over gaudy, fancy-weave and well-soiled trousers; red or blue shirts, also well-soiled, with an eagle, anchor, or other device worked in braid on front and back; and slouched, hats decorated with brass stars and goose feathers, over very long, very greasy uncombed hair and unshaven, unwashed faces with desperately fierce expressions.

Their garb, however, was only a background for an astonishing variety of personal armament. The handles of large bowie knives projected from boot tops. Heavy leather belts supported one or even two large-caliber revolvers, and usually a sword as well, while rifle straps and bandoliers crossed their chests.

"What . . ." breathed Elizabeth. "Who are those men?"

"In Italy they would be known as *banditti*," Jason replied. "Here in Missouri they glory in the name of—well, read for yourself." He pointed toward the road down the face of the bluff. A two-horse omnibus was rattling down to the levee to meet the steamboat. Its side was decorated in scarlet and crimson. The smaller letters announced 'Kansas City & Westport Omnibus,' and the larger capitals flamed out the name of the coach: BORDER RUFFIAN.

"Those are the men who—"

"Hush," Jason said quickly. "Whatever your thoughts, keep them to yourself until we are farther on our journey. The reason they are here is to make sure their enemies don't get to Kansas Territory. For the next few minutes you must be my wife and stepbrother, understand?"

She nodded, looking scared. Her brother took a step away from them and sulked.

Jason grabbed his bag and Elizabeth's and led them down the gangway toward the omnibus. As he expected, one of the Ruffians stepped in front of them and put a grimy hand on Jason's chest. Jason stopped short, looked down at the hand, then met the other's eyes. After a moment the

Ruffian dropped his hand and took a half-step backwards.

"Who are ye and whar ye be headed?" he growled. His left hand toyed with the butt of a .44 revolver.

"I, sir, am Jason Lowell, of New Orleans, and we are going to Kansas to look over some property I own there. And you, sir? Your name, and the source of your interest in my affairs?"

"Never you mind my name, and my interest is keepin' a lot o' nigger-thievin' polecats out o' my neck o' the woods. And if'n you be one of 'em, you'd best just git back on that boat afore some o the boys git rowdy."

Jason drew himself even straighter, and his face hardened. "Sir, if not for my admiration for your valor in defense of our way of life, I would be obliged to require satisfaction from you for daring to make such a suggestion."

"Talk purty, don't you?" But beneath his bluster, the man was uneasy. Jason was not his usual prey, and his manner suggested reservoirs of dangerous strength. "Wall, I reckon you can pass along. But if'n I was you, I wouldn't be so highty-tighty. Next feller you meet might take it amiss."

Jason continued to be the New Orleans gentleman, veteran of a dozen affairs of honor and touchy as hell, until the three of them were five miles from Westport in their hired buckboard. There he stopped at a fork. "The Santa Fe Trail to the left and the California Road to the right. This patch of country has seen its share of history."

Elizabeth looked around with new eyes. The land was beautiful, deep in rich grasses and fenced with stands of walnut, hickory, elm and oak. Wildflowers bloomed everywhere—pale evening primroses, bright yellow compass flowers, pink running roses, blue lupine. Warmed by the late spring sun, the westerly breeze carried a hundred intertwined aromas. Even the black thunderhead that loomed on the western horizon had a majestic beauty of its own. She took a deep breath and thought that there might be some joy in the world for her after all.

Jason studied the distant thundercloud for a moment, then gave the reins a shake. Lawrence was still better than thirty miles away, and a storm on these barren plains was no light matter.

The first fat drops darkened the dusty road when they were still an hour from their destination. Jason and Elizabeth, on the wagon seat, shared two slickers, one across their shoulders and one on their laps. Charlie huddled under the third slicker in the back of the buggy. The flash of lightning, the crash of thunder, and the sudden downpour both frightened and excited Elizabeth. She moved over until she felt Jason's thigh warm against her own. His free arm came around her shoulders, supposedly to adjust the oilskin, but she noticed that it stayed there. Leaning over, she nestled her head in the hollow of his shoulder and allowed her hand to rest on his thigh. Was she acting the harlot again? She discovered that she didn't care. She began to stroke the full length of his thigh, and she felt his arm tighten convulsively around her.

Lawrence, K.T., stood on the open prairie just south of a line of timber that marked the course of the Kaw River. A steep bluff commanded the town from the west, and Mount Oread rose to the south. As Jason urged the tired horse down the muddy road toward the town, the first thing to catch his eye was an imposing structure of stone, fully three stories high, that made the mud-chinked log cabins and shacks of sun-curled cottonwoods planks around it seem even cruder than they were. On the outskirts of town, a circular earthen fort was slowly melting back into the prairie.

"Uncle Dan lives out west of town someplace," Elizabeth murmured. "It's so late already, I think Charlie and I ought to take rooms at the hotel and look for Uncle Dan's farm in the morning. Will you be staying in town for a while?"

"A few days, I reckon." The horse instinctively turned onto a wide street that led through the center of town. Now Jason saw that the big stone building wore a sign that proclaimed it the FREE STATE HOTEL. He pulled up in front.

After an indifferent supper, Elizabeth, tired by the day of traveling, went to her room. Jason sat downstairs for a while, reading the recent issues of the two local newspapers, the *Herald of Freedom* and the *Kansas Free State*. Both seemed to spend half their space attacking the pro-slave 'Bogus Legislature' and the other half denouncing each other. The reasons for their mutual hostility were very obscure, at least to a stranger in town, and Jason was soon bored by paragraph after paragraph of inflammatory rhetoric. He tossed the paper down and climbed the stairs to his room.

He was sitting on the bed in his shirtsleeves, wondering if he should tap on Elizabeth's door, when he heard a soft knock. He slipped on his coat and checked that the two-shot Deringer was in the inside pocket, then turned the latch. Elizabeth stepped in and hurriedly closed the door. Her face showed a mixture of exhilaration and doubt. Instead of speaking, Jason took her in his arms and gave her a long, passionate kiss that left her gasping for breath.

"I wanted to—"

He stopped her words with another kiss, as his fingers deftly unfastened her dress. Moments after she entered the room, she was completely naked. She pulled away from his embrace. Fixing his gaze with her own, she reached up with both hands to release her long, lustrous hair. Posed so, her body was something out of a painting by the Old Masters. She knew it, and held the position, silently demanding his admiration.

He gave it freely, and he reached out to pull her back into his arms. As his lips explored her breasts and belly, she threw her head back and stared blindly at the ceiling while concentrating every tendril of awareness to follow and receive his caresses. Her fingers twined in his hair and pressed him closer to her. When his lips at length found what they were seeking, she let out a strange, forlorn cry that blended ecstasy and despair. She had never imagined such an experience, and she knew that later, in her solitude, she would wonder if her enjoyment was the sign of an incurably depraved nature. But, for now, the sensation itself filled her whole world.

Jason, too, was caught up in an experience that created powerful, but disregarded, doubts in him. The mere appearance of Elizabeth in his doorway had aroused him to a high pitch of excitement, and each moment since had further stoked the already overheated furnace. His safety valve was tied down, and unless the pent-up energy was converted into action soon, the boiler was destined to explode.

He pulled back, panting for breath, and Elizabeth fell on him, bearing him backward onto the narrow bed.

"You must think," she gasped, "I'm an utterly wicked, wanton girl. I don't care any more." Sliding to the floor, she tore at his fly, her mouth gaping to receive and engulf him. Only moments later, the explosion occurred.

She did not seem to notice the change in his mood. Her hunger was unappeased; why should his be sated? She continued to toy with him, to exult in her control over the weapon that had terrified her only days before, and soon he began to respond again. Reaching down, he grabbed her by the arms and pulled her up level with him, then rolled onto her. The merging was so easy, so natural, that Elizabeth had to concentrate to be sure that it was happening. Then the insistent rhythm of their coupling found its way into her blood and with growing force pounded until she thought her heart would burst.

Moved by some unknowable impulse, she raised her head and fixed her small white teeth in the muscle of his shoulder. He groaned, and his fingertips dug into her back. Her legs were so wide apart, and the blows to her center so urgent, that she started to wonder if she would split into two pieces. Then, from somewhere near the base of her spine, the heat of a glowing fuse moved through

her, adding strength as it moved. Her mouth fell
open and her head pushed against the mattress,
arching her whole body irresistibly. Had she cried
out? Or had he? For a long space of timelessness,
the distinction between them seemed swept away.

Then, inevitably, she returned to herself and her
doubts. She looked at him sidelong. Was that
scorn she saw in the curl of his lips? She had
shown so clearly that she was dominated by her
animal nature—how could he possibly respect her?
No, she had 'tossed her cap over the windmill,' as
the saying was, and she could hardly hope to find
it again.

Daniel Church was a worried man. "I sent a
letter to St. Louis," he told Elizabeth when they
met the next morning. "I guess you didn't get it.
The Ruffians aren't above intercepting our mail
these days. That's one of the things that made me
think you and Charlie should stay on in St. Louis
for a little while, until the dust settles. Still," he
added with a nod to Jason, "I'm glad you found
an escort. You have my thanks, sir."

Charlie was miffed by this speech. Didn't his
uncle think he was an adequate escort, and one a
damn sight better than some slick gambling man?
But his opinion didn't count anyway. Uncle or
not, Dan Church was a double-dyed Yankee Abolitionist scoundrel who polluted the earth he walked
on.

As a matter of fact, Church *was* a confirmed
believer in abolishing slavery, unlike most of the
Free State Party who merely wanted to keep the
institution out of Kansas. He had grown up in

Jamestown, Rhode Island, across the channel from Newport. The most important day of his life occurred when he went to a sermon by the famous Brooklyn preacher, Henry Ward Beecher. He went mostly from curiosity, but by the end he was ready to sell his cabinetry shop and move to the Kansas Territory to battle for the Lord.

His dedication was rewarded. The plot of land he bought sight-unseen from an agent of the New England Emigrant Aid Society turned out to have a fine stand of black walnut growing on it. He was already studying the planks in his drying shed, planning the tables and cupboards and highboys he would craft from them, once the Territory was at peace.

Sometimes he thought that time would never come.

"We hear rumors," he continued. "Now that it's warmer, we expect to be attacked. The Ruffians surrounded the town last year, you know. They bullied and blustered about wiping us off the face of the earth. In the end they were too afraid of our Beecher's Bibles." He patted the stock of his Sharp's rifle. "I don't expect the spell to last, though. It's even said that some of the Ruffian bands are armed with Sharp's guns, and are drilling and training like Regulars. It's a notion to give a body chills. That's why I'd have rather you'd stayed away for a while, my dear. And you, too, Charlie, of course."

The boy scowled. "I can take care of myself, Uncle Dan. I don't know what you're so worried about anyway. From what I heard, all those fellows want is to make sure the laws are enforced. The only ones that's likely to hurt are the criminals.''

"That's one way of looking at it, I know. Of course, the laws they want to enforce were passed by a bogus legislature, elected through criminal fraud and intimidation. When I met you this morning, Mr. Lowell, you were leafing through one of our local papers. Do you know that you are liable to a heavy term in jail for that terrible crime? Why, Charlie, even you may have glanced at the *Herald of Freedom* making you one of the criminal class those fellows are likely to hurt.'' He clapped his sulky nephew on the shoulder. "Never mind, son, you'll see the way of it soon enough, now you're here. Folks back East just don't understand what we're up against.''

The sound of a wagon rattling down Massachusetts Street drew Jason to the window of his room. No supplies had come to Lawrence for three days, and the rumor was that the Ruffians had declared an embargo against the town. If so, the move wasn't likely to do much harm in the short run, but it was a sign of how bold their enemies were becoming.

The blanket-covered form in the back of the wagon and the riderless horse tied to the tailgate made it plain what cargo had just arrived. Jason hurried downstairs to join the growing crowd around the wagon.

"Found him just east of Franklin,'' the wagoner was saying, "still setting his horse, but too far gone to know they weren't moving any. Don't know who he is, but someone sure put a hole through him. Let's get him inside where the doctor can take a look.''

Struck with foreboding, Jason crowded forward to see the features of the injured man. He couldn't get close enough, but as four men lifted the injured man from the wagon bed, he saw his boots. They were nothing like the ones Gus had been wearing. Light-headed with relief, he followed the crowd into the lobby.

''Come on, folks, stand back! Give me some light here!''

The throng reluctantly parted, leaving Jason at one end of an impromptu aisle. At the other end, slumped in a chair, was the wounded man, who opened his eyes and met Jason's gaze with a look of recognition. For a long moment Jason did not place the face. Then he realized that he was looking at the man he was supposed to be hunting, the Abolitionist agent Duncan Sargent.

As he took an impulsive step forward, someone grabbed Jason's arm. ''Easy, friend. We all want to hear just as bad as you do. Hey, Doc! Is he in shape to tell us what happened?''

''Absolutely not,'' the doctor said.

But Sargent struggled a little higher in the chair and said, ''Yes. You deserve to know. I was on my way here from Kansas City when I was stopped by a Ruffian band. Once they heard my accent, they told me I was their prisoner. Not the only one, either. Another poor soul was tied up, no one I knew, whose crime was refusing to swear allegiance to the Bogus Legislature. I saw how they treated him.''

He stopped to take a sip from the waterglass the doctor was holding.

"Tarring and feathering—it sounds like a prank, doesn't it? But have any of you seen it? Have you heard the way a man screams when the boiling tar is poured over his bare skin? And the mocking howls from the devils who are doing it to him? After that they tied his hands behind him, straddled him over a split rail with his feet tied together, and gave him a ride around their camp. Every step they took was crushing his privates against that splintery wood. Before they'd gotten halfway around, there was a trail of blood on the ground. About then the poor fellow fainted. They decided he wasn't much sport any more, so they tied him to a two-log raft and pushed him out into the river.

"About then I made up my mind that I'd chance their marksmanship before I'd trust their mercy. They were all looking at their other victim and yowling like fiends from the pit, so I knocked down my guard and got to my horse. I would have gotten away, too, but one of them had a Sharp's rifle and hit me as I topped a rise, three hundred yards away." As he mentioned the rifle, he met Jason's eye and gave him a wry look. Then he coughed twice, three times. At the end, a narrow red stream ran from the side of his mouth. The doctor wiped it away.

"That's all. They're stopping everyone coming this way, and woe to any they think is a Free Soiler."

A buzz of worried voices filled the lobby. The wounded man sought Jason's glance once more, and beckoned. Jason walked over and gave him a cold bow.

"I'm glad your boat wasn't badly damaged," Sargent began.

"Badly enough, sir. You could have caused the deaths of hundreds of people."

"I acted to prevent the deaths of hundreds of people. All that keeps the men who shot me from slaughtering this town is their superstitious fear of the Sharp's repeating rifle. If those guns had reached their hands, the massacre would have followed within days."

"Are you asking my foregiveness, Mr. Sargent?" Jason asked stiffly.

"No, sir. Your understanding. I detest wanton destruction. If I could have had those crates quietly dropped into the river, I would have. But the enemy was too strong. I acted only as my principles and concern for the safety and welfare of my comrades dictated." His voice was growing weaker. The doctor was looking with concern from one man to the other.

Jason gave a snort of disdain. "Have you thought that the men who shot you could say the same? You speak of principles, but what I see is blood."

"We do not waylay travelers at random."

"Not yet, perhaps, but if this goes on as it has, you will."

Sargent closed his eyes for a moment. "No," he said when he opened them again. "No. We are making our homes here. Bringing our wives and children. Civilizing the land. They are wild men, rootless men, violent men. They have no place in our world. They see that, and seek to destroy it.

They may succeed. But not without a fight.'' Each sentence ended with a gasp. By now the doctor was actively alarmed.

So was Jason. Though he wanted revenge for the bomb on the *Argo*, he had no desire to torment a dying man. ''Well, sir,'' he said in a gentler voice, ''you may be right. But we must continue our discussion at another time.''

Sargent glanced over at the doctor and saw the truth in his eyes. ''No, Mr. Lowell,'' he replied, ''in another world.''

CHAPTER SEVENTEEN

Once the sun went down, the land cooled quickly. The northwest wind still carried the memory of distant snows. In a little hollow, sheltered from the wind by a thicket, a campfire flickered. Its gleam, a tiny spark in the immensity of the darkened prairie, revealed a man and a woman. The woman was seated on a folded blanket, hugging her knees, and the man was in the act of handing her a steaming cup of coffee.

She glanced nervously from the coffee to his face, as if she half-expected the beverage to be dosed with laudanum. "My goodness," she chattered, "I do hope it doesn't keep me awake. Do you think it might? If I have to lie awake listening to the wolves and bears crawling through the bushes, I believe my hair will be pure white by morning!"

He said nothing, but buried his face in his cup.

She studied him doubtfully. Was he tired of her

288

already? She was trying to be lighthearted and amusing, but it was very hard work, and the harder she tried, the less responsive he seemed to be. Still, she knew that it was a woman's place to take men's minds off serious matters. The problem was simply that she hadn't found the right approach yet.

"What a pity that you didn't have a chance to meet Mrs. Frazer. You would have found her so ridiculous, I know. I do believe she had her shirt-waists cast in iron, she was so stiff and solid! Once when Uncle Junius passed some little compliment—you know the way he does—she looked at him as if he had asked her to desert Reverend Frazer and live with him in sin! I never saw him so flustered before. And that awful Shuttlesworth, she talked to him as if he was the bad boy in her Sunday School class. After the first time or two, he stayed away from us altogether."

Her companion made an inarticulate sound that reminded her of her fear of bears.

"I just about died when she told me she would be going on and leaving me when we got to Leaven-worth. I even begged her to stay, silly me, but she said the Reverend needed her at Fort Riley. And when I said I'd like to go along and see the fort, she told me it was no place for a young girl, as if Leavenworth City was! I declare, Mr. Lowell, if I hadn't known I could turn to you for help, I believe I would have committed a rash act. You've been my own perfect gentle knight!"

He muttered something else, which she interpret-ed as a disclaimer.

"Now nonsense! You have, and you know it, so

don't be an old silly about it! And another thing—I just can't go on calling you Mr. Lowell all the time, as though we just met at a tea party. Do you mind if I call you Augustus? And you must call me Melissa, or even, if there's no one about to hear, Missy. That's what my dear daddy used to call me.''

In fact, he hated the name Augustus, but in her voice even Nero or Judas would have sounded sweet to him. He cleared his throat and said, ''No, I don't mind,'' then, after a pause, added, ''Missy.'' He knew that she might misunderstand his taciturnity, but he couldn't help it. Did she realize the gravity of what he had done? In the eyes of the world, he had abducted an underage girl, and an heiress at that, from the protection of her guardian, a distinguished statesman. If they were caught, the odds were very good that he would swing from the nearest tree. While she kept up her girlish prattle, he was constantly listening for the hoofbeats of a posse on their trail. As soon as they finished their coffee, he kicked dirt over the fire.

''Oh, must you?'' she exclaimed. ''It was such a comfort!'' Then, in a different, more serious voice, she added, ''You expect Uncle Junius to send people looking for us, don't you?''

''From what you've told me, he badly needs your fortune. He won't give it up easily. That's why I brought us so far off the trail to camp. We'd better turn in—I want to be on our way at first light.''

Two or three hours later, a slight rustling sound woke him to instant alertness. Hand on revolver, he strained his ears. Was it an animal? A pursuer?

"Augustus?" Panic tinged her whisper. "Augustus, where are you? I can't see you?"

He reached out, touched a shoulder. "Here I am. What is it? What's wrong?"

She drew closer. He could feel violent shivers wracking her frame. "I'm so cold," she moaned. "Cold and scared. Hold me, keep me warm. Please. Keep me safe, Augustus. I'll die if you don't."

He pulled her to him and wrapped his arms around her. Gradually her shivers subsided, and she wriggled still closer to him. Sternly he reminded himself that he was her perfect gentle knight. He tried to think if any of King Arthur's men had had the sort of difficulty he was having. Sir Lancelot, of course, but he wasn't sure how that applied to his case.

"Augustus?" she said in a very small voice.

"Mm?"

"Will you . . ." For a moment her courage failed her and she fell silent.

"What, Missy?"

"Will you pretend that we're married? It wouldn't be right to be like this if we weren't, would it? So as long as we've come this far, I reckon we ought to go the rest of the way."

"What? Melissa, you don't know what you're talking about!" He pulled away and raised himself on his elbow to look into the darkness in her direction. All he could really see was a darker area against the night sky.

"Well, of course not! I've been gently raised, you know. But I know that once a man and a woman are married, there's no way to put them back to the way they were before, especially her.

And that's what I mean. I want us to be married in the eyes of God, right now, so Uncle Junius can never make me marry that terrible Luke Shuttlesworth. Is that so awful of me?'' His silence weighed on her. "You do *want* to be married to me, don't you? I'm not too ugly or too ignorant and childish for you?''

"Of course not!'' But internally he was asking himself, not if he wanted to marry her, but if he was ready to marry at all. There wasn't much time to decide—about half a minute at most. He gulped and took the leap. "I love you, Melissa, and I want you to be my wife.''

"My goodness, that took long enough! What do we do next? Do we have to take off our clothes? All of them? I surely am glad it's dark, or I don't know if I could do it! I'll tell you—you help me with my dress, and I'll help you with your suit, and then we won't feel so far apart. You're sure this is what we're supposed to do? It seems almost indecent, but I suppose you know best.''

Once they were naked, she ran her hand gingerly down over his chest and belly. When she reached his groin, she held her breath for a long moment, then broke into a fit of giggles. "My," she said when the paroxysm subsided, "but aren't you *fancy*! I never knew the like!''

The next morning, while Melissa and Gus were still following a faint trail southward from the Big Stranger Creek, Jason rode out to Ben Church's house, high on the side of Mount Oread. Elizabeth came to the open door with rolled-up sleeves and flour all over her hands and arms. There was a smudge of flour on one cheek that Jason had an impulse to lick off.

"Up with the sun, I see."

She didn't return his smile. "Jason, I'm worried," she said abruptly.

"Yes?"

"It's Charlie. He's been acting most peculiar the last few days, smug one minute and sullen the next, until I can hardly bear to speak to him for fear of getting my head snapped off."

Jason was of the view that this behavior, from Charlie, wasn't a bit peculiar. A more unmannerly cub he never hoped to meet. But he knew better than to say that to Elizabeth, who stuck up for her brother all the more fiercely as he showed himself all the more unworthy of her loyalty.

She looked at the ground and smoothed down her floury apron with both hands. "He . . . rode off yesterday, without a word, and didn't come back. If we were in New Orleans, I'd know what to think, but here. . . . Charlie's a city-bred boy, he could get into difficulties without knowing the way out. I keep thinking of him lying out there somewhere with a broken leg. He's crying and calling for me to help, but no one hears him. It's terrible!"

For a split-second Jason thought of flour stains on his black broadcloth coat. Then he urged her to him and put her head on his shoulder. As he stroked her hair, he said, "I'll ride out and look for him if you like. Do you know which road he took? There's a few million acres out there."

"Back toward Missouri, I'm sure. I shouldn't let you do this. I shouldn't feel so jittery. But the whole town is that way, talking about Ruffian attacks and ambushes all the time. I think Uncle Ben is sorry he invited us here, but how could he have known of the danger to come?''

Jason suppressed the comment that Ben Church, with his outspoken views on slavery, was one of the men who had helped to create the danger Elizabeth was speaking of. There was no point in alarming her more than she was already.

"I shouldn't worry," he said easily, patting her back. "The Border Ruffians are about as likely to make a real attack on Lawrence as I am to sell the *Argo*."

She leaned back to look up into his face. "You love that boat, don't you? I can see why you were so furious with that poor Mr. Sargent. Do you think you could ever leave the river and settle in one place?''

He shrugged. "Someday, perhaps. Sooner or later the fast packets will be put out of business by steam trains. But that's ten or twenty years away. I'll worry about it then. For now, the *Argo* is my life. It's one I enjoy.''

"Yes." There was sadness in her voice, and understanding, too.

"I'll get along then. If *my* brother should turn up in town, you'll tell him where I am? I suppose I'll be back tonight, or tomorrow noon at the latest.''

Finding Charlie Brigham turned out to be remarkably easy. About four miles east of Franklin village, on the great California Road, Jason saw a lone rider approaching. He reined in at the top of a rise and waited, automatically sweeping the tail of his coat free of his holstered .41 revolver. The times were troubled in Kansas Territory, and strangers were not always friendly.

The approaching rider saw him and slowed his pace, but soon Jason could tell that it was Elizabeth's brother. He waved his hand, and Charlie nudged his horse up the slope to meet him.

"Afternoon," said Jason amiably.

"Unh. What are you doing here? Did that durned sister of mine send you spying on me? She's got a nerve, treating me like I was five years old."

Jason thought it best to ignore the question. "How about you? Enjoying a leisurely look at the countryside?"

The lad had blue smudges of exhaustion under his eyes, but his manner was as elated as if he had been drinking. "Not likely," he said belligerently. "There's big changes coming, and I mean to be part of them. I know you think I'm just a kid that you can brush out of your way, but you'll find out different before the week is out."

Who on earth had been so unwary as to trust this cub with a secret? Elizabeth was being overly generous if she did treat him like a five year old; three was closer to the mark. Still, even the hungriest fish will slip the hook if the bait isn't quite right. "Is that right?" Jason said casually. "I've heard a lot of talk around these parts, but I can't say much seems to come of it. I reckon most of these grand plans come straight out of a grocery store keg of white lightning, all brag and bounce with nothing behind it."

"You think so?" the boy blazed out. "By golly,

you wait 'til the Cavalier Legion comes riding down this road, with music playing and banners waving and the sun glinting off cold steel! You'll see deeds done then that aren't just brag and bounce, dang me if you don't!''

Jason's slightly bored expression did not change, but Charlie had succeeded in interesting him. Someone else had recently mentioned the Cavalier Legion—someone on the boat to Kansas City? It was connected in some way with Senator Junius Stephenson, that he recalled. The best hope of learning more, he suspected, was to seem to know it all already.

"Don't mistake me, sir, I have the greatest esteem for the Senator. But action, significant action, calls for more than stirring speeches and compelling arguments. I have given up hoping to see the day when he is able to lead his followers into battle instead of merely talking about the battles to come on some future date.''

"Have you, now,'' said Charlie triumphantly. "Well, you went and gave up just one day too soon then! By this time tomorrow the Cavalier Legion will have flung the torch of liberty into that nest of vipers called Lawrence! There'll be nothing left but the scorched earth! And that's just the start!''

"Tomorrow, eh?'' Suddenly the boy looked guiltily aware that he had betrayed the secret he had been so eager to pass on. Jason hastily added, "Well, I'm sorry I won't be here to see it. Is the Senator up ahead somewhere? Maybe I can pay my respects to him if it's along my way.''

"You're going away? I figured you'd go on hanging around Lizzie 'til the cows came home."

Jason was thinking fast, testing one possibility after another. It seemed to him that he faced a twisted maze of paths, most of which led ultimately to one form of disaster or another. But the weighing of choices and probabilities was his profession, and the willingness to back his judgment with his entire stake as his gift. Elizabeth, and through her the whole town, must be warned, and Stephenson's Legion must be delayed. Both tasks were his, and he could not do both himself.

"Why, yes," he said in a casual voice. "A matter of business, I'm afraid. In fact, Mr. Brigham, you can do me a small service if you will. I had no opportunity to take leave of your charming sister this morning. Would you be so kind as to tell her you met me on the road, and that I was on my way back to St. Louis to sell the *Argo*?"

Charlie stared. "You're going to get rid of your steamboat?"

"Yes, the Cause always needs funds, and if I sell now I'm likely to get a better price than after the Revolution begins."

As he hoped, the boy was visibly impressed by this mixture of dedication and shrewd self-interest. He would be certain to repeat to his sister that Jason Lowell was planning to sell the *Argo*, but would Elizabeth recall their conversation that morning? And if she did, would she be able to decipher the warning? If she didn't, he could only hope that Charlie was as indiscreet with others as he had been with him.

Jason touched the brim of his hat. "I'll be

getting along then. Where did you say the Senator is camped?''

Charlie guffawed. ''You don't need to look none. You stay on this road, and I guess they'll find you!''

Brigham's prediction proved to be correct. Late in the afternoon, a man stepped into the center of the road just where it entered a small grove of trees. There were brass bars pinned to the shoulders of his blue shirt, but he derived most of his air of authority from the carbine in his hands.

''Hold up there, stranger!'' he called. ''Who air you, and where you headed?''

''My name's Jason Lowell, and I'm looking for the encampment of the Cavalier Legion.'' As he spoke, Jason carefully scanned the area ahead, catching a glint of light on metal to the right and a small branch that trembled in the still air off to the left. Were there more than three of them? It didn't really matter—he didn't aim to try to fight them, however many or few they might be.

''That a fact? Well, maybe I'd better just pass you along to a feller who might know what the hell you're talking about, mister. Bobby Lee!'' A frontiersman in butternut trousers and a deerskin shirt ambled out of the woods, carrying an old-fashioned Kentucky rifle nearly as tall as he was. He looked Jason up and down, then spat an arc of tobacco juice into the underbrush. ''Bobby Lee, you take this feller along to camp and see what Luke thinks about him.''

''Shore.'' He turned and walked up the road, confident that Jason would follow him. Jason did, partly because it fitted his plan and partly from respect for the fearsome accuracy of the antique long rifle. About a quarter of a mile along, a path turned off the road into a dell screened by trees. The trees did not hide the complex smell of the camp, a mixture of woodsmoke, horses, meat that was past its prime, and unwashed male bodies.

His escort led him through the curious clumps of men to a canvas pavilion in the center of camp. As they drew near, the scar-faced man Jason recalled from the *Argo* stepped out of the entrance and stared at them. "Well, I'll be a whore's breakfast," he exclaimed. "You caught you a big one this time, Bobby Lee! Where abouts was he?"

"Comin' up the road bold as brass. Said he was lookin' for the Legion, so Wilson figgered you'd want to see him."

During this exchange, Jason dismounted, tossed the reins to the nearest bystander, and walked calmly toward the big tent. "Mr. Shuttlesworth, I believe? I have news for Senator Stephenson. Is he free to see me?"

"Oh, he'll see you all right. He'll see you dancing in a noose! Though by the time I'm done with you, I don't know you'll be moving all that easily."

Jason looked at him coldly. "Sir, you are laboring under a strange misapprehension of some kind. Please inform the Senator that I am here to speak to him."

"He doesn't need to, Mr. Lowell," said a familiar voice. "Here I am. You seem to think that I'm likely to welcome you, even though you have hampered my plans a good deal. Maybe you would like to explain that to me. And while you are about it, you might explain why you are here in Kansas. I was told that you were in St. Louis.''

"Why I'm here? Do you have to ask me that?"

"Whether I have to or not, I have asked you. Have the kindness to answer, sir!"

"Certainly, Senator. I came west to find the snake who nearly sank my steamboat—the same man who destroyed those fine rifles of yours.'' Shuttlesworth let out a strangled curse and moved toward Jason, but he ignored him and concentrated all his attention on the Senator. "Did you think I was going to sit by and do nothing while some damn Yankee Abolitionist tried to ruin me? No sir!''

"To whom do you refer, Mr. Lowell?"

Jason laughed shortly. "He called himself Duncan Sargent. Claimed to be writing a book. But one of my men saw him set the bomb and light the fuse. He couldn't get to it in time. Sargent said he was from Boston, so it wasn't hard to work out what was going on.''

Stephenson rubbed his cheek thoughtfully. "Sargent—yes, I recall talking with him. An Abolitionist agent, of course. Where is he now?"

"Pushing up daisies. I caught up with him near that pesthole Lawrence and put lead through his belly. He took a long time dying, too, I can tell you. I watched the whole time. No bastard tries to sink the *Argo* and gets away with it.''

Shuttlesworth pushed forward. "Are you going to let this damned Yankee gambler talk his way out of a fix? What about Melissa? It was that pig-fucking brother of his who was sweet on her. Maybe he knows where she went.''

Stephenson gave no sign that he had heard his follower's outburst, but his next question to Jason was, ''Are you acquainted with my ward, Miss Wainwright, sir?''

''I have not had that honor, Senator.''

''Or with a Mr. Cooke, from Kentucky?''

Jason pretended to consider the question, then shook his head.

''Your brother—where is he now?''

''I left him in St. Louis to oversee the repairs to the *Argo*. This was a private quarrel I came west on.''

''A moment ago you told my lieutenant that you had some news for me. What might that be?''

So far the exchange had gone much as Jason had hoped it would, but this was by far the trickiest stretch, as well as the most crucial.

''I have been staying in Lawrence for a few days, waiting for Sargent to show up, and I learned something of the Free Soilers' plans. It seemed to me you might be interested.''

''I, sir? I wish to have nothing to do with those nigger-thieves and slum-boys who have raised the flag of treason over the sacred soil of Kansas.''

''Well, in that case—'' Jason adjusted his posture as if he was on the point of walking away.

''Still,'' the Senator continued quickly, ''it is as well to know what the minions of the Great Adversary are about. What did you mean to tell me?''

''Anyone can see the place is indefensible, for all that they built earthworks on the three roads into town, so what they plan to do is take most of the able-bodied men and dig another set of entrenchments some miles west on the road from Topeka. They seem to think that's the most likely line of attack. After that, there's talk of doing the same on a ridge between Lawrence and Franklin to cover the eastward approach.''

"You are remarkably well-informed," Stephenson said suspiciously.

"The Yankees talk of nothing else," Jason replied with a shrug. "The lobby of the Free State Hotel is their military headquarters. Anyone can sit there and learn what there is to learn.''

"And yet—I am not without my own sources of information in Lawrence, Mr. Lowell. And this is the first I have heard of this plan you describe.''

So that was the reason for Charlie Brigham's absence from home. "I first heard of it myself yesterday afternoon. The local militia was told to be ready to go by tomorrow noon, though my guess is they'll make a late start of it. They didn't look very well organized, for all their new Sharp's rifles.''

This time the Senator rubbed both cheeks at once, the left with his forefinger and the right with his thumb. "I see. Then, sir, it is your belief that anyone meaning to bring Territorial law to that rebellious town—if there is anyone of that description—would prevent unnecessary bloodshed by waiting until after tomorrow. Is that correct, Mr. Lowell?''

"Exactly correct, Senator.''

"Hmp. Well, sir, you have done me, and our nation, an important service. In return, may I invite you to partake of the hospitality of our camp for a day or two? We are rough, sir, and our manners are unpolished, but you'll find that for anyone who knows the meaning of the word Liberty, we are the salt of the earth! Luke will see to your accommodations. No, no," he added with grim humor, when Jason opened his mouth to decline the invitation. "Really, sir, under the circumstances I positively must insist!"

As Jason turned to follow the scarred man, the Senator called after him, "Perhaps after supper you would favor a few hands of cards as an agreeable way to pass the time!"

The poker game that evening remained in Jason's memory as one of the strangest he had ever played in. As the jug of Missouri corn liquor continued to circle the table, the Senator started to talk about his goals and aspirations. Jason, fascinated, used all his card-playing skills, not to win, but to keep the game involving for all the players, because the longer they played, the more revealing Stephenson became.

"Cotton is King, sir," he said at one point, "and any white man with spunk can become one of his noblemen. Riches to rival Peru and the Indies, and all you need is some prime field hands and some land that isn't played out. Look at the wealthiest men along the Mississippi today. Oh, they'll talk about Old Virginny and cavalier blood and horseshit of the kind, but in fact there isn't one whose daddy wasn't pure white trash without two red cents to rub together. They made their own fortunes, and anyone else can go do the same—*as long as we have room to grow!* Once we lose that, our entire way of life begins to die.''

Jason deftly dealt a seven to Shuttlesworth, to fill out his two pair, and a third king to a black-haired man with a wooden leg named Wegg. "Yes, I see, sir. But I shouldn't have thought that Kansas is very good cotton land.''

"It isn't, son. That's not the point. (I'll go you an X higher, Luke.) No, sir, Kansas is no more than the fuse. We are tempting the Abolitionists and Black Republicans to try to coerce us, and once they do, the whole Cotton Kingdom will rise up in defense of its rights. We have nothing in common with Yankee tradesmen and mill-owners, and it is time we shook off their yoke and took our rightful place in the world.''

"Dissolve the Union, you mean?''

"If pushed to it,'' Stephenson said calmly. "Why not? If we had had the say ten years ago, we would have held onto Mexico and gone on to take Cuba from the Dagos. All of the Caribbean could have been the private lake of the Cotton Empire— yes, and still can be if we all pull together! But someone must dare to strike the first spark. For some time now, Mr. Lowell, I have known that I am that Child of Destiny. What we do here is the beginning of a new world order that will last for a thousand years!''

CHAPTER EIGHTEEN

The day was perfect, sunny and clear, and the warm air was scented with the tang of wild verbena. Senator Stephenson, armed with writs and warrants signed by a compliant Territorial judge, rode into town first, with a small entourage. Jason, at the Senator's polite insistence, was part of it. He knew even before they reached the foot of Massachusetts Street that his warning had been understood. Occasionally a face peered momentarily from the window of a house, but the streets were empty. Lawrence was a deserted village.

"You see that, gentlemen?" the Senator proclaimed as they reined in beside the Free State Hotel. "Those walls are solid stone, three feet thick! They may call it a hotel, but it is nothing less than a fortress of defiant treason! Before the day is out, I mean to see a pile of rubble in its place. As great Cato was wont to say, Carthage must be destroyed!"

His lieutenants looked at each other doubtfully, as if wondering where they were to find this second town they'd never heard of.

"Summon the men! Fling the torch of Liberty into this nest of vipers!"

Jason noted with sour amusement that his guess about the source of Charlie Brigham's rhetoric had just been confirmed. As if in response, Charlie himself came pelting down the hill, whooping and hallooing. One of the Senator's guards raised his rifle, but Shuttlesworth pushed it aside. "Don't be a fool, the whelp's one of ours!"

Stephenson was still issuing a string of commands. "Tell the boys to give special attention to the two seditious newspapers that have spread lies and calumny about our precious way of life! Any records are to be seized and brought to me! And any of the men on the list, but don't harm them unless they attack us—we'll give no aid and comfort to the slanderers of our great cause!"

No one noticed Jason side-stepping his horse to the corner of the hotel and then around it out of sight. Nor was there an outcry as he continued, at a walking pace, down toward the river. Soon he was hidden in the trees, where he tied up his horse to a limb and stepped cautiously to the edge of the wood to watch.

The Cavalier Legion was approaching the town in a nervous clump. When no one shot at them, the men began to spread apart and walk a little taller and faster. Some started to holler and yelp in barbaric cries more or less borrowed from the Indians of the Plains. Soon the main body was running down the center of Massachusetts Street, while little splinters broke away to investigate the attractions of one or another building along the way. The sounds of splintering wood and shattering glass carried all the way to Jason's vantage.

The Sack of Lawrence was on.

Jason shrank back out of sight as half a dozen Ruffians staggered toward the river with trays of type from the *Kansas Free State* and *Herald of Freedom* offices. One of them had pulled an elegant brocade waistcoat over his greasy blue shirt, and another had a silver candlestick protruding from his hip pocket.

A flat *crack!*, like distant thunder in a treble key, resounded from the encircling hills and was followed closely by another. Stephenson had brought up his prize toys, two six-pound brass howitzers, and trained them on the hated Free State Hotel. He meant to carry out his pledge to raze it to the ground. In slow alternation the cannon fired round after round at point-blank range. But the stonemasons from Massachusetts had done their work better than the amateur cannoneers from Missouri could. The iron balls left bright scars on the stone, but the walls were as solid as ever. Wild with balked fury, the men dragged sofas and damask curtains into the street, rolled kegs of gunpowder into the hotel, and set the building afire, then cheered as the flames spurted from glassless windows and again when part of the parapet, weakened by the cannon fire, collapsed into the street. If anyone noticed that one of their band had been directly under the falling masonry, he didn't think it worth calling attention to.

By now no house in town, however poor, had

escaped looting. Kegs of whiskey from the hotel bar and the grocery store had been rolled into the middle of the street and smashed open. Men drank by the dipperful, spilling the fiery liquid over their chins and down their shirtfronts and cursing those who took the dipper from them. With no visible enemy, they emptied their revolvers into the air for the pure joy of making a loud noise. Someone with a feeling for symbolism had set fire to Ben Church's house, high on the side of Mount Oread. The column of flame and smoke signaled the destruction of the Free Soil stronghold to the entire countryside.

By now a few men were beginning to drift away. Someone, made edgy by the too-easy victory, started the rumor that the town was a trap. The Abolitionists were planning to move onto the heights that commanded the town and use their dreaded Sharp's rifles from a distance that made return fire impossible. Most of the Ruffians scoffed at the rumor, but they did so looking over their shoulders at the hilltops. Soon a steady line of them was streaming eastward, toward the familiar border country. Some of the women of Lawrence, emboldened by the change of mood, came out of hiding to watch them silently from the side of the road. Others began to sort through the wreckage of their looted homes.

Senator Junius Stephenson was one of the last men to leave. Seated proudly on his gray charger, he surveyed what he had done and called in an orator's voice to the empty windows, "Thus always to traitors! The South will fight for Southern rights!" As he rode off down Massachusetts Street, one of the women flung a fresh cow pattie at him that splattered his clothing and his haughty horse. As a statesman, he declined to take any notice of the incident.

Slowly, cautiously, the residents of Lawrence returned to their ravaged town. Jason, who had watched it all from nearby, was helping an old lady carry her furniture back into her house when he heard a familiar voice shouting his name. He turned just in time to catch Elizabeth as she stumbled into his arms. Then his brother was pounding his back and shouting incoherently. His young lady was holding back, smiling shyly.

"Oh, I was so frightened for you," Elizabeth was saying. "When Charlie told me what you had said, I knew it was a warning to us, but I was sure those terrible men would capture and kill you. Then your brother arrived and told us how strong they were, and we decided to save ourselves and let them have the town."

"Today we have gained a great victory!" Elizabeth's uncle had joined the little group. "The whole world will know what sort of men these Border Ruffians are! Can anyone doubt, *now*, which is the side of liberty and justice and which the side of treason and disunion? Hallelujah!"

Gus was pulling Melissa forward. "Jason," he said, "I've got something to tell you. Melissa and I are going to get married."

Jason's poker face fell into place automatically. "Um-hm. Congratulations. But she's not of age."

"I will be in six weeks, Mr. Lowell, and"—she smiled a knowing smile at Gus—"I think we can

wait that long if we have to. I've already written to
my Uncle Louis, explaining how terribly Uncle
Junius treated me and all. I just know he'll understand and keep Uncle Junius from doing anything
else.''

''Yes, I'm sure he—''

''*No!* Oh dear God, NO!'' Jason whirled around;
that was Elizabeth's voice, but where was she?
Then he saw her, lying full-length in the dust of
the street next to the fallen parapet of the burnt-out
Free State Hotel. Her fingers scrabbled at the shattered masonry, from which a scrap of shirt peeped
out. Suddenly he understood. Striding over, he
picked her up and held her close, trying to dampen
the hysterical shaking. She fought him, struggled
to crane her neck and stare back at the pile of
bricks and stones. Some of the men of the town
were hurrying over now and began lifting the rubble with a strangely tender haste, though everyone
knew that nothing could be done.

As the ruined body emerged from the dust,
Jason covered Elizabeth's face with his hand. She
was sobbing freely now, stammering out words
between gulps for breath. ''He was so changed. I
could have saved him, if I'd known how. Was I a
bad sister? Lately there were times I hated him. I
mean it! I damned him in my heart, and now—!''

She leaned back from the waist and stared up
into Jason's face. ''When he was little, sometimes
I carried him down to the levee. We watched the
boats go by and talked about all we would do
when we were big. I was very happy then. Do you
think I can ever be happy again?''

Because he knew that whatever he said would

mean a great deal, Jason was silent. Her eyes searched his face fearfully; then, with a sudden cry of utter loss, she tore herself from him and ran after her uncle, who was following Charlie's body to the undertaker's shop. Jason watched helplessly. For once he was unable to assign odds to his choices and act by the light of his calculations.

Gus took his arm and squeezed it sympathetically.

Jason looked at him. "It's time we were back in St. Louis. Clement should be bringing the *Argo* upriver to the yard any day now. I won't have her pawed over by strangers."

Gus looked around, met Melissa's eye, and seemed to draw strength from it. "We can't," he said simply. "We can't risk getting within Stephenson's reach until we're married. Legally he's still her guardian. Here we're fairly safe."

"Oh." Jason tried to think of an alternative plan, but his mind was moving more slowly than usual. "All right. I hate to leave you behind, but I suppose you've the right of it. Let me know when the wedding is; I'll bring some of the gang with me and we can all go back together. Hell, little brother, we'll charter our own boat to take us back!"

Melissa moved over to nestle under Gus's arm. A wrinkle appeared between her brows, as though she were willing Gus to speak up. He did. "It's not that easy, Jason. We . . . well, the river isn't much of a place to bring up a family, is it? And we've grown sort of fond of this place. The town has a great future, and with what I've put aside and some of the money Melissa inherited from her daddy, we can start our own business. A trading company to begin with, but it will grow with the town. What do you think of the idea?''

"Business? What do either of you know about business?" Fueled by hurt, his tone was more scornful than he intended. "The idea is asinine!"

"What did you know about steamboats four years ago? I can't go through my whole life being somebody else's little brother, you know!"

"Oh please," said Melissa tearfully, "we're all upset by everything that's happened. Don't let's make it worse by quarreling! I just don't think I can stand it if you keep on like this, indeed I don't!"

Gus looked at Jason, ready to apologize and make up, but he found no encouragement in his brother's face. He had seen that steely mask often enough, but it had never been directed at him. His own expression hardened. "I'll write you at the Planters to tell you when the wedding will be," he said evenly. The unspoken, but understood, second sentence was, *Come if you like, if you don't, go to hell.*

"Thank you." He bowed coolly to Melissa, stared for another moment into Gus's eyes, and turned on his heel.

The rest of the day he plunged himself into the effort to repair the damage to the town. Disregarding the danger of injuring his perfectly cared-for hands, he carried charred beams from the shell of the hotel, nailed boards over shattered windows, and shoveled rubbish into gunny sacks. His conscious goal was to tire himself so thoroughly that he would not be obliged to think or feel, but he did not succeed.

The editor of the *Free State* offered him a place to sleep in return for an interview about Senator Stephenson and his ambitions. Jason's only condition was that his name not be used; the *Argo*, after all, depended entirely on trade from the slave states her route passed through. He took it to be a futile gesture anyway. No one was going to take seriously the report that a statesman of Stephenson's eminence meant to wreck the Union and found a new empire based on slavery.

Charlie Brigham was buried just before sunset. The preacher spoke briefly, eulogizing the dead boy as a martyr to the cause of Free Soil. Jason was the only one who knew that he had been a Ruffian spy, and he thought it best to keep the knowledge to himself. After the funeral he walked Elizabeth up the hill to her uncle's farm. The remains of the house were still smoking, but when they turned their backs to look out over the valley, the prospect was peaceful and lovely. The land was darkened, but the immensity of sky was still a bright blue. Far off to the right, near the horizon, the newly risen moon gleamed palely.

They had so much to talk about, and so much to avoid, that there was only silence left. Elizabeth had spoken to Melissa and knew of the quarrel, though not the reason for it. She also sensed that Jason did not want to speak of Charlie or of the raid by the Cavalier Legion.

He was examining, with gloomy amazement, his blistered, grimy hands and their chipped and broken nails. Weeks would pass before he could deal cards with his usual control. He allocated the blame two-thirds to Stephenson and one-third to Gus, though he had the added dissatisfaction of knowing that, in truth, the fault was entirely his own.

"I imagine you'll be leaving soon, to return to St. Louis." As she spoke, she looked at him briefly, then returned her gaze to the distant scene.

"Yes." He wanted to explain, to ask for her sympathy, to lay her down and make love to her right there in the grass. He did none of these things. Instead, in a voice whose evenness made the request seem of trivial interest to him, he said, "Would you like to come with me?"

"Oh, I couldn't!" She spoke without thought, then tried to justify her impulse. "There's Uncle Dan, and rebuilding the house, and . . . I couldn't leave Charlie so soon. How could I?"

"Of course," he replied, bowing slightly. "Forgive me for suggesting it; it was insensitive of me at such a time."

The apology confused her, because it seemed somehow to mean more than it said, but before she could try to clarify it, he added, "I have much to do if I am to get an early start in the morning."

"In the morning! So soon?"

"There is nothing to detain me here and much to do in St. Louis. I expect I'll be away before you're up, so I'll say good-bye now."

He held out his right hand and refused to meet her eyes. To Elizabeth, this was the final proof of what she had feared all along: he had lost all respect for her and considered her no better than a hussy. She knew her behavior merited that judgment, but even so it cut her deeply. Couldn't he have seen the difference between someone whose passionate attraction overmastered her and someone who had lost all moral sense? But perhaps the difference was insignificant; perhaps she was already well on the road to being a loose woman.

If so, she would as soon be hanged for a sheep as a lamb! Disregarding his outstretched hand, she flung her arms around his neck and kissed him as ardently as she knew how. He was responding, too; she knew he was. But suddenly he pushed her away quite roughly, then strode down the hill without a single backward look. Elizabeth sank slowly to her knees and watched his form disappear into the dusk. The day had numbed her; one more loss, however great, could add little to the sum of her pain.

In Kansas City they told him that a steamboat downriver might come in a day or two. The bar nearest the dock offered as good a haven as any. He sat at a table off to one side and worked his way through his grievances as steadily as he did through the contents of a bottle. No one could be trusted. Love was an illusion or, worse, a trap to snare the unwary. The world was divided into wolves and sheep; sheep flocked together by instinct and called it community, but wolves knew that every other wolf was a rival and possibly an enemy. One saw clearly only from the peaks, above the fogs of sentiment, but the air was very thin and the view was bleak.

At one point he thought of traveling. He had

never seen Constantinople, or the Pyramids, or the pampas of the Argentine. He could sell the *Argo*, or leave her for Captain Clement to run, and resume the ancient quest of the Golden Fleece. It was his birthright, wasn't it, the destiny that waited just beyond the horizon? But the next shot of rye told that Cairo, Egypt, was no different under the surface than Cairo, Illinois. What point a change of scene when people stayed the same?

He slept with his head on the table, and when he woke, he bought another bottle. The boy who swept up brought him a plate of ham and eggs from the cafe up the street. The smell of the food nauseated him, but he forced himself to eat, then rinsed the taste away with raw whiskey. He missed the forests on the coast of California, where he had hidden himself after Benita died. There he had seen trees taller than a cathedral spire and as old as the mountains themselves. Afterward he had spoken of those trees once or twice, but he could tell that no one believed him.

"Excuse me, sir; would you like to join us in a friendly game of cards?"

Incredulous, Jason looked up. There, wearing an ingratiating smile, was a gambler. Not a very successful one—the diamond 'headlight' pinned to his shirtfront was glass; the gold plating had worn thin on his massive watchchain; and a close look at his brocade waistcoat revealed that the design was cleverly painted on. For an instant the very fabric of reality seemed to tear, and Jason knew that he was seeing his *Doppelgänger*, the outward manifestation of his true inner self—slick, seedy, and rapacious as a hungry shark. His soul sickened within him, but still there was the lure of a game.

"Why, certainly, a hand or two." Picking up his half-full bottle by the neck, he walked with exact precision across to the poker table and fell into a chair.

After losing on three hands in a row and dropping a couple of hundred dollars, Jason realized that at least two of the other players were in league to cheat him. His first impulse was to shout with laughter, and his second was to go for his revolver. He set both aside; if they wanted a dishonest game, he would give them one to remember. On the next deal, he folded early for the sake of holding out the ace he had been dealt; on the one after that, he added a queen to his cache. Then it was merely a matter of waiting for a hand that he could improve into a winner.

His three aces, two hands later, pulled in less than fifty dollars, but more important, they brought him the deal. In principle, what he meant to do was simple: he would give the two crooks good hands, then improve them significantly on the draw. He, of course, would be holding an unbeatable set of cards. Simple in principle, but practically it meant that he must totally control the deck. The one advantage he had was that the other players did not know who he was. They would not be watching for sophisticated passes and false shuffles.

The deal went just as he meant it to. The tinhorn gambler, holding three sixes, bet heavily, and his partner, with pairs of jacks and fours, kept raising him back. Jason rode with them, knowing that each of them was destined to draw a full house and see it go down in defeat to Jason's four tens.

The betting wound down, and the gambler tossed his two discards onto the table. Jason dealt him two and looked questioningly at the partner.

"Hold it!" The bartender was standing just to Jason's right, pointing a scattergun at his head. "Atkinson, you fool, this son of a bitch was second-dealing you! You done suckered a sharper into your game! Get up, mister, real slow, and keep those hands in sight!"

What had happened? He knew those moves better than his own name, had practiced them a thousand times, yet some backwoods barkeep had spotted him. It was the drink, of course. At his secret core he was a drunkard and an incompetent. He had hidden it well, with his taste for fancy wines, but he hadn't been able to change it. Now that the secret was out, the road ahead was clear enough: liquor and cards, disgrace and ruin. So thorough-going was his self-disgust that he made no effort to resist when three of the men marched him out of the saloon and threw him in the river. His first thought as the muddy water closed over his head was that ends and beginnings were the same. He and his father were not so different after all.

The river was cold. After a moment he began to struggle against its hold. Choking and gagging, he crawled onto a sandbar and rolled over to face the sky with his arms stretched to either side. There, drunk and wet, he slept. When he woke, the sky was almost dark and he was almost sober. His assailants had cleaned out his pockets, but they hadn't found the money belt. Bedraggled as he was, he was going to the best hotel in town, eat a good meal, with water to wash it down, and sleep in a bed that night. He would wait until morning to decide whether to embark on a new life or end this one.

He was three bites into a tough steak when he became aware that the waiter was hovering near his elbow. He looked up. "Sorry to bother you, but a lady wants to share this table if you don't mind."

The dining room was half-empty. Before Jason could puzzle it out, the waiter was holding a chair for Elizabeth. Her tremulous smile told him that she was not sure of a welcome. And he—he was not sure that he deserved her.

"I didn't think you would be here," she said in a small voice. "I was going to St. Louis."

"And now?" he asked gravely.

"Now I'm going where you go. If you'll take me."

"Didn't they ever warn you not to follow a gambling man?"

"Of course. But I must not have been listening." Her smile became more assured, though it consorted oddly with the tears on her cheeks.

"Are you going to listen to me any better?"

"Not if you tell me to leave you."

He stared at her so intently that her smile began to waver again. Then he stood up, crossed deliberately to her side of the table, and pulled her up into his arms. The waiter was scandalized, but three townsmen across the room started cheering. Jason waved to them with one hand.

"Dear?" she said breathlessly a few minutes later.

"Um?"

"Do you think we can be happy together?"

He gave her a smile of pure delight, unmarred by cynicism, and said, "I'm ready to bet on it!"